MURDER at the CAIRNCROFT FAIR

A.J.A. GARDINER

Contents

1	1
2	13
3	21
4	28
5	37
6	48
7	66
8	78
9	88
10	95
11	105
12	113
13	125
14	134
15	143
16	149
17	158
18	158
19	182

20	192
21	202
22	210
23	220
24	230
25	237
26	245
27	252
28	262
29	270
30	279
31	287
32	300
33	307
34	314
35	320
36	335
37	342
38	352
39	363
40	368

1

'No.'

'Aw, c'mon Sam. It isn't *that* high...'

'Absolutely not. And it *is* that high.'

In a moment of weakness, I gave in to Daisy's plea—and here we are at the Cairncroft fair, a yearly event since time immemorial. (Well, as far back as *I* can remember.)

Rivalling as it does Disneyland (okay, I haven't *been* to Disneyland, but this fits the picture in my head) you'd expect McNab's travelling fair to base itself in Donstable—from which a majority of its patrons travel, anyway. Logistically, however, Cairncroft has an enormous grassed field on its outskirts which boasts easy traffic access and whose owner—a farmer named Struthers—gives the fairground a deal they can't refuse. (Including discounts at his farm shop.)

Daisy wants me to go on the big wheel.

She can go on wanting.

'You're no fun.'

'Hey—I went on the dodgems.'

'Sam, I have never known anyone get through an entire dodgem session without a single collision—until now. Like I said, you're no fun.'

I barely hear her over an all-encompassing cacophony of pop music backed by screaming air sirens. (At least it drowns out the clanks and bangs that cast doubt on how safe these rides actually are.)

Oh—better show willing. 'I *might* give the waltzers a try. Although I seem to remember getting sick on them once, but that was years ago...'

'Look—there's Mr M. Didn't expect to see him here.'

She's right—Mr M, our solicitor and adopted "uncle", is strolling along arm in arm with—a woman?

'He's got a girlfriend,' is Daisy's gleeful conclusion.

'Don't be daft. She can't be more than thirty—half *his* age.'

'Mm. She's carrying a soft toy—he must have won it for her. What does that say to you?'

Somehow, the idea of Mr M firing a rifle at plastic ducks is impossible to visualise—but still more likely than a romantic entanglement with someone our age. (Well, my age.)

As we watch, a youngish man whose eyes are riveted on his iPhone walks straight into Mr M. His female companion shrieks as Mr M staggers and looks about to fall, but iPhone-man reacts quickly and reaches out a steadying hand.

After clapping Mr M's shoulder and delivering a gush of apologies, iPhone-man strides off. Oh well, no harm done. I turn to Daisy and ask: 'Shall we wander over and... where are you going?'

But I'm speaking to Daisy's back as she vanishes into the crowd.

'YOU HERE BY YOURSELF, M'DEAR?' MR M ASKS, LOOKING puzzled.

'No. It was Daisy dragged me along, but she just took off somewhere. She does that—you get used to it. Anyway, are you going to introduce us?'

'Of course, where are my manners? Samantha, this is Kat, my... um, friend. Kat, I think I've mentioned Samantha and Daisy.'

Kat coos. (She really does—I've read about people who "coo", but up until now only ever heard babies and pigeons doing it.) 'Oohh, you're the private detectives? Em's told me *such* a lot about your exploits.'

Em? Who's "Em"?

Kat giggles at my double-take. 'Em said *you* call him "Mr M" and he is awful like James Bond's boss—don't you think?—so I call him "Em".'

Kat must have missed Judi Dench's stint as "M"

'And have you known each other long?'

Okay, I'm being nosy

She simpers. (This woman has all the "cliché" sound effects down to a T.) 'Must be a couple of months now. Wouldn't you say, Em?'

'Around that,' Mr M replies—quite primly.

Then his expression melts into relief (at an easy opportunity to change the subject?) and he points. 'Here comes Daisy.'

Daisy trots up with a big, soppy grin on her face. 'What have you been up to?' I ask—suspiciously.

'Nothing. Hi, I'm Daisy. You and Mr M together, then?'

Did I mention subtlety isn't one of her strengths?

Kat snickers and flaps her fingers. 'What do you think, Em—are we "together"?'

Mr M's blushing redder than a brake light and, uncharacteristically, struggling to find words when Daisy takes pity on him. 'Mr M, got a new client for you. Can I have a business card to pass on?'

'Of course, m'dear.' Mr M reaches inside his jacket, then freezes. He pats the side pockets, looking more confused by the moment. Confusion gives way to astonishment when Daisy bursts out laughing and hands him his wallet.

'Where did you get that?' he asks weakly, holding up the wallet in disbelief.

'The bloke that walked into you—he lifted it. Very professionally done, I have to say… you need to be more careful, Mr M. Don't you know fairgrounds are a favourite hunting ground for pickpockets?'

'But… how did you retrieve it? Um… and is the chap all right?'

Daisy has a black belt in judo and sometimes carries a taser, hence Mr M's concern for the welfare of his pickpocket. He's also likely doing a mental reshuffle of tomorrow's calendar in case she needs his representation in court—after the body turns up.

Daisy looks smug. 'Oh, he's fine. I lifted it back, see? Pulled the same trick on him. Eyes glued to phone, wham... apologies, brush down the mark, then offski.'

'Where did you learn to do that?' is my first thought, and her ears turn pink.

'Well, it's a useful skill to have so I did this course...'

'Course? Where do you go for a course in pickpocketing—Perth Prison?'

'Naw, it was online—right enough, the bloke running the course *has* got some form, but you expect that.'

Online?

'You've been on that dark web again—haven't you?'

She looks at her feet. 'Well, there weren't any ads for pickpocketing courses in the Donstable Courier...'

I exhale in exasperation. 'Daisy believes in fighting fire with fire,' I explain to Mr M and Kat. 'One of these days, she's going to get herself in real trouble—there are contract killers and all sorts on that dark web.'

Mr M shakes his head. 'I can't approve your methods either,' he says sternly. 'But I am very grateful, nonetheless. All my personal ID and credit cards are in this wallet and replacing them would be a nightmare—not to mention, this being a cash venue, I'm carrying more than usual.'

His polished expression splits into a rare beam. 'I've discovered myself to be rather handy with a rifle—can I get you a soft toy?'

Daisy winks at him. 'I was thinking more a round of candy floss.'

MR M AND KAT DISAPPEAR TOWARDS THE CAR PARK—I THINK Mr M has had enough excitement for one night. While we ate our candy floss, (which, as anyone who knows Mr M will appreciate, was a sight to behold) he was careful to focus on harmless subjects like the upcoming church flower show, deftly deflecting any attempts to probe into Kat's raison d'être.

'Enough excitement for one night?' Daisy echoes with a sly look when I repeat the thought out loud. 'You don't know what Kat has planned for him.'

My almost reaction is a "two fingers down the throat" mime, which reminds me of somebody else doing that. Lena—otherwise known as the Bus Stop Killer.

After the inevitable shudder, I pull a face instead. 'Didn't you think he seemed a tad—overwhelmed? I think the poor guy's out of his depth.'

'Hm... I wonder how they met. If it was through a dating app, well—you get a lot of predators on those sites. I might do a little checking up on this "Kat" when we get home.'

I have to laugh. 'Daisy, you know nothing about her—where the heck would you even start with running a background check?'

'Want to put money on it?' she challenges.

'Okay—twenty quid says you won't get past first base. C'mon, Daisy. All you have is her Christian name—on second thoughts, even that's probably a nickname—and the fact she's going out with Mr M.'

Daisy smirks. 'You're on. Now, you said something about the waltzers?'

'Nah, let's just go find Paul. I'm dying to meet him.'

I have to suppress a grin as she colours. Paul is Daisy's new boyfriend—only the second I've known her have. Truth be told, getting a look at Paul is the reason I let her talk me into coming tonight. But now it's Daisy who grins. 'Okay, follow me. As it happens, Paul's working the waltzers tonight—so I can guarantee you extra spins.'

Outflanked *and* outmanoeuvred, I put on a spurt and catch her up. 'How did you two meet, anyway?'

'It was the fair's first night—I came with Rebecca. She was feeling down because Alan's tied up in Edinburgh and I took pity on her. Anyway, Alan notwithstanding, it was Rebecca who started flirting with Paul—but turned out the guy had more sense, so him and me ended up going for a drink.'

'What happened to Rebecca?'

'No idea—she must have gone home.'

Bet she's grateful you "took pity on her"

'You already said Paul's the fairground owner's son. 'Does he have any brothers or sisters?'

'A sister—Tina. Bit of friction there because it seems carnival folk work things the same as farmers when it comes to succession—meaning Paul's going to inherit the fairground, leaving Tina with zilch. The ironic part being she has degrees in marketing and accountancy, and it sounds like she turned the business around a couple of years ago.'

'That doesn't sound very fair.'

'Too right—it's old-time misogynistic culture at its best. Not my problem, though—they'll be moving on soon.'

I feel a burst of despair for my friend. 'Daisy, you're doing it again. First Terry—the mummy's boy—and now a travelling fairground man. What is this issue you have with commitment?'

She steals a glance at my left hand. 'You can talk—set a date for the wedding yet, have we?'

'That's completely different—there's a lot to consider before Davy and I finalise things. Difference is, neither of us are going anywhere. Unlike Paul.'

Before Daisy gets a response out (her expression making it plain one was on its way) a commotion breaks out all around. Even over the frenzied, banshee-wailing atmosphere of a normal night at the fair, it's obvious something's changed. A suddenly urgent tone replaces excited chatter as comfortable ambling gives way to agitated movement.

Daisy points. 'Look, there's Wilson. Something's happened.'

I try to keep up (not easy because my left leg's a prosthetic from the knee down) when she takes off towards Inspector Wilson of Donstable CID. He's marching purposefully, flanked by his usual Stepford sergeant and two uniformed constables. Whatever's going on is more serious than someone caught cheating at hoopla.

'Oh—it's you,' Wilson acknowledges with a sidelong glance when Daisy attaches herself to his side. 'Listen—this is police business. Go away.'

An exceptionally brave constable grabs Daisy's arm and holds her back while Wilson's entourage tries to repeat Moses' Red Sea trick on an increasingly anxious crowd. I can imagine the conflict raging in Daisy's head—if that constable did but know it, the only reason he's still standing is because some part of her acknowledges the poor beggar's only following orders.

Still—I'd say it was a close call.

Then she shrugs herself free and yells: 'Paul.'

A lanky, denim-clad youth wearing specs that are totally the wrong shape for his face (am I the only one who knows how to dispense specs? I don't even do it anymore) stops in his tracks. 'Daisy—did the police tell you what's happened?'

'Nope—I tried to ask, but they were having none of it.'

Paul grits his teeth. 'The word flying around is somebody's been shot—dead. Listen, I need to go...'

Paul takes off at a run, leaving Daisy and I with our mouths hanging open.

I jump when an elbow lands between my ribs. 'Sam—what're you waiting for? There's been a murder—let's go.'

2

Somebody's been shot?

I was resigned to the fact fairgrounds are wild places, but wasn't expecting *that*. Predictably, my nose-ringed little friend is in clover and desperate to get in on the action—unlike me, who just wants to go home by the shortest possible route.

It's obvious, from the locus of police hi-vis jackets, where the "incident" took place—and equally plain we won't be allowed anywhere near.

The music stops, lights start going out, and before long we're in the fairground equivalent of a ghost town—except for ongoing activity at the far end, around the fair folk's caravans. Eventually, even Daisy accepts it's futile trying to gatecrash this particular party, so we make our way to the car park (and my Fiat Panda) where a gaggle of disappointed thrill-seekers seem intent on exiting all at the same time. 'What's *he* doing?' I wonder aloud.

Daisy squints out the window at a hi-vis-jacketed pensioner checking everyone's registration number as they go past. 'He's making sure we've paid.'

'I wasn't expecting organised car parking out here.'

'You wouldn't—but old Struthers never misses the chance to make a few bob, and this is his field.'

'Ah, that explains it.' (Old Struthers makes Del Boy look like a philanthropist.)

Back at the cottage we share, Daisy grabs a can of beer from the fridge and pops its top. 'Want one?'

My sights are fixed firmly on the vodka bottle, but I ask her to bring through some ice. Comfortably ensconced on the sofa with our drinks, Daisy starts to speculate. 'D'you think it was a terrorist incident?'

'In Cairncroft? Get real, Daisy.'

'Hmpf... well what, then? Armed robbery?'

'I'm sure there are juicier targets than a fairground—mind you, there was a lot of cash changing hands. Look, just hold your horses until we get some proper information—I'm assuming there's nothing back from all those texts you sent Paul?'

'Nope—not yet. Whatever's going on must be keeping him busy.'

She takes out her phone and paws at its screen—probably checking the news channels to see if they shed any light. Which suits me fine—after an hour of having my eardrums assaulted by over-amplified pop music and hooters, not to mention what the rides Daisy *did* talk me into have done to my blood pressure, nestling on a comfortable sofa in total silence is sheer bliss.

The restorative calm lasts a full five minutes before Daisy shouts: 'Got her! That's twenty quid you owe me.'

Sighing, I get up and make myself a second drink. 'Are you talking about Kat? Have you actually found her? How?'

She's nodding happily. 'Yep, wasn't so hard. Used Google image search—took a candid snap on my phone, you see—and here she is, at a Law Society dinner in London. Kat—Katherine Dewhurst—is a solicitor down there, and a merry widow to boot. She's lost two husbands in the last five years.'

'That was careless of her. Daisy, if Mr M wants to keep Kat private, maybe we should respect that.'

'But you saw him, Sam. He wasn't acting himself. I'm guessing she's latched onto him somehow, maybe at a law conference, and he's too much of a gentleman to give her the push. We need to have a wee chat and find out exactly what's going on.'

He'll love that

Still... She's right, he did look—discomfited is the sort of word *he'd* use—and after all he's done for us, I couldn't see him in a sticky situation and not try to help. 'Okay. I'm sure we can think of an excuse to talk to him and...'

I'm interrupted by the front door bell (well, actually a rendition of Rossini's "William Tell Overture" but that's something of a sore point between Daisy and me) and Daisy leaps to her feet.

A moment later, she leads Paul in. He looks terrible—specs askew, mussed hair, and if his face were any redder it'd be on fire—but there again, I don't know how Paul normally looks. Probably safe to say nothing like this, though.

Daisy seats him in an armchair and fetches another two cans of beer, one of which Paul accepts gratefully. He takes a long draught and swirls it behind blown out cheeks while Daisy vibrates on the sofa next to me. 'C'mon, Paul—give. What's going on?'

Paul's bleary eyes take a moment to meet ours. 'There *was* a shooting—somebody shot my dad. He's dead.'

His voice breaks, and even Daisy freezes into immobility. Then: 'But how—why?'

Paul suddenly remembers I'm here. 'Oh, nice to meet you, Sam. Wish it weren't under these circumstances. Yeah, um—Dad must have surprised intruders in his caravan, because Eric from the darts stall came looking for change at around nine o'clock and found him lying on the floor. Dad had two heart attacks last year, so Eric assumed this was a third—until he saw the bullet hole.'

Paul tries to stifle a sob. 'Ironically, the bullet went straight through Dad's heart. The police said he would have died instantly.'

Daisy goes over and slips an arm around Paul's shoulders. 'I'm *so* sorry, luv. Have the police any idea who...?'

'No, they don't—but I do. That's why I'm here. Daisy, I need your help.'

DAISY COMES BACK TO THE SOFA WHILE PAUL TELLS US what's happened. 'Tina's been kidnapped?' she repeats in disbelief.

Paul nods sombrely. 'Yeah, when I went back to my caravan there was a note pushed under the door. Said they want a hundred grand, or I'll start getting body parts through the post. And they threatened to do away with Tina if I involve the police. Dad must have tried to stop them from snatching her—so they shot him. Which proves they aren't bluffing.'

'Did they say how you're to deliver the ransom?' I ask.

'Not yet. Their note says I've to get the money ready and wait to hear from them.'

Daisy frowns. 'Do you *have* a hundred grand?'

Paul throws out his arms. '*I* haven't got that kind of money—but I've no idea what cash reserves or credit lines the fairground has. With

Dad gone, the business passes to me. What I don't know is how soon the bank will let me access its funds.'

'And the police are unaware of all this?' I confirm.

He nods—so hard, his hair flies forward. 'Yes, they are—and it has to stay that way. I won't risk Tina's safety by involving the rozzers. I'll get the money somehow, but what if I pay them—then the kidnappers don't give Tina back? That's where you come in. I need some backup—like knowing your detective agency is looking for Tina, while I see about raising the ransom in case you can't find her. Will you do that? Please...'

Daisy and I exchange a glance—I shake my head. 'For a start, there's only two of us. The police would put an entire task force on this...'

'Yes, but that's the problem. The more people involved, the likelier word will leak out that I've gone to the police—which the kidnappers warned me not to. A ton of coppers from Aberdeen descending on Donstable will be obvious to anyone. They'd only have to look in the car park behind the police station—it'd be packed tighter than a sardine can. You and Daisy, on the other hand, can cover your tracks—the kidnappers won't know you're looking for them.'

Daisy grimaces. 'I'm pretty sure it'd be illegal if we took this on, Paul—obstruction or something. And I couldn't live with myself if anything happened to Tina because you were relying on us instead of the police.'

'Look,' he says, eyes wild now. 'I am NOT going to the police—with or without you. In fact, if you don't help me, Tina's chances are a lot worse because then it'll all be down to me finding a hundred grand and the kidnappers keeping their word about returning her.'

Daisy sighs. 'Oh, if you put it like that—I'll *have* to help. But I can't ask Sam to get involved...'

It's Hobson's choice—for both of us.

I give her shoulder a squeeze. 'Don't worry, you aren't asking—I'm offering.'

3

Next morning, I awaken to the smell of bacon frying.

Which is puzzling because, awhile back, my erstwhile housemate conned me into an agreement whereby I cook breakfast—every day—in return for Daisy clearing up after. I'm still not quite sure how she managed that...

My eyes are scratchy from sleep. Rapid blinking clears the haze sufficiently to spot my prosthetic leg in a far corner where it landed last night. Sometimes, I lose the heid with it.

After playing hopscotch across the room and back, I have to wait out an enormous yawn before strapping on the peg-leg. Last night, we were up until the wee small hours rehashing our decision to help Paul.

Of course, the longer you worry at a problem, the more circular its arguments become and my best recollection is of finally concluding we're stuck with this—even though it's likely to backfire on us.

That is *definitely* bacon I'm smelling...

In the kitchen, my eyes confirm what their neighbour down under's been saying. 'Daisy, am I dreaming or what...?'

'Ha. Ha. Oh, couldn't sleep. This was just something to do...'

Good grief—she's even made bread (In the bread maker)

'You should get insomnia more often,' I comment, ripping off a piece of French baton and spooning scrambled eggs on it.

Daisy tuts. 'What?' I mutter, chewing. (We all have our quirks, and scrambled egg butties are one of mine.)

'Anyway...' I go on, settling myself in front of a loaded plate '... got any new and brilliant insights into our latest case?'

Daisy slumps opposite and lifts a fork, then starts moving her breakfast around. 'Only that I'd rather not be within a million miles of it—but what can we do? Like Paul said, if we don't help him, Tina's chances go even further down the toilet.'

'Mm. We went over all this last night. There's no question we *have* to get involved, despite all the reasons against it. All the same, let's keep trying to change Paul's mind about bringing in the police.'

She shakes her head. 'Stubborn beggar's rock solid on that—and I see why. The kidnappers thought nothing of shooting his dad. From the sound of it, that was a carefully placed kill-shot.'

'Did you meet Paul's dad? And what about his mum? Nobody's said anything about her,' I suddenly realise.

Daisy's only been going out with Paul for a few days, but they seem to have fallen head over heels for each other. Which is worrying because, being a fairground worker, Paul could be hundreds of miles away this time next week.

Typically, of course, Daisy's leaving the worrying to me. Her own attitude can be summed up by: "When Paul's gone, he's gone."

Unquote.

But I wonder if she'll find it so easy when the crunch comes…?

'Paul's mum died years ago. I only ran into his dad once, and then briefly. He was nice enough, but a bit old school—couldn't really have a laugh with him.'

'What about Tina?'

'Yeah, she was there the day I saw his dad. The atmosphere between Tina and the old man was lethal—maybe that's why he came across so staid. I told you his dad was leaving the fairground to Paul?'

'You did—has that all blown up recently, then?'

'Uhuh. Paul says Tina assumed the old tradition was defunct—until she mentioned it to the old man and he set her straight. I see Tina's point—she was some kind of high-powered marketing consultant and gave it all up to rescue the family business. Two years on, the poor lass discovers she's getting zip for her efforts.'

Something's been puzzling me, but I didn't want to go into it while Paul was here. 'I gathered Tina's married, but neither of you seem in a hurry to tell her husband what's happening?'

Daisy grimaces. 'His name's Ivor—Ivor Patterson. According to Paul, the guy's a total waster. His permanent daytime address is the nearest pub, and Paul suspects he knocks Tina around. Oh, and Ivor's also got something of a reputation with the ladies—although, according to Paul, "ladies" might be too grand a term for the skanks he hangs about with.'

'Sounds a right charmer. But surely Paul *has* to bring him in at some point?'

Daisy laughs mirthlessly. 'To hear Paul talk, you wouldn't discount the possibility of Ivor being *behind* Tina's kidnap.'

'Seriously?'

'Naw, Ivor's too small time for that. But he has been mixed up in some shady business—small-time drug peddling, burglary—though nothing's ever been proved. I met him just briefly, and it was pretty obvious he's a poser and little else.'

Pushing back my clean plate, I rip off another piece of bread. 'Okay, maybe Ivor's best left out of it. So—we're doing this. That's decided. Next question is how? What's the plan?'

She gets up and tips half her breakfast in the pedal bin—for Daisy, a red flag in the "being rattled" stakes. 'I've been thinking about that—how d'you get a handle on phantoms? Which is what these kidnappers are—we know nothing about them. All we *do* know is they shot Paul's dad and snatched Tina, then took her away somewhere. I vote we look at the "took her away somewhere" first—if we could get a lead on the vehicle they used, that'd be a start.'

'But how? We don't have access to traffic cameras—even if there were any around here. Plus, they took Tina from the middle of nowhere—meaning no shops or houses that might have caught them on security cameras.'

'I've had two thoughts—one is the parking attendant. Remember, last night, we had to park in an adjacent field and pay for the privilege? That bloke strutting about in a yellow jacket checked our number on the way out to see we hadn't gone into extra time—so he must have had it noted down. Hopefully, the kidnappers' vehicle is on his list'

'That's a good thought—I'll give Struthers a ring. He's in Mr Entwhistle's snooker club, so I know him vaguely. You said two thoughts?'

'Yeah, my second leads from the first. Everybody's got dashcams in their cars these days...' she screws up her face '... well, everybody except you. Anyway, using Struther's records, we can find people who were there last night and get a look at their dashcam footage. Maybe...'

'How will you locate them, if all you've got is their car numberplates?'

She taps her nose, forgetting about the nose ring. 'Ooh, that tickles... all a matter of having the right connections, Sam. But first, we'd better pop into the detective agency and clear everything outstanding to let us work full out on this. Luckily, we haven't much on—Rebecca can handle what there is.'

I feel a grin form. 'Bet you're glad now about giving Rebecca a chance—she seems to get more indispensable all the time.'

Daisy decides to ignore that. 'Let's drop off at the hotel on our way and have a quick catch-up with Jodie.'

'Hah. Any excuse to play with that baby, eh?'

She smiles a soft smile—something you don't often see. 'That's a bonus, but I also want to find out what Mr M's goddaughter can tell us about his new squeeze.'

4

'She's growing like a weed.'

Jodie squints at Daisy. 'I think there might be a better way of putting that. "Getting bigger" would do or, if you insist on being flowery, how about "blossoming"?'

Baby Alanna's lying on the sofa in a nest of cushions, with Daisy knelt beside her waving a furry rabbit around tiny, grasping fingers. My working theory is extra-terrestrials have beamed up the real Daisy and replaced her with this watered-down version.

Jodie catches my eye, lips twitching—she thinks so, too.

We've dropped into Jodie and Logan's flat on the hotel's top floor en route to the detective agency. Logan, my co-owner, is downstairs somewhere and it appears Jodie's still on maternity leave from Donstable CID. 'When *are* you going back, Jodie?'

She pouts. 'Monday—two days from now. Oh, don't get me wrong—I'm chomping at the bit, but a big part of me dreads leaving her. Caron's got an amazing résumé though, so at least I know Alanna's in capable hands.'

Daisy glances over her shoulder. 'Who's Caron?'

'My new live-in nanny—didn't Sam tell you about her?'

I snort. 'She's not been around to tell anything to since meeting Paul.' Which, of course, turns our conversation to the shooting.

Predictably, Jodie already knows about it. 'Doesn't make sense,' she muses. 'Armed robbers targeting a fairground—nope, not buying that. *Must* be more to it.'

My stomach clenches and I notice Daisy's mouth tighten—while hoping Jodie doesn't.

Luckily, it seems she didn't—or, if she did, is way off base on why. 'Sorry Daisy, but let's face it—you haven't known Paul very long. I reckon his dad was involved in something heavy, and this is the result. What happened last night smells more of a "hit" than opportunist thievery.'

We need to be careful around Jodie until Tina's kidnap is resolved—she's a dear friend and not above bending the law for the right reasons, but I'm pretty sure if Jodie got a sniff of what's really going on she'd (with the best intentions) rat us out to CID.

Daisy's face is pure innocence. 'As you said, I haven't known them very long. But I can't believe Paul would be mixed up in anything unsavoury.'

Jodie frowns. 'You only met him last week, though. Daisy love, are you sure this thing with Paul isn't going too fast? Don't take it the wrong way,' she adds hastily. 'I'm just worried that after being single so long, you're confusing relationship-building with bungee jumping.'

Daisy shrugs. 'Naw, I see where you're coming from—been getting the same from Sam. But Paul's only here for another week, and we clicked, so... live in the moment is what I say. Anyway, we didn't come to talk about me.'

Alanna screeches angrily and Daisy demonstrates an instinctive understanding of baby psychology by tickling her tummy.

Alanna responds with a happy gurgle.

'If Caron quits and you get tired playing detective, there'll be a job here for you,' Jodie observes drily. 'Yeah, okay—this Kat person. Nope, never heard of her and he hasn't said anything to me.'

'We thought Mr M looked jumpy,' I offer.

Jodie laughs. 'If she *is* pursuing him romantically, he'll be more than jumpy—no, I think you've got the wrong end of the stick. Mac was devoted to Alanna and I can't see him ever accepting a substitute.'

Jodie and Logan named baby Alanna after Mr M's late wife, Jodie's godmother. 'How long is it since his wife died?' I ask.

'Getting on ten years—so okay, it wouldn't be *that* surprising if he found someone new to share his old age with. But you know my godfather—he'd want somebody just like him. Taking up with the sort of lassie you're describing isn't Mac at all.'

Daisy nods. 'That's what we thought—I'm worried she's forcing herself on him and he's too polite to give her the boot.'

Jodie laughs. 'He comes over all mild-mannered—which he is—but Mac's a successful solicitor. He hasn't any problem with plain speaking when it's needed. No, there'll be an innocent explanation—tell you what, I'll drop in on him this afternoon and find out what it is, then get back to you.'

'Cheers, Jodie.'

I feel better hearing that—Mr M's such a lovely person, I couldn't stand to think of anyone giving him grief. 'Right, Alanna,' I announce. 'Sorry, but I'm taking your playmate away now...'

THE DETECTIVE AGENCY IS SITED IN SPACIOUS GROUNDS behind the hotel; back in olden days, it was a stable block. A few months ago, Graham—our hotel gardener—laid a track from the hotel so detective agency clients can bring their cars right up. Daisy and I only live five minutes down the road, so we walked over today—leaving Rebecca's Audi sole occupancy of our makeshift parking area.

I originally had the paved courtyard earmarked for an all-weather tennis court, where I planned to give pro-tennis lessons while Daisy taught judo and yoga in the old stables. Then an "all bells and whistles" health club opened in Donstable and (to Daisy's delight) we ended up with a detective agency—now, complementing Graham's efforts, the courtyard's become a car park.

Rebecca's nominally our receptionist, but recently she's been getting more involved in the detective side—to the extent we helped her buy the Audi so she could take on surveillance work. At the rate Rebeccca's role is growing, I think we'll soon be looking for a new receptionist.

I go in first and Hector, the office cat (really Rebecca's now), greets me with a warm purr. When he sees Daisy, Hector spits angrily before burying his head in two fluffy paws.

It's an improvement—he used to swipe his claws at her, then leave the room.

Daisy calls Rebecca through for a confab on the technicalities of clearing our calendars so we're free to help Paul. In Daisy's office, Rebecca sits in front of the desk and I take my usual chair to one side. I have to smile when Rebecca pulls modestly at the brightly coloured bandanna she mistook for a skirt this morning.

Just, please—DON'T cross your legs

'So,' Daisy finishes, 'It's really only pretend-clients—the hotel's murder mystery guests—you'll have to cover. There's nothing else pressing—and this *thing* Sam and me are doing should get wrapped up fairly quick. One way or the other.'

'Big case, is it?' Rebecca probes, eyes sparkling, obviously desperate to muscle in on whatever it is.

'Favour for a friend,' Daisy replies flatly, and Rebecca takes the hint.

'You don't have to worry—I can deal with anything that arises. Oh, I'd better tell you though—somebody phoned this morning about a new missing person case.'

Daisy smacks the desk. 'That's all we need. What're the details?'

'Um… woman says her husband went out last night and didn't come home. Isn't answering his phone, either. The police did their usual checks—hospitals, traffic accidents, etcetera—and came up blank. She reckons they lost interest then.'

'Most missing persons turn up within 48 hours,' I explain. 'So CID won't review it sooner unless they classify the person as high risk—an old dear who went out wearing thin clothing in winter, for example.'

Daisy claps her hands. 'Spot on. You been reading my textbooks again?'

I feel my cheeks glow. 'Well, I keep getting drawn deeper into this, so it seems only sensible to try and make myself competent.'

Rebecca's eyes pop. 'Textbooks? There are textbooks? Can I borrow some?'

Rolling her eyes, Daisy turns back to Rebecca. 'I'll look something out for you—anyway, other side of the coin with missing person cases is the first 24 hours can be crucial in tracking them. Here's what we'll do. Sam and I will go have a quick word with the client—leaving you to handle last night's murder mystery punters on your own?'

Rebecca nods happily.

'Okay, then we'll refer this woman to an agency in Aberdeen if urgent action's warranted. Otherwise, we'll take her case and leave you a blueprint for getting started while Sam and I get on with… the *thing*.'

Rebecca shrieks. 'My own case. Oh, wonderful. I can't wait.'

Smiling, I remind her: 'You'll only get the case if we judge it routine—and likely end up with a lot of boring drudgery. Checking with known contacts, scouring social media—stuff like that.'

'Doesn't matter—it's real detective work.'

The front bell jangles and Rebecca returns to her post, humming a merry tune, to rescue the first hotel guest stumped by last night's murder mystery. 'She's keen—you have to give her that.'

Daisy "harrumph"s—then looks thoughtful. 'I've just thought of a whole new strategy for finding mislaid men. If we put Rebecca's picture in the paper with a footnote saying she's looking for them, that'll bring any red-blooded male running before you can say "missing person".'

5

Liam and Keisha (yes, *really*) Simpson live in the bad end of Donstable, not far from what was Jack the Sack's scrapyard. Since being seized along with all his other assets (excluding a rottweiler Daisy palmed off on Graham the gardener), Jack's former corporate HQ is being redeveloped into a community centre. The Councillor behind this initiative has the very best of intentions—he reckons "giving" to this deprived area will inspire its predominantly criminal population to consider becoming productive members of society.

Unfortunately, the builders are well behind schedule because the locals keep nicking their building materials.

Liam and Keisha (I'm now managing to say their names with a straight face) live in a grim council terrace whose front gardens contain an abundance of "objets d'intérêt" —such as smashed up furniture, one-wheeled bikes, and black bin bags with gaping holes that exude worryingly gooey substances.

Pulling up at the kerb, I turn a dubious eye to Daisy. 'Think it's safe to leave the car here?'

She makes a face. 'Not really.'

Then hops out and puts two fingers to the corners of her mouth. The resultant whistle would make a locomotive puff with envy.

I join her on the pavement and experience a stab of panic when three teenage males detach themselves from their street corner and sidle towards us. Their jeans hang so low the "sidle" is more of a "waddle"—and they're wearing T-shirts emblazoned with witticisms I will *not* repeat here. Their leader (presumably) inquires as to the nature of Daisy's peremptory summons.

'Wotcha want?'

Daisy produces a ten-pound note and waves it. 'See that car—if it's still intact when we come out, I'll give you another of these.'

The youth swipes her tenner and shoves it in a jeans pocket—happily without exposing any more of his boxers. 'Twenty when you come back,' he mutters.

Daisy shrugs. 'Fifteen—final offer.'

He turns to his compatriots, then—seeming to decide consulting them's a pointless exercise—swings back to Daisy. 'A'right—ten minutes tops, though.'

Daisy scowls, obviously not expecting that. Her brows furrow as she calculates. 'Tell you what—*fifteen* minutes and, if we're longer, I'll pay a penalty of one pound per minute. Okay?'

That gets a frown while he mulls it over—reminds me of my laptop when I open too many windows—before nodding. 'Fair 'nough.'

Business concluded, the three stooges return to their street corner and Daisy winks. 'Bit dearer than the multi-storeys in town—but probably safer.'

When we ring the doorbell, a cacophony of barking breaks out. Nervously, I mutter: 'Sounds a big dog.'

Daisy ignores me—dogs don't worry her. Cats are a different story, but dogs—no problem. When the door flies open something small and furry rushes out and leaps around us, snarling and baring tiny teeth. Daisy looks down in amazement. 'It's a hamster,' she chuckles.

No. Definitely a dog, and notwithstanding their size those teeth look sharp, but—it is small. Very small—I wouldn't like to guess at what went into its breeding. Possible influences are Shih Tzu, rat, and toilet brush...

'Wotcha want?'

Daisy peers at the cardiganed woman staring daggers at us. Then points to the street corner and our "parking attendants". 'You related to them?'

Cardiganed-woman follows Daisy's finger. 'Them's my nephews—how'd you know?'

'I'm psychic. Are you Keisha Simpson?'

The woman's expression turns wary. 'Who's asking?'

Sighing, Daisy pulls out a leather wallet and flashes it at her. 'Cairncroft Detective Agency—you rang earlier.'

Keisha (if it is Keisha) squints. 'That's a bus pass.'

Daisy looks for herself. 'So it is—ten out of ten for observation. Alright—will a business card do?'

After examining the card I hand her, the woman (who obviously *is* Keisha) says: 'Fine. C'mon in.'

We follow her into a surprisingly well decorated and furnished house. The lounge features an "L" shaped couch unit that wouldn't be out of place in a DFS showroom a carpet so springy I feel like Neil Armstrong taking his first stroll on the moon. The wallpaper's vintage Laura Ashley and every paintable surface has been rendered resplendent by several coats of Farrow & Ball emulsion. (After refurbishing the hotel and putting my stamp on our cottage, I know about these things.)

It's a few moments before Keisha joins us—from her loud, running commentary it seems the feral Tibetan toilet brush is being shut in the kitchen.

'Sit down,' Keisha says when she returns, plonking herself at one end of the sofa unit. Two little boys playing with action figures on the floor are summarily instructed: 'OUT.'

For a moment, I panic—a sudden onset of double vision can be due to all sorts of things, some of them serious. (I used to be an optician.)

The boys are mirror images of each other, and also dressed identically—the only difference between them is one has a squint in his right eye, the other in the left. (Right and left convergent strabismus respectively—but I'm showing off now.)

With loud huffs, the boys (who must be about eight years old) gather their respective superhero dolls and slouch out of the room. I nod after them. 'Twins?'

'Aye—double trouble.' For the first time, a smile splits Keisha's face. She's about my age, and on closer inspection the cardigan is cashmere. Her voice has softened since we sat down, losing its rough, brusque edge, and it occurs to me the "washerwoman" persona is probably a necessary survival mechanism in these parts.

'Nice,' Daisy comments, looking around.

'Aye, well.' Keisha smiles again, which takes years off her. 'It was mostly bought on the never-never—but since Jack the Sack got put away, I've been able to enjoy it properly. Real bargain my makeover turned out—only had to make two payments. That's why I phoned youse—it *was* you sent Jack and Tiny to the slammer, weren't it? So you must be good.'

Hearing those names spoken out loud sends a shiver through me—the day Jack and Tiny were sentenced, I almost wept with relief. Daisy has a nasty habit of antagonising people, but they don't usually invade our home with the intention of dismembering us. Coughing to clear my throat, I ask: 'I believe your husband has gone missing?'

Keisha's face contorts and she practically spits the name. 'Liam. Yeah, last night 'e went out in 'is car and didn't come back. I thought 'e wasn't answerin' 'is phone either, then one of the kids found it in the kitchen.'

'You must be terribly worried.'

The bark of laughter takes me by surprise. 'Worried? Well, I am—but not about 'im. I'm worried 'cos the leccy's coming due, then there's the rent next month, not t'mention feedin' 'is sons.'

Daisy cocks her head. 'I'm getting the impression you don't reckon Liam's missing-missing? You think he's run off?'

'No "think" about it, darlin'. Liam's been playin' around since ten minutes after we got wed—that was with one of the bridesmaids—but 'e never took off with a floozy before. I only put up with 'im 'cos I need 'is wages—if Liam wants to shack up with one of 'is Jezebels, she's welcome to 'im so long as 'e sends me a cheque every month.'

This has got to be our weirdest missing person case yet. 'So, let me try to sum this up—tell me if I get anything wrong. Liam didn't come home last night, the police have already checked he hasn't been in an accident, and you've good reason to believe he's taken off with a... girlfriend... and want him found so he can be compelled to support his family.'

Keisha nods. 'Got it in one, darlin'.'

I feel embarrassed about having to ask, and am truly relieved when Daisy does it for me—with both feet, as usual. 'You able to pay us? Because we don't work for free.'

'How much?' Keisha responds, suspiciously, and Daisy hands her a fee schedule.

Keisha pulls a battered pair of specs from her cardigan pocket and peers at the card for a long minute.

She looks up with her lips drawn tight. 'I could manage three hundred for this "retainer" thing. But when that's gone, I'm dry.'

'Will it leave you enough for the, um, "leccy"?' I ask, trying not to sound patronising. (And probably failing.)

'That *is* the leccy money,' she says quietly. 'I'm lookin' on this like an investment—'cos what's the point in payin' the next bill if I can't manage any after that?'

I look at Daisy—she stares back, then mouths: *'Oh, blow it.'* To Keisha, she announces: 'Look, give us a hundred and we'll see how far that stretches. It might be possible to put the balance off until Liam starts forking out support.'

Big softy

If *I'd* come out with that, she'd be raging. I'm glad she did, though. Keisha might have a nice living room, but it's obvious her life isn't easy—and that she's doing her best for those kids. Keisha accepts Daisy's terms gratefully, then fetches one hundred pounds in crumpled notes from a hideaway in some other part of the house.

Daisy gets her notebook out. 'Tell me about Liam—where he works, who his friends are, family—oh, and his car registration number. We'll need a photo, too.'

Five minutes later (just as our parking fees rise to one pound a minute) we've learnt that Liam does casual labour for several building sites in Aberdeen, drives an ancient Ford Escort, and is an active member of all the major dating sites. 'Can I see his phone?' Daisy asks, and Keisha fetches it.

'Passcode's 'is date of birth,' she informs us wryly. 'Liam uses that for everythin'.'

Daisy glances back at her notes before feeding the numbers in. She fiddles for a minute, then looks up with a puzzled expression. 'He's deleted all his texts, in *and* out.'

Keisha snorts. 'Don't take a genius to work out why, does it?'

'No, but—they wouldn't *all* be floozy-related, surely? I think he left his phone behind so it couldn't be used to track him—and cleared everything off it for the same reason. It seems Liam doesn't want to be found.'

'Course 'e don't—'e knows it'll cost 'im.'

'Do you know his email address?'

Keisha looks puzzled, then shrugs. 'Liam4398@yahoo.com.'

Daisy writes that down, hands back the phone, then stands. 'Okay, somebody'll get back to you if we need anything else—or have any news.'

Back at the Panda, there's no sign of our "parking attendants"—and my wing mirror's swinging from its cables.

Daisy puffs in exasperation. 'They must have found some pensioners to mug.'

'You do realise getting that fixed will eat up most of Keisha's retainer?'

She purses her lips. 'Repairing it *should* go on her final bill, under expenses, but...'

'I know. It's alright—I'll cover it. We'll have to call this one pro bono anyway—she can't afford what it'll end up costing.'

Daisy looks thoughtful. 'We're going to shift the donkey work onto Rebecca, remember? Maybe we can write this off as a training exercise?'

That's actually quite smart

'Something didn't sit right with you about Liam's phone, did it?'

She shakes her head. 'Why's he worried about being traced through his phone? Only the police can find somebody that way. Makes me wonder just what Liam's up to.'

At that moment, Daisy's own phone buzzes and she checks the screen. Her face falls. 'It's Paul—there's been a complication. Think we'd better get over to the fair and hear this first hand.'

6

'The police have arrested Ivor.'

When we got to Paul's caravan, it was to find him pretty worked up—and no wonder. First, someone shoots his father, then he discovers his sister's been kidnapped, and now...

'That's Tina's husband—your brother-in-law?' (I like to be clear on these things.)

Paul nods numbly and Daisy asks the obvious question. '*Why* have the police arrested Ivor?'

'They found the gun that was used to shoot Dad, in Tina and Ivor's caravan—with Ivor's fingerprints all over it.'

I say what seems self-evident. 'Ivor must be behind Tina's kidnapping.'

Paul looks at me as though I'm daft. 'Ivor? He can barely find his way home at night, far less mastermind a kidnap. What I *could* see is him shooting my dad—they weren't exactly on the best of terms and Ivor's got a nasty streak.'

Daisy frowns. 'What's Ivor saying?'

'That the gun was payment for a "job" he did—and his intention was to sell it on.'

'There was no reason for them to search Tina's van—the police don't know she's been kidnapped.' Daisy turns to Paul. 'Have they searched everyone's caravans?'

'No, just Tina and Ivor's.'

'Mm... must have been a tip-off. This smells of a frame-up.'

'You think the kidnappers framed Ivor?' I ask.

'A falling out amongst thieves, you mean? No, not likely—the kidnappers would have to know that when Ivor realised who set him up, he'd return the favour. But he *is* being framed—can you really see Ivor shooting somebody, then tossing the gun in his sock drawer? First thing *anybody* does is get rid of the murder weapon—it's pure instinct.'

She's silent for a moment, then: 'Paul—was Ivor even around last night?'

'Never laid eyes on Ivor the whole evening, now I come to think of it. I went over this morning to tell him what had happened—that was when the police turned up.'

'How did he react to the news about Tina—do you think he was surprised?'

'I didn't get a chance to tell him before the bobbies whisked him away.'

'Oh—good. He won't be blabbing about it to Inspector Wilson, then.'

A horrible thought strikes me. 'Paul, if you're wrong and Ivor *was* behind the kidnapping—on his own—that would mean Tina's locked up somewhere with nobody to bring her food and water.'

Paul pales, but rallies almost immediately. 'No, Ivor's a lackey through and through. He's incapable of planning and executing a kidnap by himself.'

Daisy puts her arm around Paul's shoulders and squeezes, then steps back. 'So that's one less thing to worry about. Let's get back to the matter at hand—have the kidnappers been in touch about delivering the ransom?'

'No. Why are they taking so long—do you think they've done something to Tina? Maybe she tried to escape and they…' What she lacks in stature, Daisy makes up for in volume. 'Paul, STOP IT. You falling apart won't help Tina. My guess is they're ratcheting up the tension to keep you in line. This is exactly what the kidnappers want—you going to pieces and making it easy for them.'

Paul takes a deep breath. 'How does my falling apart make it easier for the kidnappers?'

'Well, for a start, I'm going to suggest you ask for "proof of life" before giving them a penny. That's the sort of thing they want to freak you out of thinking about.'

'What—you think Tina's dead?'

'No, no, no. I don't think that at all. But making them give you proof of life is only sensible—*and* gives Tina a layer of protection. Knowing you could ask for updates at any time means they *can't* get rid of her.'

'Not before they've got their cash,' Paul amends glumly. 'After that...'

'Talking of which—any progress with raising the ransom?' Daisy cuts in.

Paul flops on an armchair and breathes out heavily before answering. 'I spoke to your man MacLachlan and he says it'll be weeks before I can draw money out of the business. But I've found a way around that. A couple of years ago, another fairground owner—Dougie Dobson—was on at Dad to sell him the fair. We were barely turning a profit then, but Dobson's a shrewd operator and wanted to absorb us into his own operation—he's got several fairs and they're doing very nicely, thank you. Dobson offered what the rides would fetch second hand, less the finance on them 'cos he'd have to take that over. Have you any idea what fairground rides cost? No? Well, it's a lot, believe me. Even "used". But that was when Tina stepped in and worked her magic with budgets and marketing.'

He's starting to wander, so I try and bring him back on track. 'Paul, have you struck some kind of deal with this Dobson fellow—is that what you're trying to say?'

He nods, looking sick. 'Yeah. It was Dad he was calling for, so I explained what had happened… then we got talking and, well… he's agreed to front me the money in exchange for a contract stating I'll sell him the fair when I get control of it. For net asset value, less the advance he's giving me.'

'You didn't tell him about Tina…?'

'No, 'course not—said Dad left some debts I had to deal with. Oh, and the advance is 100 grand in cash.'

Daisy throws out her arms. 'But surely that'll leave you with next to nothing.'

Paul shrugs. 'Dobson says he'll give me a job… doesn't matter so long as we get Tina back.'

'Sounds to me like this Dobson's taking advantage,' Daisy growls, but Paul shakes his head.

'There's no other way I can raise the cash.'

Daisy fumes some more, but it's obvious Paul's made up his mind. 'Okay, I guess... right, let us know the moment you hear from Tina's kidnappers. Sam and I are dropping everything so we can concentrate on finding Tina.'

She turns to me. 'We'd better go brief Rebecca on her missing person case.'

Making our way back through the fairground, I have to ask: 'What if Paul's wrong about Ivor, and he is Tina's—only—kidnapper?'

She nods, her expression sombre, and pulls me between two stalls. Once we're around the back of one, its heavy canvas mutes the fairground noise slightly—enough to hear ourselves talk. 'I didn't want to panic Paul more than he already is, but... we can't discount the possibility. Even if it does have Ivor practically convicting himself. He *is* thick, by all accounts—and whoever tipped off the police *could* just have been doing their civic duty. What we need is for the kidnappers to contact Paul about delivering the ransom—now he's banged up, that would prove it isn't Ivor working alone. Question is, how long can we afford to wait—until six, d'you think? That's getting on for a whole day since Tina was taken—surely we'd expect the ransom demand to come in by then?'

I should have known her apparent indifference to the possibility—however remote—of Tina being trapped without food or water was a blind to stop Paul going off the deep end. She was right to play it down—anyone can see Paul's on the verge of cracking up. 'Sounds a good compromise. It's only a few hours—there would still be time for the police to locate her. I'm assuming you mean we'll go to Inspector Wilson if the kidnappers don't get in touch by six?'

'Absolutely. If Ivor *has* magically transformed into a master criminal, Wilson putting the frighteners on might be enough to make him spill where Tina is. If not, the police can start looking for whatever hidey-hole he stashed her in.'

'They could even put out a public appeal to have farmers check their barns, all that sort of thing. Okay, agreed—six, but no longer.'

I hope it isn't *too* long—the thought of that poor helpless girl locked up without food or water makes me shudder. But equally worrying is if we go to the police and Ivor *isn't* the kidnapper—who knows how the real ones will react? What they'll do to Tina…

When I put that last into words, Daisy shakes her head. 'You're crossing bridges we'll never see, Sam. It won't come to that—I'm sure of it.'

Wish I had her confidence

Daisy must see I'm struggling to wrap my head around all this because she punches me lightly on the arm before leading the way back out from our impromptu conference space. 'Look, we can hypothesise until we're blue in the face—but it's more important to stay sharp for whatever comes next. I think we should try and clear our heads. Tell you what, Rebecca can wait—let's take five and go on a ride. What d'you fancy?'

Going straight back to the car

'Um—dunno.'

'Alright, I'll choose—big wheel.'

'Absolutely not—Daisy, you know how I feel about heights.'

She nods, reluctantly. Then points. 'Hey, what about that? Looks just your style.'

I follow her finger to a huge boat swinging languidly from its frame. 'That looks harmless enough.'

'It's called the "Pirate Ship",' Daisy throws over her shoulder as we join a short queue.

Mm. I'm quite looking forward to this. From what I can make out, it's a larger version of those rocking cradles you see in swing parks. Daisy's right—we need a chill out, and this is just the thing.

It's bigger than I'd realised—so tall we have to enter via a stairway. Once on the ride itself, we find its seats arranged in blocks of three on either side of a centre aisle. Since it isn't busy this early in the day, Daisy and I have a row to ourselves. A fairground worker comes around and makes a show of ensuring our lap belts are fastened— reminds me of air hostesses doing similar checks on the (very few) aeroplanes I've flown in. He also swings up a metal rail which locks in front of us— seems kinda overkill for a ride this tame.

Finally, the boat starts swinging—and the feeling is delicious. In fact, having slept fitfully last night, I almost nod off.

Something makes me snap open my eyes—and I blink, disbelievingly, because all I can see is blue sky? Then we swing backwards and my stomach struggles to keep up with the rest of me as I realise something's gone wrong.

A thunderclap of comprehension explodes in my head—when we were approaching it, the beggar must have been powering down.

Now it's threatening to loop the loop. In a full-blown funk, I elbow Daisy.

'Ouch—what're you doing?'

'It doesn't turn upside down—does it?'

'Naw—nowhere near. They don't usually get higher than 75 degrees.'

Seventy-five degrees?

'You besom—you KNEW, didn't you?'

Her smirk is answer enough and my knuckles whiten on the rail in front (now I see why it's needed) even as Daisy thrusts both arms vertically.

'Are you crazy?'

She's not the only one trying to commit suicide—it seems to be some primitive rite of passage, demonstrating one's courage (stupidity) by making a show of not holding on. Well, if she falls out, it'll be her own fault.

Another swing back and this time, on the plunge forward, we keep going—or should that be climbing? I don't care what Daisy says—it's obviously about to turn upside down, at which point the flimsy lap belt will snap and I'll be left dangling by my fingertips from the safety rail.

At the last possible moment, and with a shudder that makes me worry about its structural integrity, the Pirate Ship stops dead. The problem now is one of physics—because suddenly I'm weightless. My bottom is floating up out of the seat. Halfway through my terrified scream we plunge into reverse and the gravitational pull inverts—not only am I back in my seat, it feels like I'm going to burst right through it.

Mid-swing, I wrench at my lap belt—seized by a sudden need to know it's secure.

Yep, still tight. Better check Daisy's.

'Sam, gerroff. What're you doing?'

'Making sure your safety belt's on properly.'

'The guy checked that...'

'Yes, well, I'm re-checking... Aahhh.'

Okay—that had to be the highest it goes. Seventy-five degrees—sounds right, so it should start slowing now.

No—it's going higher still. Daisy squeezes my arm. 'Get a grip, Sam.'

'Daisy, I assure you, I am gripping onto anything and everything...'

Finally, an eternity later, our swinging torture chamber slows and I'm treated to about thirty seconds of the sedate rocking I signed up for. When we (blessedly) come to a stop, Daisy reaches over and unclips my belt. 'Cool, huh?'

Tonight, while she's fast asleep and snoring, I am going to sneak into Daisy's room and dribble cayenne pepper under her nostrils...

WE DECIDE LUNCH AT THE HOTEL IS CALLED FOR, IN THE spirit of not sitting around brooding. Not to mention I need sustenance after my ordeal on board "The Pirate Ship".

Daisy surprises me by including Rebecca. 'I've decided she needs to know about the kidnap. Rebecca's either a bona fide member of the team or she isn't—we don't want the hassle of Chinese walls. Anyway, she's come a long way since I laid her out in the stable block.'

I gape—coming from Daisy, that's praise indeed.

Which is why we're sitting in the hotel restaurant, waiting-off ordering until Rebecca arrives. Daisy glares at her watch. 'I told her 12.30.'

'Probably got caught by a latecomer from the murder mystery,' I placate.

Staging murder mystery weekends (and then mid-week murders) saved this place from bankruptcy. Since Daisy came up with that gem, the hotel never looked back. But the hotel belongs to Logan and me, and Daisy had her own ambitions—which crystallised in the Cairncroft Detective Agency. Having her agency in the hotel grounds lends authenticity to the whole murder mystery atmosphere while generating extra income from guests who want help to figure out "whodunnit".

The company staging murder mysteries for us rotates a series of scenarios, and the detective agency has a stock of "surveillance reports" and other "investigative results" — "clues for sale" at its barest, but the guests love it.

'What're you having?' Daisy asks—I can't think why because she never has what I do. It's almost like she wants to make certain hers is something different.

'I'm between fish and chips, and lasagne.'

Sounds pretty typical lunch fayre, but it isn't. Louis, our foreign chef (nobody's worked out exactly what his nationality is—all we know for sure is he isn't French) is a culinary genius. We seem to attract them—his predecessor, Maggie, practised herbal witchcraft on her food. Occasionally, in my dreams, I still taste some of the exotic flavours she magicked. If only Maggie hadn't been a murderer...

With Louis, it's harder to pin down why his food's so good. His signature is authenticity, whether it be Malaysian curry or Scotch pie—then he goes on to inject the dish with something fresh and vibrant that makes your taste buds scream for more. (Yes, even his Scotch pies.)

So I know Louis's fish and chips will transport me to the seaside, while his lasagne offers a cheap alternative to visiting Rome. Who knew menus could double as travel brochures?

'Still nothing from the kidnappers,' I point out, the thought of Tina being abandoned in some dank hole suddenly destroying my appetite.

'We *will* hear from them,' Daisy says, decisively. 'I'm convinced Ivor was set up—nobody is that stupid. Wonder if Jodie could find out who called in the tipoff that got Ivor's caravan searched?'

'Jodie won't start snooping for you—not when she's just back from maternity leave. Anyway, she isn't. Back. Not until Monday.'

'She knows everybody in the Donstable nick...'

'Daisy, Jodie definitely won't risk a blot on her copy book this soon after being away.'

'Okay. Might ask her anyway...'

Sometimes I think talking to a brick wall would be more productive

'Do you really want to start her thinking about why we're so interested?'

'Mm... s'pose. Maybe it is a bit risky—*would* be good to know, though.'

Probably fortunately, Rebecca's red-faced appearance interrupts our verbal volley. 'Sorry, guys—got a woman who's convinced Lord Edelford did it, despite my putting him two counties away when the murder went down.'

Daisy wrinkles her nose. (Which makes her nose ring do strange things.) 'Lord Edelford? How could anybody think...?'

'She says it's a *feeling.* I ended up inventing stuff to steer her towards the real killer. Hey Daisy, what's with the super-duper hairdryer sitting on your desk?'

I think it was Nietzsche who said: "If looks could kill?"

'It's a drone. A sort of miniature helicopter.'

'Oh—well, it *looks* like a hairdryer. I thought all those fan-bits were for drying your hair different ways...' Wisely, Rebecca clocks her boss's expression and gives up trying to equate Daisy's new toy with a Dyson-esque hairstyling innovation. 'What's it for?'

Daisy's sudden glow is almost maternal. 'Surveillance. Dougal has a built-in high-spec camera and microphone for snooping. Picture the scene—our wayward husband meets his mistress in the middle of a park where he reckons nobody could possibly eavesdrop, while unbeknownst to him Dougal's hovering two hundred feet up recording every word.'

'Dougal?' I put in.

'That's his name,' Daisy says dreamily. 'He's going to revolutionise our surveillance capabilities.'

Rebecca pouts. 'Should I be worried? Sounds as though Dougal could put me out of a job.'

One's as bad as the other

'No,' I answer for Daisy. 'It's just another tool—which still needs a human to operate it. The worst that could happen is having to do your job from some Houston-style control room—but that day's a long way off. Thankfully,' I finish, with heartfelt vehemence. (While nonetheless privately acknowledging that at least in a control room, we wouldn't have to worry about Rebecca standing out to the target like a sore thumb.)

Daisy frowns, finds nothing in my statement to argue with, and nods her agreement.

Rebecca sighs with relief. 'And *can* you use it for hair drying too...? Only joking. You ordered yet?'

'We were waiting for you,' I explain, passing over the menu.

'Oohh—I'm going to try his paella.'

Once the waitress is out of earshot, we tell Rebecca about Tina's kidnapping. Her reaction is a mix of shock and envy. 'Okay, I'll deal with all the other stuff while this is happening. But if you need me...'

'We'll holler,' Daisy dismisses her. 'Right, Liam the lech—I reckon your best approach is to check all the dating apps. You're also the ideal person for that, seeing as it's your specialist subject. When you locate the ones Liam's using, make a list of the women he's been talking to—there's a good chance he's taken off with one of them.'

Rebecca pouts. 'But how do I find that out? The sites don't tell you who's talking to who.'

Daisy holds up a hand. 'We've got Liam's email address and Keisha says he uses his date of birth as a password for everything. Just log into his account—username is normally email address—and have a shufty through the mailbox.'

Rebecca's palms land on her cheeks with an audible slap. 'Oohh, hacking. Great—I can do that.'

Daisy rolls her eyes as our food arrives. By unspoken agreement, we eat in silence—sensing quiet moments will be few and far between over the next few days.

7

On our way out, Daisy's phone rings. 'It's Paul,' she mouths, striding ahead for privacy. My heart leaps—could that be the kidnappers?

Unaware of the sudden tension, Rebecca flounces off to start her "hacking". She's come on in leaps and bounds since Daisy agreed to give her a chance in the agency, and proved herself on a number of occasions—notably an Oscar winning performance as "Esme" when we worked a "sting" on local moneylender Jack the Sack and also, if less dramatically, with several successful solo surveillances. Course, we had to overcome a huge hurdle before Rebecca could work undercover.

Rebecca's appearance is the antithesis of a private investigator's need to blend in. Watching her slink under the arch to reception in an almost backless top (it's practically frontless as well) over the microskirt I mistook for a bandanna earlier and thigh-high boots any dominatrix would die for only reinforces what I already knew—one thing Rebecca *isn't* is unnoticeable.

Which is why we helped her buy the Audi.

Even paid for tinted windows...

Daisy pounds back in, her eyes shining. 'Paul's heard from the kidnappers.'

'Oh, thank goodness.'

My immediate thought, that Tina's safe because she has a bunch of kidnappers with her, feels paradoxical—but the alternative if Ivor *had* been working on his own was too terrible to contemplate. 'What'd they say?'

'He's to deliver the ransom tomorrow afternoon. Paul asked for proof of life and after some toing and froing, they agreed. They're going to send him a picture of Tina holding today's newspaper.'

'Great—at least we'll know for sure she's alright. How do they want the ransom handed over?'

She shrugs. 'They're playing that close to their chests. Paul's to have the ransom ready to go at noon—and his phone turned on.'

'Talking about phones—am I right in thinking the police could triangulate the kidnappers' calls in a matter of seconds and pinpoint their exact location? And does Paul know? Surely that would convince him we need them involved.'

She shakes her head. 'You *are* right, but I already told him. Maybe shouldn't have, but in the interests of full disclosure I also pointed out that any kidnapper with an ounce of sense makes their ransom calls from somewhere far, far away from wherever they're holding the victim.'

Hadn't thought of that

'Yeah, alright… did Paul say what the kidnapper sounded like? Male, female, young…?'

She interrupts, grimacing. 'Would you believe—a Dalek? Beggars were using an electronic voice changer.'

'Oh.'

'Yeah, we're not dealing with amateurs—which is okay, because neither are they. Right, that leaves us a little under 24 hours to find Tina—let's start with old Struthers. See what we can glean from whatever information his parking attendant recorded. I know you were going to phone him, but he's a cantankerous beggar—we might get further face to face.'

'Why *were* they recording registration numbers—how does that work?'

'They charge for parking by the hour. So the attendant notes your number and how many hours you've paid for, then refers back to that when you leave. If you've overstayed, he slaps on an excess charge. Meaning there should be a list of plate numbers with arrival and departure times for us to peruse. The attendant had his phone out when we passed, so he was probably recording it all on that.'

'We've no idea *when* they took Tina—so that'll be an awful lot of numbers to go through.'

'I know. Just have to make our best guess at where to start, then work through them until we run out of time. But it's all we've got.'

'Okay, let's pay old Struthers a visit.'

Daisy's brows knit. 'We should go in separate vehicles. That way we can split up if need be, to make best use of the time left.'

Sounds sensible—although she still hasn't said how we're going to turn registration numbers into names and addresses

Before I can try asking, Daisy's on the way out. 'I'll see you there,' I call after her.

She sends me back "the look". 'Yeah—try not to keep me waiting *too* long, wilya?'

DAISY DRIVES A MOTORCYCLE, WHICH SHE'S CHRISTENED "Bessie". I use the term "drives" loosely—do you talk about TT racers "driving" around the Isle of Man?

Bumping up a potholed farm track, I see Daisy and Bessie (in my mind's eye) skimming along the grass verge at 60. Well, I'm not ruining my Panda's suspension for the sake of making Daisy wait a few minutes less.

Retirement gave old Struthers time to embrace his inner entrepreneur. A (seasonal) Xmas tree business and one, isolated self-catering log cabin are his main ventures to date. Even back in the days he was busy running the family farm, Struthers couldn't resist an opportunity to turn a quick buck—as evidenced by the deal that's brought Paul's fair back to Cairncroft all these years.

The track I'm currently negotiating at 20mph leads through dense woodland to a custom-built abode Struthers erected to house himself and Mrs Struthers in their retirement. Following a time-honoured tradition (which, it appears, also applies to funfairs) of handing the farm over to his elder male issue, it's usual for a seceding farmer to vacate the farmhouse in favour of said issue and their family.

Struthers' retirement retreat occupies a picturesque spot, but is very isolated—at least a couple of miles from his old farmhouse. My fiancé is a surveyor and confirmed the veracity of rumours suggesting Struthers' son paid off key planning department officials to ensure permission *wasn't* granted to build nearer the farmhouse.

Finally, I drag the Panda around a hairpin bend (at 10 mph now) to be faced with a sprawling ranch-style house that somehow reminds me of army barracks.

An ancient Jaguar is parked outside the front door. Struthers', I presume—looks his style. I pull up at the extreme edge of a vast, monoblocked front yard bounded by forestland, where Daisy and Bessie are independently leaning against opposite sides of the same tree. Predictably, Daisy's irritated.

'You'd have been quicker walking,' she snaps as I get out.

Before I can think of a good throwback, the sound of another car arriving draws our attention and an orange Mini bumps off the track. It tucks in beside the Jaguar and a young woman emerges. She makes no attempt to pull down her skirt, which there anyway isn't enough of to make the effort worthwhile.

Daisy sniggers. 'Didn't know Rebecca had a sister.'

Yes—going by her dress-style, the newcomer has a lot in common with our recently promoted staff investigator. Looking like she's come straight from a department store makeover (if more "Superdrug" than "Frasers") it isn't so much *what* Rebecca's clone is wearing as what she *isn't*. As for the heels—well, think stilts and you're halfway there.

She glances over and waggles red-taloned fingers at us, then teeters up the path to an oak front door and—without knocking or ringing the doorbell—just opens the door and walks in.

Daisy chuckles. 'Are they putting something in the water around here, or what? First Mr M, now old Struthers.'

'But Struthers has a wife,' I point out.

'He does, doesn't he?'

After a moment's thought, Daisy dips into Bessie's pannier and pulls out a short length of stiff wire and a strip of flat, rigid plastic. Then takes off at a run towards the cars. Befuddled, I nonetheless follow—you get used to being befuddled around Daisy, and going with the flow is generally easier.

My prosthetic leg imposes speed restrictions that have me arriving well behind my friend, who's now up against the Mini with her plastic strip (which is effectively a plastic crowbar) wedged in its passenger door's top edge. She applies leverage, and a gap appears.

'Daisy...?'

She ignores me, intent on feeding her wire through the opening thus created. I didn't notice the wire has a loop at its end, whose purpose becomes clear when Daisy neatly snags the locking knob and pulls it up.

'Are you crazy?' I hiss as she opens the door. Daisy's voice comes back muffled because her head's under the dashboard.

'... taking a quick look... Ah, what's this? Oohh—great. Just what I was hoping for.'

A stentorian bellow makes us both jump. 'HOI—YOU. WHAT are you doing?'

Daisy withdraws fast and slams the door, then we both turn to face old Struthers as he marches towards us. He's a big man, decked out in his customary tweed shooting outfit, and currently has a crimson face. With small eyes and a long jaw adding to the impression of a charging bull, he stomps to a stop in front of us.

Daisy smiles sweetly—which scares most people, but Struthers seems unimpressed. 'Your friend left her car door open—I was just closing it.'

'On the passenger side?'

Daisy shrugs. 'She must have gone 'round to get something out.'

Struthers looks unconvinced. 'If you weren't lassies, I'd detain you and call the police.'

'That's discrimination.'

Daisy sounds genuinely insulted. 'I'm as capable of getting up to no good as any laddie. As for detaining us, well, I'd like to see you...'

Then breaks off, obviously realising this isn't exactly productive, and pulls out her bus pass. 'Cairncroft Detective Agency, Mr Struthers. We need to ask you a few questions.'

Struthers surprises me when he takes a step back, looking… frightened? Maybe he's got a bus phobia?

'Wh… what sort of questions?'

'We're helping the police with their enquiries into a murder at Cairncroft fair—I expect you've heard about it?'

Struthers nods weakly, but looks relieved?

'We understand you were running a car parking concession at the fairground and need its records from last night—specifically, registration numbers together with times of arrival and departure.'

Unfortunately, Struthers seems to have recovered from his initial reaction. 'I can't see the police asking a private detective agency for help.'

'Well, them and the owner's son,' Daisy concedes. 'Anyway, it's no skin off your nose to give us the information—hardly confidential, is it?'

'That's where you're wrong—all data concerning other people is covered by data protection laws. If I gave out people's private information willy-nilly, it could land me with a massive fine—not to mention the "betrayal of trust" issue.'

'Private information?' Daisy scoffs. 'Licence numbers are there to be read. How can you call that…?'

'It's not the licence numbers per se,' he interrupts. 'Those records say where their owners were at a given time—that's private information, and I can't divulge it. I have to say, Miss Chessington, it's very surprising to see you involved with whatever game your friend's playing... anyway, I'd like you to leave now, please. I'm busy.'

Looking at the house with a smirk, Daisy says: 'Yeah—that's obvious.'

Is there a "redder" adjective than "crimson"? If so, that's the colour Struthers' face just turned. 'I don't know what you're implying, but that young lady is my niece—and you're interrupting.'

'I bet we are,' Daisy mutters, but I think it was only me caught that. In a normal voice, she says: 'Is *Mrs* Struthers helping you entertain the young lady?'

Momentarily, Struthers looks poleaxed—but recovers quickly. 'My wife is shopping in Aberdeen today, as it happens—which means looking after our niece falls to me. Something you are currently preventing me from doing.'

'And her "looking after" you, I expect,' Daisy murmurs.

Before Struthers can react, she leans closer—her face suddenly grave and filled with concern. 'Mr Struthers, there's something I have to tell you.'

He falls for the dramatic pause. 'What?'

Pointing at the house, Daisy drops her voice to a whisper. 'That woman who's pretending to be your niece—she's nothing of the kind. When I was closing her car door, I noticed these business cards...' she holds one up '... and according to this, that young lady is "Cute Candy" who gives her address as a strip joint in Aberdeen. Now...' she raises a palm against Struthers' desperate bluster '... we're obviously dealing with some sort of con woman here. Is it enough to warn *you*? Or should I make *Mrs* Struthers aware also?'

For a long moment, Struthers looks as though he's about to pop. Then deflates in a prolonged, whistling exhalation. When he speaks, it's in a low voice containing not a little pleading. 'Thank you so much for making me *aware*. Em, no, I will deal with this—there's really no need to involve *Mrs* Struthers. Now, perhaps I was a tad hasty before—what was that information you wanted?'

8

Having given us everything he can (which turned out to be precisely nothing) Struthers strides off in the direction of his Ponderosa-like abode.

'Beggar,' Daisy explodes. 'We don't have time for this.'

Struthers confirmed that his parking attendant—a local odd-jobber called Stanley Watson—records the registration numbers of arriving cars on his smartphone, and does indeed note their arrival and departure times.

Snag is, Stanley was rushed into Aberdeen Royal Infirmary early this morning with suspected appendicitis.

'We could break into Stanley's house and get the phone,' Daisy declares.

Frighteningly, she's serious

'Daisy, while I've no doubt your burglary skills are far better than they should be, there's two problems with that. First, five gets you ten Stanley took his phone with him. Second, everybody's phone these days is password protected—or even fingerprint protected—so the phone wouldn't be any good without Stanley.'

She muses that over. 'You're right.'

Then hoicks out her own phone. 'Nothing more from Paul—so, far as we know, nothing else is happening until tomorrow. Sam, this is our best chance of getting a lead on the kidnappers. I agree Stanley would have taken his phone with him—so let's go to Aberdeen and visit him in hospital.'

'He won't give us the records, same as Struthers wasn't going to until you…'

There she goes again. With a sense of déjà vu I hobble behind, back to Struthers front door, where she slams a thumb against the bell push—and keeps it there.

It's a full minute before the door's flung open and I can't help noticing Struthers' tie is askew. 'What is it now?'

'I need written authorisation from you to Stanley, so he'll give us those records.'

'But Stanley's in hospital.'

'That's where we're going.'

Struthers tuts, and Daisy holds up "Cute Candy's" calling card. 'Oh, very well—wait there.'

'Clever of you,' I observe, pointing to the card she's stowing in her jeans' pocket.

'T'be honest, after seeing "Candy", I was more thinking it's only a matter of time before *Mrs Struthers* comes knocking at our door wanting the "wandering-hubby" package—I was just getting ahead of the game.'

'If she does, though—Mrs Struthers, I mean—you can't use "Candy" now. Not after making a deal with him.'

'Course I will—when his wife twigs what he's up to, the old goat deserves everything he gets. Anyway, we shouldn't *have* to make deals for information pertaining to a murder. Shh—I hear him coming back.'

Struthers whisks open the already ajar door and thrusts a sheet of headed paper at Daisy. 'There—that tells Stanley to give you his records from last night. Now—will you *please* go away?'

A LITTLE OVER AN HOUR LATER, WE'RE TRAMPING ALONG A corridor in Aberdeen Royal Infirmary headed for the surgical ward. Before setting out, we detoured from Struthers' place to Cairncroft so Daisy could drop Bessie off. While her first instinct was to shoot over here on her own (which admittedly would be significantly faster than travelling with me in the Panda) Daisy decided, for a journey of this length, saving a few minutes wasn't worth sacrificing the relative comfort of enclosed transport in a country with no compunction about unleashing drenching downpours (even in June) without prior warning.

We confirmed Stanley's location at a front desk and having arrived at his ward, are now required to buzz the nursing station for permission to enter. There's a wall-mounted intercom outside the ward for precisely that purpose.

Daisy shakes her head. 'Naw, makes it too easy for them to tell us "no". Hang about a minute.'

It's actually *three* minutes before a porter ambles up and jabs at a keyboard, put there for the benefit of those hallowed few in possession of its code. Daisy squints over his shoulder and when the lock clicks open, whisks back around and mouths "2674".

In her normal voice, she says: 'I think we'll keep her on a drip and maybe increase the dose of... oi, hold the door.'

The porter starts, then obliges. Daisy leads us past our newly appointed doorman and once inside, pulls me into a huddle—still speaking loudly. 'Of course, it's important to watch for side effects. Too much of that stuff and internal organs start popping like... okay, he's gone.'

In front is a long corridor studded with doors on both sides. Peeping out at its far end is a counter, presumably attached to the nurses' station—which a large sign advises all visitors must report to. 'So what next, *Doctor* Daisy?'

'Hah. Fooled the porter, didn't I. Got us in, *and* the entry code in case we need to come back—be handy for getting out, too.'

Daisy reaches past to a wall-mounted cabinet whose open ports facilitate the dispensing of masks, gloves, and plastic aprons. She whisks out two sets of each. 'These could be useful. Here, stick them in your bag.'

'What will we say?' I mutter as we approach the nursing equivalent of Checkpoint Charlie.

'Play it by ear,' is all I get back.

A nurse nested behind the desk is on a telephone call. She throws a few curious looks our way, but doesn't seem in any hurry to finish her conversation with someone who might be in the hospital's catering unit, or equally could be the maître d'hôtel where she's dining with her boyfriend at end of shift. Finally, she replaces the receiver and welcomes us to her ward.

'Yes?'

Daisy sniffs and makes her lower lip tremble. 'My Uncle Stanley was brought in this morning with a burst appendix. Can I see him?'

Nurse (Susan Simpson, according to her nametag) softens slightly and taps at a keyboard before peering at the screen behind it. 'Stanley Watson?'

We both nod.

She shakes her head. 'Mr Watson's still in theatre, so... oh, here he comes now.'

A trolley rumbles past, containing an elderly man with his eyes closed. An accompanying nurse pushes open the door to a side room and the porter wheels Stanley into what must be his room.

Daisy manages a single step, but Nurse Simpson is quick to set her straight. 'You can't see him yet—he's going to be woozy for a while, and we'll be busy doing "ob"s. Maybe tonight, if you want to come back then?'

'But...'

The nurse's expression is enough to convince even Daisy she's wasting her time. 'Alright, we'll do that.'

We turn to leave, and Nurse Simpson calls after us. 'Oh, you'll need the code to get out. It's 2674.'

OUTSIDE THE WARD, DAISY USHERS US INTO A CONVENIENT stairwell. 'Take your jacket off, Sam,' she orders, tossing her own into a corner.

'What? Why...?'

'Never mind, just do it. Then bring the masks and stuff out of your bag.'

A minute later we're masked, gloved, and plastic aproned. Daisy also demanded I hand over the plastic rain-mate I always carry (what? I don't *like* getting my hair wet), which is doing a reasonable (if "almost") job of hiding the distinctive blue skunk-streak that runs over her crown. 'We can't leave our jackets and my bag here—they'll get nicked,' I protest.

'Don't be daft—it's a hospital. C'mon, hurry up.'

Yet again taking the path of least resistance (story of my life it sometimes feels) I trail along as Daisy marches back to the ward entrance. She punches in 2674 and slams through the doors. 'Just follow my lead—I know what I'm doing.'

Passing by the nursing station, I'm (very) conscious of Nurse Simpson's head rising—but she returns Daisy's cursory wave before returning to her computer screen. We crash into Stanley's room like Clint Eastwood entering a Wild West Saloon, making two nurses hovering over Stanley look up in alarm.

'S'okay, we're with surgical census,' Daisy declares from behind her mask.

One nurse is very short and very young, and develops a sudden fascination with the floor. The other is older, taller, and obviously in charge—she doesn't appear chuffed. 'You're with WHAT? Never heard of it.'

Stanley's still out cold and both nurses are on the other side of his bed. At our side, lying forlorn on Stanley's bedside locker, a silver iPhone draws Daisy's gaze—which stays locked on it, for a moment, then she looks sharply at a window behind the nurses and exclaims: 'WHAT is THAT?'

Little and Large both turn to the window (as do I) and when we look back, I'm the only one who notices there's no longer a silver iPhone on Stanley's locker. Daisy struts to the bedside, eyeing two confused nurses. 'Aw, just a pigeon. Yeah, surgical census *is* kinda new. See, a few folks recently got the wrong operation, so we're sort of a task force trying to limit the damage when that happens.'

As she speaks, Daisy lifts Stanley's limp hand and presses his thumb against the silver iPhone.

It beeps.

The senior nurse snaps: '*What* are you doing?'

'Well, we have fingerprints on record for the patient who was *supposed* to get an appendectomy, so now I'm checking whether this guy's match. If not, I'll send him back to theatre for whatever op he should have had... oh, and go looking for the poor beggar with appendicitis.'

With that, she turns away from two sets of goggling eyes and makes a quick exit—with me on her heels.

When we draw abreast of the nurses' station, our old friend Susan Simpson gives us another and this time more appraising glance. Since she doesn't dial 999 or call security, I deduce the penny still hasn't dropped.

Back in the stairwell, Daisy pulls down her mask and gets out both phones—her own and Stanley's. She swipes and jabs at their screens until a long beep emanates from both. 'Right, that's the parking file transferred via bluetooth,' she explains, then points. 'And look, our jackets and your bag are still here—told you they would be.'

My head's spinning. I open my mouth, but nothing comes out.

Daisy strips off the various medical accoutrements and shrugs on her denim jacket, hands me back my rain-mate, then makes for the door. 'Just be two ticks, Sam—need to give Nurse Simpson my uncle's phone what I brought and forgot to leave. Poor old soul might want it when he wakes up.'

9

'Anything?'

We're five minutes from Cairncroft and Daisy's spent the journey studying Stanley's parking records. She scribbles something in her notebook, then sits back with a sigh. 'I'm wracking my brains because one of these numberplates seems familiar—I've definitely seen it recently.'

'Go and read it out—maybe I'll recognise it.'

She does, and I don't. 'Nope, sorry.'

'Oh, that's so frustrating. I'm going to kick myself when we find out who it is. Interestingly, they only stayed 30 minutes—*highly* suspicious—although the timing's on the early side. Right—that one goes top of the list for checking out. I'll add another three for now and we'll get all their details, then go visit them.'

'Talking of details—how? Can we get that sort of information from DVLA?'

'Naw. I've looked into this before—the legal route's a form V888. If you've got what DVLA calls a "just cause" for knowing who the driver is, they'll tell you. Collecting parking fines falls under "just cause", so theoretically we could... um... persuade old Struthers to sign the form, but the downer is DVLA takes four weeks to process it.'

'I didn't like the way you said "legal route".'

She grins. 'We'll get Alan to run the plates on his police computer.'

"Alan" is a detective inspector (recently promoted to *chief* inspector) with the National Crime Agency. He's also Rebecca's boyfriend. 'Wouldn't you be better asking Rebecca to try and persuade him?'

She shakes her head. 'I've got more pull with Alan than Rebecca has. It's down to me they gave him that promotion, remember?'

I'm not sure Alan would entirely agree. His promotion *did* come hot on the heels of Alan arresting "the Bus Stop Killer", it's true—and this *was* shortly after Daisy tasered her—but Alan might argue he was already on his way and that Daisy's antics didn't change the inevitable conclusion. But it *was* us who figured out where to find Lena—and there *was* a back road none of us knew about, down which she planned to vanish, so I suppose...

I look dubiously at Daisy. 'How many numbers are on that list?'

'Aw, I'll give him them in dribs and drabs—we haven't got time to investigate many, anyway.'

Daisy's phone beeps in time with the taps she delivers to its screen before holding it up to her ear. 'Alan—hi, mate. How's it going? What do I want? What makes you…? Oh, alright. Need some plates run….

Look, Detective *Chief* Inspector, you owe me…

Aw, c'mon Alan. It's only four plates…

No, I won't make a habit of it—definitely a one-off—cheers. I'll read them out.'

One-off? Those are just the first four

After ending the call, Daisy performs a series of wriggling contortions until her phone's safely back in a jeans pocket. She puffs with frustration. 'Alan's gonna do it—but he's out of the office. Says it'll be a few hours before he gets back to us.'

'I think you're lucky he's helping at all. Daisy, did your mother ever mention the word "please" to you?'

Then regret the quip, because Daisy's family life was as far from "The Waltons" as it's possible to get. 'What'll we do while we're waiting?' I add hastily, so she doesn't have to answer.

She smiles tightly, acknowledging my belated attempt at tact. 'Let's swing by the fairground and see if Paul's heard any more from the kidnappers. Particularly the proof of life picture—I'll feel a lot happier after seeing that.'

WE'RE SURPRISED TO FIND THE FAIRGROUND UP AND running. Paul, however, is in his caravan rather than spinning waltzers. 'I've still got wages to pay and the crazy thing is we've never been so busy—Dad getting shot seems to have attracted everyone and his dog.'

I can understand that—my Aunt Claire's murder was instrumental in launching the Cairncroft Hotel to a level of profitability she could only dream of before her death. All down to Daisy's idea of running murder weekends (and mid-week mysteries) on the site of a murder scene. Part of that "rebranding" was a new name—"The Murder Hotel"—which works well for marketing but hasn't caught on with the locals, especially Daisy's

"Cairncroft Cowboys". To them, we'll always be "The Cairncroft Hotel."

Being honest, I'm a bit the same

Looking around Paul's caravan, I comment: 'This is dinky.' Then, noticing the lit digital display on a tiny microwave, I add: 'Where does the power come from?'

'It's a serviced pitch,' Paul explains. 'That's just one of the reasons we keep coming every year—this end of the field has connections for mains power and water. There's even a septic tank for emptying our chemical toilet cartridges.'

TMI, Paul

Daisy hands back Paul's phone. She's been studying an image sent by the kidnappers in response to Paul's "proof of life" demand. 'Well, she doesn't look too clever, but that's today's "Press & Journal" in her hands so...'

'Doesn't look too clever?' Paul explodes. 'Tina has a black eye and is obviously terrified.'

Daisy hangs her head. 'Sorry—didn't mean to be disrespectful. My point is she's alive and relatively unharmed—is that better?'

Paul reaches out a trembling hand. 'No, *I'm* sorry—you're only trying to help, I know that.'

Daisy holds out her phone. 'Paul, do you recognise any of these registration numbers? They're from cars that were parked in the field last night.'

Paul studies the screen and his brows furrow. 'No—'fraid not.'

'Okay. I'm sure that first one rings a bell, but it's driving me crazy trying to figure out why...'

'Have you got the ransom ready?' I ask.

Paul nods. 'Yeah—Dobson sent one of his guys over with it an hour ago. Tell you the truth, I'm kind of nervous about having it here—probably sit up looking at it all night.'

Daisy frowns. 'You could have something there. The kidnappers will expect you to have the cash ready, and might decide collecting it by force is an easier option. Right, you're staying at the hotel tonight. Sam'll comp you a room and that cash can go in the hotel safe.'

Oh, Sam'll comp him a room, will she? —alright, of course she will

'The fair's open until eleven—I can't leave until then. That's the other problem—I should be out there, but couldn't bring myself to leave all this money lying around.' He waves at a canvas holdall on the floor.

Daisy strides over and picks up more money that she's seen in her life. 'We'll take this away now and put it in the safe.'

"Brilliant, Dais.' That'll let me get on with running the fair meantime. Will the hotel still be open after eleven, or do I need to ring a bell?'

Daisy looks thoughtful. '*If* the kidnappers were planning anything, they might be watching—and follow you. Tell you what, I'll come back for you at eleven on Bessie—no way can they keep up with her. Then we'll go with you in Sam's Panda to make the ransom drop tomorrow.'

Poor Paul—I don't envy him experiencing Daisy's countersurveillance tactics while perched on Bessie's pillion

But the poor lad obviously doesn't have sufficient imagination to comprehend what lies in store. 'Thanks so much—hey, who knows? I might even get a few hours' sleep tonight, after all.'

Don't bank on it, Paul—think your fairground rides are scary? Hah—sleep won't come easy after a "Bessie special"

10

Back at the hotel, I breathe a sigh of relief after placing Paul's 100 grand inside our safe, which lives underneath the reception desk. It isn't a big safe, and I did worry there'd be enough space, but we obviously haven't any jewellery-bedecked film stars staying tonight because the holdall only has to share with a single, flat cardboard box. Leaving plenty room for the bar takings when Jeff or Logan brings them through later on.

'Which bank did you rob?'

We both jump violently—Daisy regains her balance faster than I do. 'Sorry,' Logan adds. 'Didn't mean to scare you—but it does look like the stereotypical bag of money.'

'DON'T sneak up on people,' Daisy snaps from beside me, and Logan colours.

He can't help himself, though. 'So—what IS in it?'

'It's legal stuff my friend Paul is worried about keeping in his caravan—you know, to do with his dad's estate.'

One thing about Daisy—she thinks on her feet

'I was sorry to hear about that. Are they any nearer finding out who did it?'

'No. Oh, and by the way, Paul's staying in the hotel tonight—but we want that kept quiet.'

Logan looks puzzled. 'Why?'

At which point I step in. 'He's getting a lot of hassle from the press and needs a wee break. I've already briefed Hazel, but just pretend Paul isn't here.'

Hazel, our hotel receptionist, nods in agreement. She's behind the counter with us, scrunched up at one end to give us room. Daisy pulls out the cardboard box and shakes it. 'What's this, Logan.'

'Put it back,' he breathes, looking around as though expecting the box's owner to materialise out of thin air. 'It belongs to Caron—our new nanny. She says it's family heirlooms—seemed paranoid about whatever's in it.'

'Jodie said she was live-in,' I remember.

'Yes—with Jodie starting work again, and my hours, it was the only solution. She comes with gold-plated references,' he adds proudly.

Daisy's still fiddling with Caron's box. 'Doesn't feel as though there's anything in it?' she comments.

Logan grabs it out of her hand. 'Well... maybe it's old photos, I don't know. Caron treasures it, though, and insisted I lock it up in the safe.'

Daisy's thinking. (You can always tell, it makes her look constipated.) 'You *did* check her out properly?'

'I told you. We phoned her last family and yes, Jodie checked *them* out too—made sure it *was* them she was speaking to. They couldn't praise Caron highly enough—we're lucky to have her.'

'Mm—alright.' Daisy takes the box back and tosses it on top of Paul's holdall, showing little respect for whatever aspects of Caron's heritage it contains, and I close the safe. A winking red light tells me it's secure and can only be opened by someone who knows which numbers to feed its keypad. 'So—is Jodie busy polishing her handcuffs for Monday?'

Logan laughs, then lowers his voice. 'Monday can't come soon enough for Jodie—she's becoming grumpier by the day. Don't get me wrong, she loves being with Alanna and that's the only thing giving her second thoughts, but Jodie won't be happy until she's back out there arresting people.'

Daisy peers at her watch. 'I need to drop into the agency and touch base with Rebecca before she knocks off. See you at the cottage, Sam?'

'Sure,' I agree as she shoots off, wondering what she needs to "touch base" with Rebecca about. Then, turning to Logan: 'You know, I never thought about this until now, but Rebecca's doing a lot more unsociable hours for the agency these days—poor Hector must be fed up.'

'The cat?'

Logan makes a show of mopping his brow. 'Oh, the cat's *fine.* It stays with us when she's out doing whatever you've got her doing.'

'Do I detect a touch of... something, there? Don't you and Hector get along?'

Logan exhales heavily. 'No, he's well behaved and Alanna loves him. It's just—sometimes he looks at me and I think: "Wouldn't fancy being on *your* bad side, mate."'

He turns his head to where Daisy exited into the residents lounge, en route to the kitchen where she regularly enrages Louis by using his domain as a shortcut, and nods. 'Bit like her...'

IT BEING A LOVELY NIGHT, I DECIDE TO LEAVE THE PANDA AND walk back to our cottage. We're only five minutes away and my left leg's cooperating (i.e. not hurting after today's demands) so I take the chance to lose myself in birdsong and that feeling of space—peace—only a country walk can impart.

Daisy arrives shortly after—and her eyes settle on the gin bottle. 'Uh, uh,' I remind her. 'You're driving later—Paul. Remember?'

'I know—it was just wishful thinking. Also, when Alan gets back with those plates, we might be going out again—with so little time left, any leads need following up straight away. Want a coffee?'

'Brill—macchiato, please.'

We finally invested in a Krups coffee machine for the cottage—and haven't regretted it. Daisy brings my macchiato, then picks up the landline. 'You've got a voicemail from Davy.'

Ouch

'I was supposed to ring him today and make plans for the weekend, but with everything...'

'Doesn't he have your mobile number?'

'Yes—but I forgot to charge it.'

'Again?' she says with an eyeroll. Her finger hovers over the speaker button. 'Shall I play it?'

'NO.'

I grab it from her and turn away, putting the handset to my ear.

'Hi, Sam. Suppose you're caught up with something to do with national security—or something Daisy THINKS is. Listen, no prob—I'm meeting Leslie, an old friend from uni who's turned up out of nowhere, for a drink. Catch you tomorrow. Bye... oh, I phoned your mobile, but it went straight to voicemail. Think it's out of power again...'

Hmm. Part of me's relieved he's taking it well—but I'm not so sure about this "Leslie". Problem is, it's one of those unisex names. Leslie Phillips springs to mind—but so does Leslie Ash. There's no way of telling whether Davy's "Leslie" is male or female—which is worrying.

Oh, for goodness' sake—listen to me. I sound like a possessive fiancé—though anyone who knows me would laugh at the idea—and how would *I* feel if our positions were reversed and Davy started wondering about me?

'Everything okay, Sam?'

Daisy's concerned tone cuts through my inner turmoil and I swing back. 'Yes, of course. Good news is Davy's meeting Leslie, somebody he knows from his university days, for a drink—so he won't be playing Cinderella after all.'

'Leslie? Is that a woman?'

'Probably not—I mean, it could be, but not necessarily. Anyway, he didn't say—but it wouldn't matter if she was.'

Daisy gives me a searching look. 'Sure you two are alright?'

'Of COURSE we are.'

She recoils slightly and I realise that was a bit full on. 'I'm just tired and yes, maybe I expected "Where are you—I miss you" rather than "No worries—I've found somebody else to go for a drink with". Which is totally unreasonable. It's me who stood him up—I'm *glad* he's not sat twiddling his thumbs.'

'You don't sound glad.'

Daisy's great. Her total lack of tact and empathy never fails to distract me from whatever issue I'm fretting over—which sometimes isn't a bad thing.

'Saw Jodie on my way over—she'd been down at the village with Alanna.'

To my relief, Judge Judy grants the motion for a change of subject. 'She still excited about Monday?'

'Yep—and then some. She's raving about Caron—says it wouldn't have been workable without her. There's a day-care place in Donstable, but Jodie looked sick at the thought of leaving Alanna with strangers.'

Daisy giggles. 'Bet Alanna would love a day-care centre. All the attention, other kids…'

'Possibly, but Jodie's happier knowing she's safe at home. They're lucky to have found Caron—seems the lass is qualified up to her eyeballs. Anyway, what were you rushing off to "touch base" with Rebecca about?'

She sips at her coffee. 'Oh, just stuff… making sure she's alright with her missing person case, checking whether anything else needs seeing to…'

I always know when she's up to something—but never manage to get it out of her before whatever it is happens

'Did Jodie manage over to see Mr M?' Daisy asks suddenly.

'Yes—I was coming to that. Mm... he's giving nothing away, but Jodie reckons this "Kat" person has moved in with him.'

'No!'

'Well, maybe it's temporary, but Jodie says Kat's definitely staying there—she went to the loo and clocked two pairs of knickers drying on a towel rail.'

'Oh-oh. Mr M wasn't for admitting it, then?'

'Nope—Jodie says he brushed off every attempt to get at how serious their relationship is. And thought the same as us—he seemed really awkward about it.'

'Well, if the old fool's doing a "Struthers and Candy", then he would—but I'm worried Kat is manipulating him somehow. Or worse—those dead husbands worry me. Sam, we need to dig deeper into this. Isn't Jodie concerned, too?'

'She is—and at the same time, isn't. Jodie has enormous confidence in Mr M's ability to sort his own problems—but yes, she's obviously uneasy about the situation.'

Daisy slams her head against the sofa-back. 'We're totally committed with Tina's kidnap right now—but soon as that's wrapped, I intend taking a long hard look at this "Kat" woman. If she's messing Mr M around—I'll make her regret it.'

Remembering Logan's thoughts about the wisdom of getting on Hector or Daisy's bad side, I see where he's coming from.

Daisy's phone bleeps and she pulls it out, reads the text, then groans. 'Oh, no.'

'What?'

'Alan got tied up with whatever he's doing and won't be back in the office until tomorrow. Which means he can't run those plates until then. Aarrgh—that's too late.'

11

After that, the evening became something of an anti-climax. With nothing better to do, we tried (and failed) to get into various rubbish programs on the telly. Daisy was in a foul mood because of Alan "letting her down". Not being able to have a drink didn't help, either. I was quite relieved when eleven finally loomed and she roared off on Bessie to collect Paul.

Part of me wonders whether I'll see her again before morning until just before midnight (late for me, but I'm too agitated for sleep—which is solely because of Tina, and nothing whatsoever to do with Davy and his university friend) when the front door bangs behind her.

She makes straight for the drinks trolley. 'Boy, do I need a drink.'

'There are helplines for people who feel that way...'

'Ha. Ha. Is there a helpline for private detectives plunged out of their depth who've just been comforting the brother of a kidnap victim?'

Wow—this must be getting to her. Daisy admitting she's out of her depth is like Ant & Dec confessing to stage fright

'It's the personal aspect,' she explains, collapsing on the sofa beside me and miraculously not spilling a drop of the largest G&T I've ever seen. 'It's easy to be objective about clients, but this is Paul—and Tina. Second-guessing yourself all the time is exhausting, but I'm terrified of getting something wrong.'

'That's why they don't let doctors treat family,' I sympathise. 'But Dais', I'm not seeing anything you could have done differently. Listen, what are we going to do about Mr M?'

I *am* concerned for Mr M—but have to admit I'm using him to distract Daisy from her panic attack.

She makes a face. 'You're right—we can't just let that ride. Anyway, this Paul and Tina mess *should* be over tomorrow, after we deliver the ransom, so yeah—a little strategizing wouldn't go amiss. If "Kat" has moved herself in with Mr M, the situation's urgent.'

'I wonder if we should have a word with Miss Dobie? She has her ear to the ground where Mr M's concerned.'

Daisy looks uncertain. 'Maybe—but Miss Dobie's been his secretary for a long time and she's fiercely loyal to the old goat. She might not even talk to us… there again, surely she'll realise we're only trying to help. Mm, okay. Let's give it a whirl.'

'We can't speak to her at the office, though—need to get her on her own.'

'Agreed. Any idea where she lives?'

I shake my head, and Daisy flaps her fingers. 'Jodie'll know—and tomorrow being Sunday is the ideal time to catch Miss Dobie at home. I'll send Jodie a text—with any luck, Alanna'll get her up in the wee small hours and she'll see it then. That would let us drop in on Miss Dobie first thing.'

After savouring the last sip from my vodka and tonic (I'm going to call it a night now so I'll be fresh tomorrow) I put down my glass and get up. 'Leaving aside your lack of empathy for Jodie and Logan's disrupted sleep patterns, that sounds like a good idea—with the added advantage it'll give us something to do instead of kicking our heels waiting for noon.'

She's already pecking at her phone. 'I'll send the text right now—get me another drink while you're up, will you?'

NEXT MORNING, BY MUTUAL CONSENT, IT'S BACON sandwiches for breakfast. We're both up to high doh about the ransom drop and just want to get on with it. I really should phone Davy and tell him I'm tied up again, but decide to hold off in case everything resolves this afternoon. If that happens, we can go out for a nice meal 'n' chill later. I'll wait until I know—don't want to dangle the possibility, then snatch it away.

Daisy holds up her phone. 'Jodie texted me Miss Dobie's address. If we go and see her now, that should use up most of the morning.'

She wishes. By my rough calculations, unless Miss Dobie lives in Inverness, we'll be back watching Paul bite his nails by half-ten. But I keep quiet and instead ask: 'What time did Jodie reply to your text?'

'Um... here it is. Yeah, 3.30AM. See, told you.'

On our way to meet Paul in reception, as arranged previously, Daisy insists on detouring to the detective agency. She's strangely reticent about why...

Although it's not yet nine, Rebecca's at her desk sipping a travel mug of hotel coffee. (We really need to get another Krups machine for in here.) She looks... exhausted? Also—no sign of Hector?

'Anything?' Daisy demands—excitedly?

Rebecca shakes her head. 'Zilch. Zero. Absolutely nada.'

'*What* are we talking about?'

Daisy turns to me and I can tell she's *trying* to keep her voice casual. 'I had Rebecca stake out Paul's caravan last night in case the kidnappers did go after the cash.'

'You *what*?'

I must look fierce as I feel because Rebecca starts and even Daisy recoils. 'Are you out of your *tiny mind?* What if those thugs *had* turned up? *Rebecca* doesn't have a black belt in judo.'

Daisy has the good grace to blush, but it's Rebecca who speaks up. 'It would have been fine, Sam—honestly. I parked the Audi beside some other fairground vehicles, and with its tinted windows nobody could see I was inside—oh, and I kept the doors locked, like Daisy said. If anybody *had* showed up I was only to follow them, then report back.'

She pouts, looking aggrieved. 'And I might not have a black belt, but Daisy's shown me a few moves—*and* she loaned me a taser, just in case.'

Now I'm really seeing red. 'You can't hand out tasers willy-nilly—they're illegal. How many do you have?'

Daisy shrugs. 'Only two.'

Breathing heavily, I sink into a visitor chair. 'Daisy, it's one thing putting you and me in the firing line—constantly—but you mustn't do it to other people.'

Rebecca stiffens. '"Other people?" I'm not "other people", Sam—I'm part of the team. Aren't I?'

The sob in her voice chisels its way into my anger and I take a step back.

I *am* angry with Daisy for dropping Rebecca in her latest war zone, but the lass *is* desperate for an expanded role and if she really wants to crime-bust alongside Daisy, well—it sounds trite, but danger's part of the game in Daisy's world.

I should know

'Sorry, Rebecca. *Of course* you're part of the team. A *vital* part. Just be careful, okay?'

She brightens. 'Oohh, thanks Sam. I appreciate that. And yes, I'm always careful—promise.'

Daisy fills her cheeks and blows out a lungful of air. 'Cheers, Rebecca. I owe you one.'

A practicality strikes me. 'Um—it's Sunday. Who's going to man the office for any hotel guests that want us after last night's murder mystery? You surely don't expect Rebecca to, after spending all night watching Paul's caravan.'

Rebecca sticks her hand up. 'I don't need much sleep. And I meditate—it's great during long surveillances because you can rest without losing awareness of the target. Oh, and I've got caffeine pills, too.'

'Well, if you're sure...'

Swift glance at my watch. 'It's nearly nine—Paul will be waiting.'

As we turn away, Rebecca jumps up. 'Hold on. You need to know about this.'

Daisy spins back, huffing. 'Make it quick.'

'Last night, I used the time to go through a load of dating sites and you were right—Liam had profiles on three of them.'

'Great. That should help you trace him.'

Daisy starts to turn again, but Rebecca grabs her arm. 'No, you don't understand. See, his most recent online girlfriend is Tina Patterson—Paul's sister.'

Daisy looks at her for a long moment. She pulls out her phone. 'Rebecca—have you got the registration number for Liam's car handy?'

Rebecca fumbles for her own phone. After a moment's swiping and tapping, she turns its screen towards Daisy. 'Yep, there it is.'

Daisy's gaze shifts between her and Rebecca's phones, then she lets out a groan. 'What?' I ask anxiously.

'One of the cars on Stanley's list that arrived in Struthers' car park on Friday night—remember how I said its number looked familiar? That's because it was Liam's—*knew* I'd seen it recently.'

She swings to me. 'It was *Liam* who kidnapped Tina.'

12

Paul will be getting worried, but we're finally on our way—only ten minutes late. 'So, do you really think...?'

'Yep, it's obvious—Liam chats Tina up online, gets to know the family's worth a bob or two, then snatches her. Our missing person is Tina's kidnapper.'

'Sure we're not jumping to conclusions?'

She shakes her head. 'Tina's kidnapped the same night Liam's car makes a quick visit to the fairground, then the lad himself is reported missing? What do *you* think?'

'Yeah—when you put it like that. But does that help us right this moment?'

'Not without knowing where Liam is, which Rebecca's working full out on—hope there aren't a lot of "pretend" clients from the hotel to distract her.'

'Maybe I should go back and give her a hand...'

'No, it's a long shot anyway—knowing Liam's the kidnapper's one thing, locating him and where he's holding Tina quite another. Even if she gets peace to look, I'm not expecting Rebecca to find him before the ransom drop.'

Hazel's watching Paul pace up and down in front of the reception desk when we finally arrive, and his face lights up with relief when he sees us. From the dark shadows around his eyes, he didn't get much sleep after all. He looks pointedly at his watch and Daisy mutters: 'Hold your water—we're here now. Anyway, the drop isn't for hours yet. Hey—take a look at this. Ever seen him before—especially with Ivor?'

She holds up her phone and Paul studies the photo of Liam we got from Keisha. 'Nope—doesn't ring any bells. Why—who is he?'

'Never mind,' Daisy dismisses. 'Listen, Sam and me are nipping out to do something, but we'll be back well before twelve.'

Paul rubs his hands together. 'Are you sure? What if you get held up?'

'We won't.'

'Mm... I'd feel happier if you drop me off at the fairground, just in case. There are vehicles there I can use if you don't make it.'

Daisy tuts, then looks thoughtful. 'You know, maybe you're right. Just in case. Alright, and obviously you'd better take the... you know what... with you. Sam, go and get it.'

When I go around to her side, Hazel moves over to let me get into the safe. After a few moments, Daisy says: 'What're you doing, Sam—counting it?'

Slowly, I straighten—and from Daisy and Paul's reactions, the shock shows in my face. 'It's gone,' I stutter weakly. 'The bag of money—it isn't there.'

'WHAT?'

Daisy bounds around to my side and crouches, staring helplessly at the empty safe. Well, empty except for Caron's cardboard box. Then, laboriously, she stands and repeats: 'It's gone.' And adds, as an afterthought: 'So are the bar takings from last night.'

Paul emits a noise halfway between a sob and the kind of exclamation golfers make after missing a six-inch putt. Hazel holds up her hands. 'I came on at seven and nobody's been near it since then. Must have been taken during the night.'

'Somehow, the kidnappers outsmarted us,' Paul moans, and Hazel does a double-take.

'Kidnappers?'

'Um, Hazel,' I say quietly, putting a hand on her shoulder. 'Maybe ignore what you just heard—and keep quiet about it?'

She nods quickly. 'Course I will.'

Hazel's someone I trust implicitly, and it doesn't hurt she did a stint as receptionist in the detective agency when it first opened.

Daisy's shaking her head. 'No way was it the kidnappers. They couldn't have known the ransom was here.'

She stoops and plucks Caron's cardboard box from the safe. 'No, this was an inside job.'

'Daisy,' I shout. 'You can't...'

Too late—she's ripped open Caron's package and tipped its contents onto the desk.

Which doesn't tell us a lot, because said contents comprise a sealed envelope. So Daisy rips *that* open and pulls out—a Chinese takeaway menu?

Jodie steps out of the lift at the same moment, carrying Alanna in a baby sling. It's a funny thing, but our hitherto rogue elevator now behaves impeccably for Jodie. I wondered whether it had a crush on her until Logan confided that when they first moved in, Jodie kicked seven bells out of it on three separate occasions. Since then...

She looks around our stunned faces with a curious expression. Then says: 'Don't suppose any of you have seen Caron? I can't find her anywhere...'

THE HOTEL RECEPTION WASN'T AN IDEAL PLACE TO CONTINUE that conversation and if Daisy's right about Caron, we need to find out everything Jodie knows about her missing nanny.

There's no way we can keep Tina's kidnapping a secret from Jodie any longer—she's asked three times what was in the bag that's gone missing and during a couple of hurried asides Daisy and I agreed it's time to fill her in—hoping, at this late stage, she'll see the sense in letting us carry on as planned.

Always assuming we can come up with a hundred grand by noon today

So we reconvene in Jodie and Logan's flat on the top floor. Logan's busy in another part of the hotel and Jodie decides not to call him in. 'You know what Logan's like—he'll just get into a state.'

Alanna gurgles with joy when Daisy returns from checking Caron's room in the staff quarters. Unlike Hector, who huffs and puffs before uncurling himself from Jodie's ankles to slink away.

Jodie looks from Alanna to Daisy. '*Sure* you wouldn't consider a career change? Only, I'm in desperate need of a nanny...'

'You are,' Daisy confirms. 'Her room's cleared out—Caron's offski.'

Jodie throws her arms up. 'I'm back at work tomorrow—and haven't anybody to look after Alanna.'

And Paul just *has* to pipe up. 'What about the ransom money? I'm supposed to deliver it at noon.'

Jodie's face freezes. 'Ransom money?'

Hmm—thanks, Paul. I was hoping we could ease into this part of the conversation a little more gracefully, but...

Nothing else for it. We come clean—and Jodie explodes. 'Are you two finally losing it? Not only are the police far better equipped to handle a kidnapping, you've laid yourselves open to obstruction charges and I dread to think what all.'

'It was my fault,' Paul insists sharply. 'If they hadn't helped me, I'd have gone it alone. So don't blame them—now, can we get back to the small problem of Tina's life depending on my delivering money I no longer have?'

Jodie fixes Paul with a hard look. "Ivor Patterson's already in custody—if he was involved, Inspector Wilson might be able to get Tina's location out of him.'

Paul looks about to blow. 'If he even knows—which he probably doesn't. And if I don't deliver Tina's ransom, it may not *matter* where she is.'

Jodie's undeterred. 'Paul, can't you see my colleagues would handle the ransom drop better? It's tight, but there's still time to set something up.'

Paul's return gaze is equally stony. 'If the kidnappers twig what I've done and kill Tina—and let's face it, the police around here aren't exactly FBI Hostage Rescue material—how d'you think I could live with myself? Knowing I was responsible for my sister's death.'

'But if doing it your way goes wrong—surely that comes to the same. Won't you blame yourself for *not* involving the police?'

He shakes his head. 'I've gone over and over this in my head and I'm convinced the safest option for Tina is to pay up. Look at it logically—why, if we give them their money, would these people upgrade from kidnap to murder? They'd get hunted harder and go down for longer—much easier to release my sister and vamoose somewhere far away to enjoy their cash.'

Jodie sighs—then remembers and, scratching her head, says: 'But you don't *have* the ransom cash any more.'

Daisy glances at her watch. 'S'okay. We've got over two hours to get it back.'

Jodie looks at her disbelievingly. (Actually, so do I.) 'And just how will you do that?'

'By finding Caron—because it must have been her took it. Jodie, did you check her out properly?'

'I did a full background check—I *am* CID, you know.'

'And took up her references?'

Jodie nods. 'They were all bona fide.'

Daisy's brows are furrowed—you can almost hear the wheels spinning. 'The person you verified didn't do this—that's the whole point of the process. I reckon we're looking at identity theft, but *our* "Caron" must be close to the *real*

Caron. It's not like the usual scam that only involves ordering a copy birth certificate—this cookie had access to Caron's personal papers, including her job references. So could they be sisters? Or—flatmates, even?'

'If *that* were the case,' Jodie says excitedly, 'her last address—which I verified—is probably where you'll find the real Caron.'

'Who hopefully can point at us at the fake one before noon. Got that address handy, Jodie? And please don't tell me it isn't local.'

Jodie shoots out of the room and returns a moment later, sifting through a cardboard folder. 'Here it is.'

Daisy grabs the proffered sheet. 'Great. This is in Donstable.'

Jodie nods. 'It was something else in her favour—that she was local and knew her way around.'

'Hang on,' I tell Daisy as she makes for the door. 'We need to check if Jodie's going to let us carry on with this.'

Daisy spins to Jodie. 'C'mon, Jodie—I don't care what you say. Your lot doesn't have time to come up with anything better.'

Jodie exhales—a long, noisy outpouring of breath. 'Alright—I suppose. But we never had this conversation, understood? You haven't shared anything that could see me joining you in the dock if it goes pear-shaped. And also—I'm assuming that by tonight either you'll have Tina back, or be reporting whatever happened to my colleagues.'

'Deal.'

Daisy ambles over and gives Jodie a hug? (Which Jodie returns?) Then catches Paul's eye. 'You got that, Paul? Jodie knows nothing about this.'

Paul nods and offers Jodie a weak smile. 'Thanks.'

Jodie's face darkens. 'That little cow had it all planned out. She asked Logan to put her "family heirloom" in the safe—unless Chinese food played a seminal part in their history, that was a ploy to watch him entering the code.'

'What I don't understand,' I say slowly, 'is how she'd know when there'd be a worthwhile cash haul in the safe. I mean, Caron... or whoever she is... *couldn't* have known about the ransom money. And yeah, we keep the cash takings in there overnight—but with so many people paying electronically, she could have gone to all that bother for a few pounds.'

Daisy's shaking her head. 'She's obviously got a better idea of how things work in the Last Chance Saloon than you do, Sam. None of *them* have bank cards—it's all cash through there.'

Jodie sighs. 'What am I going to do? Logan has too much on to look after Alanna and I won't get a replacement nanny at this short notice. But Inspector Wilson will *not* be chuffed if I ask for more time off on my first day back.'

'You can have one of the maids,' I exclaim, in a burst of inspiration. 'Probably Rosemary would be best—she loves kids. We've got a list of local folk happy to do temp work at short notice, so covering a maid's no problem.'

Jodie claps her hands, making Alanna squeal with delight. 'Brilliant. Right, I'll get onto that straight away.'

'Talk to Hazel—she'll know if Rosemary's on today or, if not, get you her number. I guarantee Rosemary will jump at the chance to play with Alanna rather than clean rooms. Whoops... have to go.'

Daisy's already halfway through the door, and she's got a point.

The clock's ticking.

13

Paul decides he'd still rather wait at the fair, giving him access to alternative transport if we're not back in time. Quite what the point is without any ransom money escapes me, but it's easier to just drop him off—especially considering, in his current state, he'd only get in the way.

Then we head to Donstable and the real Caron's last known address. (Which hopefully still is.)

The satnav takes us to a slightly rundown area which is nonetheless Mayfair to Keisha's Whitechapel. After parking the Panda, we discover most of these crumbling mansions don't have a house number. We do find a weathered numberplate on No. 11, and a wheelie bin labelled with white paint identifies No 19—from there, it's a simple matter of basic arithmetic. (I've always been fine with arithmetic—geometry was where my problems lay. Never could get my head around that square pie thing.)

In common with every other house on this street, No 25 has been converted into flats and one of the buttons beside its front door is labelled "C. Cottrell". 'There she is,' Daisy says excitedly, and jabs the button.

A female voice answers: 'Yes?'

'Police,' Daisy monotones, and I poke her with my elbow.

'That's illegal,' I whisper as the door unlocks with a sharp click.

Daisy turns a hurt look my way. 'What? "Pizza", I said—not "police". Isn't my fault if she misheard.'

We enter a once-grand front hall with two doors off to ground floor flats and a wooden staircase on the back wall. The right-hand door is already open and a lass in her twenties steps out. 'You Caron Cottrell?' Daisy demands, flashing her bus pass.

The girl nods, her eyes wide. 'Em—do you want to come in?'

'Actually, it's your flatmate we're looking for.'

Ah—must have been her ordered the pizza.

Caron shakes her head. 'I don't *have* a flatmate now... oh, do you mean Liz? Hah—doesn't surprise me you're looking for *her*.'

Liz likes pizza?

'Why is that, Madam?' Daisy asks gently.

'She's a right villain. Nicked all my food, forever dipping in my purse—and took some of my best jumpers when she left. If the besom hadn't gone when she did, I'd have flung her out anyway.'

This "Caron" looks nothing like the one we know—ours was tall and slim with blonde hair, whereas the original version is a redhead who's (not to put too fine a point on it) short and dumpy. Daisy rattles off a description of "our" Caron and the genuine article's eyes flash with recognition. 'Yes, that's her. What's she done?'

Daisy puts on a sad expression. 'We're not at liberty to say. Can I ask—is our information that you're a nanny correct?'

'I *was*. Decided it was time to settle down in my own place though, so I've started as a nursery nurse at the day care in Donstable. That's why I advertised for a flatmate—you wouldn't believe what it costs to set up a flat from scratch—but after Liz, I'd rather live on beans. At least when I went to the cupboard, they'd still be there.'

'Yes, about Liz—it's vital we catch up with her quickly. Any idea where she is now?'

Caron frowns. 'Sorry, Liz didn't leave a forwarding address—probably afraid I'd give it to the debt collectors. They've been ringing every day since she left.'

Daisy spreads her arms. 'Family—friends—boyfriend?'

Caron perks up. 'Oh, she had a boyfriend. Right sleazeball he was, but Liz was besotted. If she hadn't been spending so much time at his place, I'd have thrown her out weeks ago.'

Imagine someone lost in the desert who looks down to find themselves up to their ankles in water—and you'll see Daisy's expression. 'Got an address for him?' she breathes, then sags when Caron shakes her head.

'But... one night, when we were still talking, Liz was over at his and they had a lovers' tiff. She rang and asked me to pick her up—the buses had stopped running, see, and as usual Liz was broke and couldn't afford a taxi. Muggins here obliged—so I've *been* to Pete's place.'

Daisy scrabbles for her phone. 'Can you show me on a map?'

Then they go into a huddle, leaving me struggling to catch the odd, disjointed phrase.

'Turned right there...'

'I remember going down Charleston Drive...'

'No, back a bit—oh, that's clever. How'd you do that?'

Daisy's voice: 'Google Street View. Do you recognise it?'

'Yeah, that's the right road. And... yes, there. That's Pete's building. The blue door. It's flats, like here, and Pete's is one up. On the right, I think. Yes, it was—I saw him looking out the window, watching us get into my car.'

'Brilliant,' Daisy tells her. 'Thanks so much.'

'That's alright—always happy to help the police.'

OF COURSE, PETE'S ADDRESS JUST *HAS* TO BE IN THE BAD END of Donstable—only a street away from Keisha's flat. To get there we have to go through the town centre and my head is so full of everything from the missing money to finding out who Tina's kidnapper is (and a certain concern for my surviving wing mirror considering our destination) that I nearly miss it. Luckily, I'm sitting beside Hawkeye.

'Sam, look... Isn't that...?'

I follow her pointing finger and swallow painfully. 'Yes—it is.'

Davy—my fiancée—going into a café. Accompanied by—Leslie? If so, Leslie is *not* a man.

Anything but.

Leslie is a twenty-something, vivacious blonde. She's got more curves than Paul's rollercoaster and her dress is tailored to showcase them. Her face is one of those that—apart from being pretty—I can only describe as "bubbly".

Fun – lively – catwalk-ready – the sort of package you don't let a boyfriend anywhere near. As she chats gaily (bubbles?) her fingertips snake out and touch Davy's arm.

As for him—well, I've never seen the big idjit look so happy.

A horn blares as I slam on the brakes. 'Sam—you were *this* close to getting rear-ended.'

I hardly hear her—it's *Leslie's* rear end I'm concerned about as I watch it sashay inside the café with Davy tailgating closer than Mr road-rage behind us. (Who's now leaning out of his window, shouting obscenities.)

Daisy rolls down her own window, leans out, and uses sign language to suggest his behaviour is unacceptable.

Mr road-rage must actually be a reasonable sort (and able to read sign language) because he goes quiet as a mouse.

My fiancée and *Leslie* have disappeared inside, no doubt cosying up over cups of latte and perhaps sharing a panini. Slamming the Panda into gear, I make its wheels spin as we rocket off.

Daisy throws me an appreciative look. 'Brill, Sam. You're finally getting the hang of this driving thing. Um... I'll keep an eye out for cop cars, shall I?'

My newfound "Dukes of Hazzard" roadcraft technique gives way to a more sedate pace and when she judges I've calmed sufficiently, Daisy puts a hand on my knee and murmurs: 'They're only going for coffee—and Davy *did* tell you about her. It's not like he's hiding anything.'

'You're right—I overreacted. It's just coffee.'

If I repeat that often enough, maybe I'll start believing it

It's a relief to arrive at our destination and have something else to focus on. In particular, the wellbeing of my already injured car.

After we get out, I press the lock button on my key and regard the hole where poor Panda's wing mirror should be with a twinge of sadness. (I had to pull it off so the paintwork wouldn't get scratched.) 'Daisy, I'm not happy about leaving the car here—after what happened last time.'

She's not listening, and I follow her gaze to the same three youths who were supposed to ensure my car stayed in one piece while we were in Keisha's yesterday. They're doing their "gangsta-strut" along the opposite pavement and seem unaware of us. That changes when Daisy yells: 'Oi. I want a word with you.'

The three stooges watch curiously as she marches up. Then two of those expressions change, abruptly, to shocked—I can't see their leader's because he's flat on his back. Catching Daisy's eye as she strolls back, I venture: 'Osoto gari?'

'Yeah—or "large outer reap," in English.'

I've been to all Daisy's black belt gradings (who knew there were different levels of black belt?) and she tests me afterwards…

Both henchmen are helping their leader off the pavement when Daisy holds up a phone—which isn't hers. Not unless she's invested in a new case, laser printed with psychedelic patterns. 'Want this back?' she calls.

Leader, who's now on his feet and (barely) standing unaided, pats frantically at a jeans pocket. 'How'd you get that?' he roars.

'Tell you what—when we come out, if our car's no more damaged than it is now, I'll give you the phone back.'

He takes a menacing step off the kerb. (Strangely, his two compatriots seem reluctant to follow.) 'What if I just *take* it back, right now?'

Daisy shrugs. 'You can try.'

Leader blinks. 'Um… okay, but don't be long.'

'We'll be as long as we are,' Daisy throws over a shoulder as I follow her into the block of flats.

14

Our destination is the top right flat. An outer door looks to be buzzer controlled, but both buzzer and lock turn out to be broken. 'So you lifted his phone mid-throw? Neat,' I comment as we head for the stairs. 'You're getting really good at this "pickpocket" thing.'

'I am, aren't I.'

Scarily so

After negotiating a set of stone steps that don't smell particularly hygienic, we find ourselves standing between two gnarled wooden doors. Daisy raps her knuckles against one.

A muffled male voice shouts: 'Go away—whoever you are.'

'Pizza delivery,' Daisy calls cheerfully and winks at me before whispering: 'See? I'm being good.'

"Hurried fumbling" noises precede the unmistakeable click of a lock turning and the door flies open, revealing a slight man in his twenties whose tongue all but hangs out as he rushes to claim a pizza that isn't his. 'Okay, give it here...'

He breaks off, studying Daisy intently—like he's trying to place her. I'm doing the same to him—I've definitely seen this guy before, just can't remember where. Daisy does, though. 'You,' she snaps, her tone a whiplash that makes him recoil.

Glancing sideways at me: 'That's the scumbag who lifted Mr M's wallet on Friday night.'

"Scumbag" (or presumably, Pete) goes to slam the door, but Daisy already has her foot in place. She reaches through the gap, grabs Pete's throat, and squeezes. Pete wrenches free and staggers back with a hand over his windpipe, trying (and seemingly failing) to draw breath as Daisy barges in.

'What's going on?'

We're in a small, square hall and those words, spoken in a familiar female voice, come from the nearest of four doorways. Its owner's hand flies mouthwards when she recognises us and Daisy says: 'Well, well. What are you doing here, Caron—or is it Liz?'

Caron/Liz turns and races back into the room she emerged from, hotly pursued by Daisy who shoulders Pete out of her way. Before I can follow, Pete staggers into me and I yelp. He holds up a plaintive palm. 'Sorry,' he gasps. 'Just a bit dizzy—still can't breathe properly.'

He emphasises the apology by backing off, palms raised, and I nod before going after Daisy. Not quite sure what she did to him, but that wasn't judo—she was into aikido a while back, but my limited knowledge doesn't suggest one-handed choke-holds fall within aikido's remit. Must remember to ask her...

The room turns out to be a bedroom. It has a standard double bed, unremarkable in itself—what sets it apart is 100 grand in used notes scattered over the surface. (Plus last night's bar takings.) The holdall they arrived in lies abandoned under a window.

Daisy's currently absorbed in retrieving a fistful of twenties from each of Liz's tightly fisted hands—presumably the bold lass made a last-ditch attempt grab what she could. She screeches when Daisy applies leverage to her wrists (now that *is* aikido) and the banknotes flutter floorward. Stooping, I gather them up while Daisy pivots Liz towards the bed. 'Right, m'lady. You've got one minute to get *all* that cash packed back in its bag.'

Liz turns a venomous face into Daisy's. 'Or what?'

I shudder—bad move, especially when Daisy still has hold of a wrist. Liz screams—short and sharp. 'Okay, okay—I'll do it. Leggo, wilya?'

Daisy releases her and it actually takes Liz more like *three* minutes to repack the cash, which isn't terrible considering the number of banknotes involved.

When she's finished, Daisy grabs the bag and hands it to me. Then she turns back to Liz. 'Who thought up this scam—Pete?'

Liz shakes her head. 'No, I did. Pete was going to turn the cash into bitcoin, so it was safe and untraceable. He knows about that sort of thing. Course, we weren't expecting so much—what is it, some kind of tax dodge?'

Daisy ignores that last and sneers. 'From the little I've seen of *Pete,* it's odds on he was planning to take off with the lot.'

'No, Pete wouldn't...'

I back off to the doorway while this is going on, holding the bag of money. Out of nowhere, a hand slams between my shoulder blades. Taking off from a standing start, my left leg quickly falls out of synch with the right and I prepare for an uncomfortable rendezvous with Pete's threadbare carpet—when Daisy appears from nowhere and grabs me. We nearly both go down, but Daisy's a lot stronger than she looks and suddenly I find myself able to stand unaided as Daisy rushes at the door.

A bang my imagination instantly transposes into a gunshot sends me whirling around, so fast I'm in danger of making close acquaintance with that carpet after all. With a shock, it dawns on me I'm no longer holding the bag of money.

'Beggar.'

Daisy's got hold of the bedroom doorhandle, yanking angrily, but it won't budge. The bang must have been it slamming. 'What happened?' I ask weakly.

'Pete. Blighter grabbed the bag when he pushed you, then locked us in.'

I look desperately at the window. 'We're one floor up—and there's no other way out. He's going to get away.'

Daisy's hand is in her jeans pocket, scrabbling around. With a grunt of satisfaction, she pulls out something resembling an Allen key and another, straight metal rod shaped like a tiny lightning bolt at one end. Dropping to her knees and leaning close to the lock, Daisy first inserts her Allen key, then probes gently with the lightning bolt.

Tasers—lock picks—the woman's a walking depository of illegal implements

Liz retreats to the bed, where she sits with folded arms and glares at Daisy. Anxiously, I check my watch—10.45. Just over an hour before the ransom drop's supposed to happen.

Daisy squeals with glee when the lock turns. 'Done it,' she announces proudly, jumping to her feet and throwing open the door. 'C'mon, Sam—let's get 'im.'

'He's got too big a start—we'll never catch him.'

'Maybe—maybe not. We can drive around in the Panda—might catch sight of him before he goes to ground.'

I do my best to keep up, but have long accepted stairs will always be a challenge. When I finally emerge, Daisy's out on the road and looking from side to side with an angry expression. 'Gone,' she spits, shaking her head.

'Well, let's try driving around, like you said. With any luck…'

I break off, seeing what Daisy's seeing—or rather, *not* seeing.

Our "parking attendants" for a start—they've scarpered. But suddenly I don't care about them any more. I'm staring at an empty patch of road outside the entrance.

My Panda is gone.

Clenching both hands into impotent fists, I state what seems obvious. 'Pete must have hot-wired it.'

But Daisy's shaking her head. 'Can't do that with modern cars. D'you maybe have one of those magnetic boxes stuck underneath, with a spare key?'

'Absolutely not,' I shoot back, hesitating to add "Do you think I'm stupid" because, in common with barristers, I baulk at asking questions when the reply might not be to my liking.

Then I pat at both jacket pockets. 'My keys—they've gone.'

Daisy groans. 'Pete's a pickpocket—he must have lifted them.'

My hand flies to cover a mouth already wide open. 'After you throttled him, he staggered into me—then apologised profusely. I thought he was just…'

Daisy's shoulders sag. 'That's when he did it—we'll never catch him now. As for those traitorous kids—they better keep out of my way.'

'But you had their phone? Oh—Pete probably shoved a handful of cash at them.'

She nods grimly. 'Outbid us—that little twerp got a free upgrade on his phone.'

'Should we report the Panda as stolen?'

'No—it would raise too many awkward questions, plus we haven't time. If the Panda doesn't turn up, you can call it in later—maybe say it was taken from Donstable Main Street, though. Meantime, we're stuck here and Paul's expecting us in not much more than an hour with Tina's ransom.'

'Which we don't have,' I remind her.

She winces. 'Okay, gonna have to improvise. Let's walk up to the town centre, find a cash machine, then get a taxi.'

'Find a cash machine? Are you serious? A cash machine isn't going to spew out a hundred grand, even if either of us had that kind of money in our account.'

She touches a finger to her nose (carefully avoiding the nose ring) and starts walking, forcing me to do the same. 'By the way,' I remember, since it's a ten-minute walk to Donstable town centre and an ideal opportunity to indulge my curiosity. 'What was that you did to Pete's throat? Some new martial art you're learning?'

She gives me the sort of look teachers save for a slow pupil—in my case, usually the maths teacher. 'Naw. That was just me getting my gander up.'

15

We make it to Paul's caravan with 20 minutes to spare. 'We'll need every one of them,' is the response when I share that information. Daisy's keeping mum on the details of whatever plan she's concocted, "in case it doesn't come off".

We managed to draw £300 each from the cash machine. For some reason, Daisy chose to have it all in ten-pound notes. I was impressed she had so much on call—we're a long way from the days when muggins here was forever fronting her bus fare to work. (Come to think of it, I never got any of that back.)

In my wildest dreams, I don't see the kidnappers settling for £600.

Paul's frantic when he comes to the door. 'Where have you been? Do you know what time it is?'

'Calm down,' Daisy tells him. 'First, do you have a vehicle we can use? Sam's... ah... misplaced hers.'

He looks at her curiously, then points at a dull-grey jeep parked beside the caravan. 'Yeah, that's one of the fairground workhorses—we can take it.'

I'm just curious. 'Don't you have a car of your own, Paul?'

'None of us do. The fair has a pool of vehicles we all use—according to Tina, it saves a lot in tax.'

Daisy sticks her head between us. 'If you two are quite finished, I need another bag like the ransom was in and a cardboard box that fits neatly inside it. And a pair of scissors... *please*.' She gives me a sideways glance as if to say: '*See?* I do know that word.'

Paul stares at her. 'I take it you didn't find the money, then?'

'Oh, we found it... but it sort of got away again.'

She raises a hand as Paul's face beetroots. 'Look, no time to explain. Will you just get me the things I asked for?'

Muttering angrily, Paul stalks back into the caravan with us following. Inside, he lifts a sofa seat to reveal storage space and after rummaging, produces a sports bag not unlike the one Pete ran off with.

'Great,' Daisy declares. 'Box next.'

Stooping to open a cupboard under his tiny sink, Paul pulls out a carton of beer. Peroni, I note absently—one of the few beers I quite enjoy. On a hot day, mainly because it's refreshing. A lot of beers aren't—there's a reason they call "bitter" bitter. Mind, I'm not normally a beer drinker…

'Sam. Did you hear me? Empty the bottles out of that box—and Paul, find me some scissors. Where are my rubber bands?'

Paul gapes at her. 'Rubber bands? You never said anything about rubber bands.'

'Didn't I? Well, I need some.'

Breathing heavily, Paul heads for the door. 'Should be able to rustle a few up from the stallholders—how many d'you want?'

'A lot,' she snaps, grabbing the now-empty Peroni box and checking it fits in the holdall. Satisfied, she removes it again. 'Sam,' she barks, and I jerk upright.

'Yes—something I can do?'

'There is—go'n open one of those Peronis. I'm parched.'

PAUL DOES A DOUBLE-TAKE WHEN HE CHARGES BACK IN, clutching several packets of rubber bands, and clocks Daisy mid-swig from a Peroni bottle. 'Please don't rush, Daisy. We've got at least ten minutes before the kidnappers expect me to set off with their non-existent hundred grand.'

He breaks off abruptly and stares at the box beside her. Daisy's laid out four rows of ten-pound notes on top. Each row comprises five piles of cash, three notes thick. Daisy does her "sweet" look. (The one she had to stop using on small children because it made them scream.) 'Paul, I'm still waiting for those scissors—but any chance you could get me a small screwdriver instead? Reckon it would work better.'

Wordlessly, Paul reaches behind an armchair and brings out a toolbox. He rummages inside, then produces an electrical screwdriver. Daisy leans over to snatch it and a packet of rubber bands before turning back to her creation.

After moving the piles of notes onto the floor, she lifts one and positions it carefully on the box, then jabs a small hole through the cardboard midway down each of the banknotes' long sides. 'Oh bother,' she exclaims. 'I *do* need scissors, after all.'

Looking like someone living a bad dream, Paul pads into the kitchen area and returns with scissors. Taking them from him, Daisy snips a rubber band—leaving her with a length of elastic. Then she threads each end through one of the holes she made before. Turning the box over while holding the banknotes in place with her other hand, she takes hold of the protruding elastic tails and pulls them tight. That frees her other hand, and she ties a knot. Flipping the box back over, Daisy breathes a sigh of satisfaction. 'Yeah, seems fine. Right, repeat nineteen times...'

When she's done (at one minute **to** twelve) and inserts her finished product in the new holdall, I have to admit it closely resembles a bag full of money. (If you don't pull the bag open too far—it'll also help if the kidnappers need glasses they forgot to bring.)

Paul nods grudging approval. 'Okay, that's clever. Two problems, though. First, what if they try to lift out a wad of notes?'

Daisy shrugs. 'It's a risk, but I'm betting they'll be in too much of a hurry to do more than have a quick keek before getting on with their getaway.'

Paul's lips tighten. 'Hm... doesn't really matter, because second thing is what's the point? The kidnappers won't release Tina until they've counted the cash—when they'll realise straight away what you've done.'

'True—but I've got a plan. It involves letting them take the "ransom" back to wherever they're hiding out, following them, then getting Tina out ourselves.'

Paul pales. 'THAT'S your plan? Follow them? Daisy—don't you think the kidnappers will expect us to try that? Which means they'll have set it up so we can't.'

A horn toot-toots outside and Daisy springs up. 'Ah, that'll be my delivery.'

At the same moment, Paul's phone rings. He looks at the screen and his hand shakes. 'It's them—the kidnappers.'

16

I'm getting shaken to bits here. Why have I spent half my waking hours since moving to Cairncroft being thrown about on roads that don't merit the title? At least this time, the strain on our vehicle's suspension isn't *my* worry.

Which brings my poor Panda to mind—I hope Pete treats her well and ideally abandons his getaway car somewhere the police (when I'm finally allowed to contact them) will easily find it.

Paul's driving, I'm riding shotgun, and Daisy's in the back seat working furiously at her phone. She has a large cardboard carton on the seat beside her—the last minute "delivery". Rather than Amazon, it was Rebecca in her Audi who dropped off Daisy's package moments before we left to carry out the kidnappers' instructions.

Daisy was expecting the kidnappers to send us on a treasure hunt of the "be at the phone box outside Donstable post office in twenty minutes" (and so on) variety, but instead Paul was given a set of satnav coordinates and told to be *there* in twenty minutes. (By sheer dumb luck, she got the "twenty minutes" right.)

Naturally, I'm consumed with curiosity about what's in Daisy's box but, when I ask, get only: 'Shush—I'm busy.'

The satnav coordinates are taking us north (Donstable's to the East) and I'm increasingly puzzled by where the rendezvous can be. My first thought was Inverurie— "twenty minutes" just about fits (albeit with pedal to the metal)—but our satnav's got us going down narrow, unsurfaced farm tracks leading only to the middle of nowhere.

Must be getting close, though—only three minutes left on the "time remaining" display. We're driving through a very flat area of raw countryside and can see for miles in every direction except straight ahead, where the meadows erupt into a conical hill. It's not unlike East Lothian's famous "Berwick Law", though considerably smaller.

Checking my watch tells me we're two minutes shy of the kidnapper's deadline for our arrival at wherever they've sent us.

'Got it.'

Paul and I both startle at Daisy's triumphant whoop. I spin around in my seat while Paul's eyes seek her out in his rear-view mirror.

Daisy waves her phone. 'I see how this works.'

She points at the hump of hillside ahead. 'From up there, the kidnappers can view this entire area laid out like a map—so if we had a police tail, they'd spot it straight away. We'll get told to dump the bag, then leave. When the kidnappers see us go and no SWAT teams appear, they'll come down and pick it up—then be offski.'

'Clever,' I mutter—because it is.

Paul exhales in a moan. 'But that means there's no way we can follow them.'

Daisy opens her cardboard carton and, with a smirk, lifts out Dougal the drone. Putting him down next to her, she swipes at his control app on her phone and a low hum fills the cabin. After winking at Paul through his mirror, Daisy winds down her window. She picks up Dougal with one hand (obviously lighter than he looks, or is that because his fans are running?) and reaches out, dangling him over the track.

Then lets go.

Instead of crashing to the ground her drone hovers in mid-air. (The drone equivalent of "treading water"?)

Then Daisy taps her phone and Dougal soars upward in the sort of smooth ascent I've long wished our hotel lift could master.

'So,' Daisy says smugly, 'even if the kidnappers are watching through binoculars, they'll just think Dougal's a big bird. After we drop off the ransom, I'll leave him hovering a couple of hundred feet up. Then, when the kidnappers collect their cash, Dougal will follow them back to wherever they're holding Tina—and so will we.'

I've got to hand it to her—some of her schemes are questionable to say the least, but this time she's really come through. Paul thinks so too—he's beaming. 'That's brilliant, Dais'. Has it got cameras, then?'

'Yep—we can watch them all the way to their rathole.'

Then her face turns serious. 'Paul, there's something else I've thought of—and you need to decide quick on this, because we're only a couple of minutes from the dropsite. The kidnappers have made one potentially fatal error—sure, they're able to see nobody's coming for them, but the very nature of this area makes it easy to trap anybody already in it. If I phone the police and convince them to act fast, they could block every exit road—all three of them—and grab the kidnappers on their way out.'

'How would they know which car belonged to the kidnappers?' I wonder.

Oops—I'm back in my maths' class, getting THAT look

'It's not exactly the A1, Sam—these roads probably never see more than one car in a day.'

Paul shakes his head. 'No. Absolutely not. What if whoever's watching her has orders to kill Tina if his mates don't return by a certain time? It's too risky.'

Daisy breathes out noisily, and for a moment I'm sure she's going to argue the point—then her frustration lapses into resignation. 'Okay—for the record, I think that's the wrong decision, but—it *would* have been tight to set up at this late stage.'

'*You have arrived at your destination*' the annoying American woman drawls and Paul brings us to a screeching halt. As he does, his phone rings. We'd already agreed he'd keep it on speaker.

Electronic voice: 'You were told to come alone.'

Paul: 'I thought you only meant the police. These are just friends of mine and Tina's. They only came along for... moral support.'

Electronic voice: 'Get out of the car. Bring the ransom with you. Then place it at the roadside.'

    Paul complies, and returns to the jeep. 'Shall we go now?' he asks his phone.
    'Not yet,' the electronic voice replies. 'The countryside code clearly states you should take any rubbish home. Please comply.'
    Paul pushes his glasses up (they're a terrible fit) as he looks at me, then Daisy. We both shrug. 'Haven't a scooby what that's about,' Daisy says slowly, her brows creased. Then a bang makes everybody duck by reflex.
    'They're shooting at us,' Paul whimpers, but Daisy shakes her head. 'No, that wasn't a gunshot.'
    Understanding floods Daisy's face and her lips twist into a snarl as she grabs at the door handle. Another loud report echoes through the air, but

this time it's much closer—and more of a "crunch".

'Dougal', Daisy screams, leaping from the car.

Paul's eyebrows rise. 'Dougal?'

I make a face that says I don't know what she's on about either and get out to follow. I find her a short distance up the road, crouched over a mass of tangled, smoking wreckage.

A pile of metal junk that used to be called "Dougal".

Daisy looks around as I approach. 'They killed Dougal, Sam.'

'Um.' I'm not sure how to comfort someone when their drone dies.

Daisy stands up, forcing a stoic expression. 'Oh, don't worry—I'll get another one, and we didn't really have time to bond. Shame, though—he was a bonny lad.'

I spread my arms. 'What happened? Did his batteries run out?'

She answers by pointing up. Raising a hand to shield my eyes, I scan between the clouds. There's *something* up there—before today, I'd have assumed a falcon, or an eagle.

'Listen,' Daisy says and sure enough, by concentrating really hard, I can just pick up a high-pitched hum.

I look from Dougal's crumpled remains back to the sky. 'You mean...?'

'Yeah—the kidnappers brought their own drone. A big one—it must have rammed Dougal and flipped him over so his own rotors sent him into a power dive. I was wrong, Sam—good job we didn't ask the police to fence the kidnappers in.'

'You think they'd thought of that—and were using a drone of their own to watch the escape routes?'

'Exactly. Either, being "drone aware", they *did* spot Dougal through binoculars, or *their* drone picked him up on its cameras.'

Paul comes up behind. 'So we can't follow them after all?'

Daisy shakes her head, then scowls. 'I'm wondering whether we should take the dummy ransom away with us. It might be safer, rather than risk them throwing a wobbly because it's short...'

Paul snorts. 'Short? That's one way of putting it.'

'... it's a question of what makes them madder—no ransom, or not enough. I mean, they *might* look on the six hundred as a deposit...'

'Do you hear that?' I thought it was just me, but the distant hum is definitely getting louder—which means closer. We all whirl, zeroing in on the source of what now sounds like a huge swarm of angry bees.

Back up the road, not far behind the ransom bag Paul left at the roadside, a monster drone hovers ten feet off the ground. It's at least four times the size Dougal was, with twice his number of propulsion fans. Jet black, it also differs from Dougal in that there's a cable hanging down. Did it get damaged in the collision, I wonder?

Without warning, the enemy drone skitters forward, losing altitude as it comes. When it passes over the sports bag, a hook on the end of its hanging cable snags one of the handles. Then the thrumming rises in pitch—becomes a roar—and the blighter streaks skyward in an almost vertical ascent, taking Paul's sports bag with it.

'Okay,' Daisy says in a dazed voice. 'Guess that's one less decision we have to make.'

17

'How'd it go?'

Eyes aglow, Rebecca cranes across her desk as all three of us walk into the detective agency. Even Hector, sitting on a pile of files, senses her excitement and lets curiosity override his usual pique at Daisy's presence.

We don't need to say anything. Rebecca's gaze flips between our expressions and she slumps back in her chair. '*That* well, huh?'

An atmosphere like a wake *and* proximity to Daisy is too much for Hector, who leaps from Rebecca's desk and makes a huffy exit into the staffroom.

Then storms back out, now looking *thoroughly* cheesed off, when Daisy goes in to dump the carton doubling as Dougal's coffin.

On her return, Daisy hustles Paul into her office while I give Rebecca the short version of our disastrous first encounter with Tina's kidnappers.

When I go through, Daisy's crouched at her filing cabinet with its bottom drawer open. She waves a bottle of Irish whisky at Paul, but he shakes his head. 'No—I'm driving, remember?'

Daisy nods. 'You're right—REBECCA. Coffee—strong.'

'When they twig what's in that bag, those slimeballs will kill her,' Paul mutters darkly.

'Won't happen,' Daisy says firmly. 'They saw we didn't involve the police, so nothing's really changed—the kidnappers still have Tina and you still want her back. They aren't going to flush all that planning and effort down the toilet when effectively all we've done is added another step to the process.'

Paul looks at her and you can see he's trying to believe what she's saying. 'You think so?'

Then his face falls. 'Even if you're right, what if they decide to scare us so we don't do anything like that again? They might cut off one of Tina's fingers and send it through the post.'

'Naw—the post takes forever these days, and half the time they lose whatever it is...'

Daisy's attempt at levity crash-lands harder than Dougall did and she pulls a face by way of apology. 'The kidnappers have put a lot into this,' she persists. 'They won't want to walk away with nothing—and I can't see them hurting Tina, either. They'd be scared of panicking you into going to the police.'

Paul's chin falls to his chest. 'But even if they do give us a second chance at handing over the cash, we don't have it.'

'He's right,' I chip in. 'And they won't fall for a mock-up this time.'

Daisy's eyes go hard. 'We need to find Pete—and fast.'

I turn to Paul. 'In case we can't—find Pete—is there any way you can raise more money?'

Paul's head comes up slowly—as though it weighs a ton. 'Maybe—I could try Dobson again. To be honest, I'm not sure how much the fair's really worth—but I doubt it's anywhere near two hundred grand.'

'Okay, here's the plan.'

Daisy's only happy when she's got a plan, irrespective of its quality. 'Get back on to Mr M, Paul—ask him for some rough estimate of the fair's value before you speak to Dobbs. From what you've said, I could easily imagine that man trying to rip you off. Meanwhile, Sam and I will see about tracking down the original ransom.'

I wonder how she intends doing that, but now might not be the right time to ask. Instead, I put in: 'It's Sunday, Daisy. Mr M's closed.'

'Oh, bother.'

Then she brightens. 'More often than not, he pops into the office after church for a catch up—let's him get stuff done without any interruptions. I'll give him a bell...'

'You've just said he doesn't want to be interrupted...'

'Pfaw.' She flaps a hand while using her other to pick up the phone. 'This is an emergency... Mr M? Hi—it's Daisy. Can I ask a huge favour?'

A minute later, she hangs up and grins at Paul. 'He'll see you at half-four in his office.'

Then she looks quizzically at me. 'I actually didn't think he'd be there today—not with Kat around to entertain him.'

'Mm... maybe he needs a rest?'

I meant because he's used to living alone and might find someone else's constant presence exhausting, but her sudden hilarity suggests Daisy misinterpreted me.

Then she puts back on her business face. 'Paul, you go and get together whichever of your dad's papers will help Mr M value the fair. Meanwhile, I...'

Just then, my phone buzzes—when I check, it's a call from Davy. 'Um, have to take this,' I apologise, waving the phone and making for the door.

Hearing Rebecca clank cups in the staffroom prompts me to keep walking until I'm outside. Privacy assured, I stab the "answer" button with a shaking finger.

'Hi, Sam. Uh—how's it going?'

'Fine. How about you—enjoy meeting your old university friend yesterday?'

'Oh—yes, it was nice. Em... thought I saw your car earlier? I was in a café at the time...'

So THAT'S why you're calling—and sound so guilty

'Yeah, I saw you too. Was that Leslie you were with?' I realise too late that adding a sing-song lilt to Leslie's name might have been a tad childish.

'It was, yes.'

Aha. Trying the old "so what?" game, are we?

'Twice in as many days—you must have *really* re-connected.'

His exasperated sigh makes my phone vibrate. 'Sam, it isn't what you seem to think. Leslie and I had business to discuss.'

'Sorry Davy, now I'm confused. Is she a former university friend or a business associate? I'm having trouble keeping up with her various personas.'

'Don't be like that. She's both, alright?'

'Ah, okay. So what kind of business were the two of you discussing?'

Silence. Then: 'I can't really say yet. I mean, it's early days...'

So early, it isn't actually happening

'Tell you what, Davy. Give me a bell back when you *can* say, because I'm always interested to hear about your *work.* Got to go now.'

Stabbing the red button with a ferocity my poor phone didn't deserve, I suck in air then let it out in a long hiss. MEN. They're all the same—untrustworthy, cheating pigs. Every one of them.

Although I did think Davy was different.

Suddenly the rage subsides and a tear trickles down my cheek. Fingers touch my forearm, startling me. 'You OK, Sam?'

It's Rebecca. 'Yes, fine,' I reply, trying for breezy—and to swipe away the tear before she sees it.

'Daisy sent me to see where you'd got to—sorry, I overheard some of that. Boyfriend problems, I take it?'

I nod. Rebecca knows all about my last boyfriend and how he cheated on me.

She should—it was her he cheated with

'If there's anything I can do…'

Working in the detective agency has changed Rebecca beyond recognition. From seeing her as my mortal enemy (because, back then, she was), I've watched her grow into someone I trust—respect, even. Hmm… maybe there *is* something she can do.

'Rebecca, I've got a job for you—in your professional capacity. But not a word to Daisy, alright…?'

GOING BACK IN, WE PASS PAUL EN ROUTE TO RAID HIS DAD'S office space. It'll be interesting to see what value Mr M puts on the fair. Daisy's right—this Dobson character sounds as though he's taking advantage.

Daisy's waiting beside Rebecca's desk, tapping a foot on the carpet. 'There you are—what took so long?'

I shrug. 'Nothing—spoke to Davy on the phone, then chatted with Rebecca for a few minutes.'

She gives me a look that says I'm a lousy liar. Tough—what I don't need is Daisy's "help" sorting out this Davy and Leslie thing. Especially since Daisy's idea of "helping" is likely to involve putting Leslie in hospital...

'I have a lead on Pete,' she declares smugly.

Now *that* I wasn't expecting. 'Great... let's go, then.'

'We don't have a car,' she reminds me. 'But it's okay—we'll borrow Rebecca's Audi.'

Rebecca colours. 'I kinda need the car for something...'

'Yes,' I put in. 'Rebecca has stuff she needs to get on with.'

Daisy sighs. 'Fine—you'll just have to ride pillion on Bessie, Sam.'

'Rebecca,' I tell her firmly, 'That thing I asked you to do can wait. Give me the keys to your Audi.'

'SO WHAT'S THIS THING YOU'RE GETTING REBECCA TO DO?' Daisy asks curiously.

'What's this lead you've got?' I counter firmly, playing Daisy at her own game and turning on the headlights when I meant to indicate right. Well—you get used to your own car.

'Alan,' Daisy says, not a little smugly. 'He owes me one, after taking so long to run those plates. I explained your car was missing and he agreed to do an ANPR search on the police computer.'

'ANPR? I know what that stands for—I do. Just can't remember exactly...'

'Automatic Number Plate Recognition. Traffic cameras read the plate number of every car they "see" and store that information in a computer. Alan put your Panda's registration in and got a hit straight away.'

'Oh, brill... wait a minute. There aren't any traffic cameras around here—are there?'

'Not locally, no—but there's one on the A96 about twenty minutes away with a layby in its field of view, and your Panda's parked there.'

I feel a thrill of relief—I still haven't gotten over losing my Škoda, but the Panda's proved a worthy substitute and I'd have hated to start from scratch with yet another car. Then the full meaning of what she said sinks in. 'Daisy, don't get me wrong—I'm thrilled about getting the Panda back. But if it's *parked* in a layby on the A96, Pete's probably long gone. That's just where he dumped it.'

'Yeah, but think about it—you don't go for a walk on the A96. If he dumped it there, someone must have picked him up in another car. Alan's trying to get the last few hours footage from that camera—once he does, and goes through it, ten gets you twenty we'll have details of the vehicle Pete's in now. Which means Alan can do a new search for *it* on ANPR.'

'But if you've told him my Panda was stolen, won't Alan just pass the other car's details to the local police?'

'I told him to run it past me first, in case it was his dippy girlfriend took the car and forgot to tell us.'

Fifteen minutes later we pull into the layby Alan's satnav coordinates directed us to, and there it is—my Panda. So overcome am I with relief that I don't see her at first...

'Sam, look. Over there... isn't that Liz?'

Sure enough, it's Jodie's renegade nanny. She's sitting against a tree trunk, sobbing her heart out. When we approach, Liz glances up. 'Oh, it's you,' she sniffles.

We already checked the Panda was empty but Pete *could* be behind a tree, perhaps attending to personal business... 'Are you alone?' Daisy asks softly.

'Very,' Liz snaps back, then bursts into tears again. Daisy looks at me and inclines her head. The unspoken message is: "You're better at this sort of thing."

It would be ideal if I could kneel beside her, but that's complicated with a prosthetic leg. Choosing the simpler route, I step forward and put a hand on Liz's shoulder until she looks up. Then speak in a soft tone. 'There, now. I'm guessing Pete's abandoned you here?'

Liz nods. 'He... he phoned and asked me to bring his car. Said we'd leave together and start a new life. But after I got here...'

Her voice dries up, and Daisy finishes for her. '... Pete took his keys and when you tried the passenger door, it was locked.'

'He... he just drove off and left me. Oh... I HATE him.'

Good thing we got here before it clicked with Liz she could go home in my Panda

Daisy must be rubbing her hands in glee. (Hopefully metaphorically—I'm scared to look.) 'Liz,' I say quietly. 'The best way to get your own back is by helping us find him. What's the make of Pete's car—and do you know its registration number?'

Liz sniffs, then her features harden. 'I can do better than that because I've known for a while Pete was untrustworthy. That's why, one night when he was asleep, I popped a tracking app on his phone. Give me yours and I'll download you a copy of the control app—it pinpoints Pete to an accuracy of ten feet.'

18

Pete fled to Aberdeen. Specifically, to a plush hotel near Hazlehead Park called "The Excelsior".

Or so the Google map in Liz's tracking app says…

Daisy took great delight in calling Alan back and telling him our "own resources" beat him to the punch.

Parking my recovered Panda on a paved forecourt, I wonder what Davy would say about this mix of traditional design with modern building materials. I know the answer—Davy's so much into modern with a capital "M" he designed himself a house that looks like something out of an Isaac Asimov novel.

Why am I thinking about Davy?

How could I not be…?

'Sam—you still there?'

Giving my head a shake to clear it (well, it worked with Etch a Sketch when I was a kid) I focus on the here and now. 'I was admiring Pete's latest hideout,' I stammer, but Daisy's not listening. Instead, she's reading a text that just came in. 'It's Rebecca—saying she got the Audi back. That's a relief.'

We made a deal with Liz, which involved letting her borrow the Audi if she delivered it to Rebecca. Rebecca would then (because Daisy phoned and told her to) take Liz home to Donstable. The snag, of course, being whether Liz would simply vanish with Rebecca's Audi. But we were desperate to get after Pete and happily our gut instincts, which said Liz was too frazzled to contemplate carjacking, turned out correct.

'So—how do we play this?' I venture.

Daisy's brows knit. 'Essentially, Pete needs to come out of his room so we can go in and nick Paul's cash back—oh, and your bar takings.'

She makes it sound so routine—as though we're planning a shopping trip

'And *how* do we accomplish that?'

'Dunno,' she admits, opening her door. 'We'll work it out on the trot.'

And trot she does, all the way up to and through huge glass doors under an opulent art déco canopy. I catch up with her in a reception area next to which the Cairncroft Hotel's resembles a cupboard. (A *small* cupboard.) *This* is more akin to an indoor version of George Square.

Open plan is its predominant feature—there's an area for casual drinks styled as a conservatory, the "shopping zone" sells whisky and tweed, and as for their reception desk—it's long enough to do ten check-ins (or -outs) simultaneously. Dotted amongst the main modules are pockets of foam-filled block seating around glass tables littered with today's newspapers and an assortment of high-end magazines.

Incongruously, sprouting from exposed brickwork, plastic animal heads wearing extravagantly carved wooden antlers watch imperiously from up high. Higher still, creepers of ivy entwine pergola-type beams set just under a glass roof.

Daisy nudges me. 'Giving you any ideas for the Cairncroft?' she asks mischievously.

I almost answer that Davy would be in clover here, but bite it back in the nick of time. Before I think of an alternative response, Daisy's on the move again—headed for a bank of elevators. (Three? Why do they need three?) Confidently, she jabs a call button and we step aboard the first to arrive.

Even the elevator is massive. An electronic voice cautions us to "mind the doors" and Daisy giggles. 'Can you imagine what *our* lift would say if it could talk?'

I can—and shudder at the thought. 'Have you thought he might not *be* in his room?'

'Oh, he will—Pete'll be like a kid on Xmas morning, busy playing with his new toys.'

'The gadgets in his room?'

'No—the used banknotes.'

We get off at the first floor and Daisy sets off at strolling pace down an oak-lined corridor studded with doors. She's peering intently at her phone. 'What're you doing?' I hiss.

'Following Pete's tracking signal. It'll be strongest outside his door.'

She points at a rectangular lock plate with a tiny red light showing. 'The doors here have keycard locks—*we* should get them.'

'Yeah, right—have you any idea what those cost?'

Fortunately, the corridors are arranged in a square configuration, so we don't have to backtrack when it becomes obvious Pete isn't on this floor—instead, we simply call the lift again. 'How many floors do they have?'

Daisy scrutinises the control panel. 'Mm... eight.'

'This'll take all day.'

It doesn't, because Pete's room turns out to be on the second floor. Daisy puts her ear to the door of number 217. 'He's in there,' she whispers. 'I can hear the telly.'

'Maybe he went out and left it on.'

'Naw—I just heard the loo flush.'

She leads me back to the lifts. 'Okay, here's what we'll do. You use one of those house phones they have dotted about downstairs. Pretend you're reception and tell Pete somebody backed into his car in the parking area. He'll go rushing out to check, and I'll be waiting to slip in and grab the cash.'

'Um... how will you get in? Those doors lock automatically.'

She jabs the call button. 'I *know*—we're going to take care of that first.'

BACK IN RECEPTION, DAISY SELECTS HER TARGET. 'THAT ONE, I reckon. She's young and doesn't seem too sure of herself. Probably not been here long. C'mon—it'll look better with two of us.'

The reception desk isn't busy right now and we approach it at an angle carefully calculated to target a female clerk in her early twenties. She's wearing heavy plastic glasses, which goes some way to confirming Daisy's initial assessment. Thin as a rake (nervous energy—good), there's also something "agitated" about her movements.

Daisy dips her head and speaks in a small voice. 'I feel so stupid—gone and lost my keycard. Will it be very expensive to get another one?'

The girl—Valerie, according to a prominent nametag on her maroon uniform jacket—relaxes visibly. It appears Daisy's right about her being a recent hire, because her unspoken reaction is "Great—I know how to do this."

Out loud, she says: 'That's no problem, Madam. I'll just run you off a replacement—and there's no charge. What's your room number?'

'Oh, how wonderful,' Daisy simpers. '217, please.'

Valerie thumps at a keyboard then freezes, eyes locked on her screen. 'Um… according to this, room 217 is occupied by a Mr Peter Mathers?'

Daisy draws herself up to full height. (Which won't impress anybody.) 'Are you aware of the Gender Reform Bill, which is going through the Scottish Parliament as we speak?'

Valerie gapes. 'I might have heard something about it...'

'And is it any concern of yours what sex I decide to designate myself—or what I choose to call myself? Perhaps you feel that despite an accident of birth imprisoning me in a body with no Y chromosome, I should simply suck it up and accept my lot?'

Valerie's now bright red. 'No, of course not... I didn't realise, you see.'

She wipes her brow with the back of a hand. 'I'll run that keycard off for you...'

'Hang on, Miss Jones.'

A white-haired man in a pinstripe suit appears at Valerie's shoulder. *His* nametag reads *Manager*. 'I booked Mr Mathers in myself... and this most certainly isn't him.'

Oops

I look to Daisy for guidance—which won't be forthcoming, because she's halfway across the ballroom-sized area of floor separating reception desk from main entrance. The manager peers after her and tuts. Then turns to Valerie. 'You really must be more security conscious, Miss Jones. We do NOT give out keycards to anyone who asks for them.'

His rather beady eyes focus on me. 'Who was that woman?'

I shrug. 'Never seen her before in my life...'

'YOU BOOKED A ROOM FOR THE NIGHT? WHY? AND HOW much did that cost?'

I found Daisy in the Panda, lying low. 'I had to explain why I was at the desk—checking in was the best I could come up with. As for what it cost—you don't want to know.'

'We *nearly* got away with it,' Daisy muses, then brightens. 'The maids will have keycards that open any room—and in a place that size, there'll always be some about. I should have thought of that first...'

'Daisy.'

I hate to disillusion her, but... 'If you're intending to use these newfound pickpocketing skills to lift a maid's keycard, there's a problem. The moment you set foot through those doors again, that manager will dial 999.'

She screws up her face. 'He will, won't he? Oh, bother—I really blew that one.'

We sit in silence for a few moments, Daisy's brain no doubt working at the speed of light, until suddenly she sits upright and points. 'Look.'

A massive tour bus pulls up at the front entrance.

Daisy's knee jigs up and down. 'They must do package holidays—and there are at least 50 people in that thing. D'you see what this means?'

'Um—the Excelsior won't go broke this week?'

'No, dummy. In a moment, all those people will try to check in—nobody'll notice me with that going on. Okay—Plan A, version 2. C'mon...'

Daisy's out of the car already and heading back to the hotel—and she's right. That bus is disgorging tourists like Heathrow's terminal one during a bomb scare and they're all making their way through the glass doors. When we follow them in, the reception desk has vanished behind a wall of bodies. Suddenly, it's apparently excessive length makes total sense.

We get to the lifts unchallenged and arrive on the fourth floor. 'Why 4?' I ask.

'Don't want to run into Pete while we're looking for a maid,' Daisy explains.

We find a housekeeping cart in the third corridor, the one that leads back to the lifts. Pretending to be absorbed in conversation we watch the maid emerge, leaving the door to close automatically behind her as she moves on to the next room. She takes a keycard from her overall pocket and touches it to the lock, which immediately beeps and flashes green.

With her theory confirmed, Daisy heads for the same room. I hang back, pretending to loiter. It feels safer out here.

Daisy's voice floats around the wedged-open door. 'Don't mind me—just pretend I'm not here.'

'Not at all, Madam,' is the immediate reply. 'I can come back later.'

Then a shrieked: 'Watch out.'

There's a sound of scuffling. Daisy's voice says: 'Oops, sorry. I tripped on the carpet.'

A rather puzzled-sounding maid points out: 'But it's laminated flooring.'

'Must be a loose laminate, then—look, I'll leave you to get on.'

Ignoring the maid's protests that she could "go and do other rooms" Daisy comes skipping out, flashing a keycard concealed in her palm. With me struggling to keep up, we arrive back at the lifts. 'Have to be quick before she realises it's missing, but by the time she does and gets up enough courage to tell snake-eyes downstairs, we should be done.'

The lift doors open and Daisy jabs "2" and "G". 'You know what to do, Sam?' she checks, and I nod.

After dropping her off on Pete's floor, I'm relieved to find reception still struggling to deal with their block booking. Making my way to the furthest-away house phone (never really figured out the point of them, although I suspect they're more for the convenience of staff than patrons) I pick up its handset and tap in "217". Long, agonising moments pass until finally a gruff male voice says: 'Yes?'

This is the bit that's worrying me. I'm not good at doing "accents", but don't want to risk Pete remembering me from our brief interaction at the flat. So, with the recent inspiration of Paul's satnav, I go for Texan.

'Howdy, Mr Mathers. I sure am sorry to tell you some idiot's run into your car out front here. Can you come down and take a look at the damage?'

I hold the phone away from my ear as Pete vents, using words I've only ever heard in the Last Chance Saloon at closing time. He ends with: 'I'm on my way.'

Hanging up the house phone, and with no small sense of relief, I skedaddle through the glass doors and back to my Panda. There's an awful moment when I convince myself that, with our luck, we'll have gone and parked right next to Pete's car.

When Pete does come flying out, I breathe again when he makes for a Volkswagen estate parked away at the back. I crane to watch him circle it twice, his frown giving way to bewilderment, then he returns to the hotel at a more sedate pace.

Pete disappears through the glass doors—and seconds later, Daisy pops out.

Carrying a holdall.

She slams into the passenger seat and wraps both arms around her prize. 'Okay, Sam—floor it.'

19

We get back to Cairncroft shortly after five. After separating Tina's recovered ransom from the bar takings, and depositing both in the hotel safe, we go looking for Paul.

Pulling up outside The Cuppa Tea, which is under Mr M's office, I ask: 'Do you think he'll still be here?'

Then bite my lip, realising I've just parked behind Paul's jeep.

'Fine detective you are,' Daisy chides with a snort. 'I'll text him to say where we are and he can join us downstairs when they finish. I'm peckish, anyway.'

'When aren't you?'

A little bell tinkles when we enter The Cuppa Tea—it always reminds me of Maisie's, a café along from CosmoSpex where Daisy and I used to lunch most days.

Good times—*not*.

At the counter, while Daisy's choosing her cream cake, I ask Doris why she stays open on Sundays. It's kind of unusual outside the city.

The Cuppa Tea's proprietor has to be in her sixties, but a cheery demeanour and apparently inexhaustible store of energy make her seem years younger. Doris's head tilts as she considers her answer. 'Thing is, luv, if I wasn't here, what *would* I be doing? Watching telly? Looking out my window counting people going past? Hah—I'd only need the fingers of one hand for that. No, better to be busy... hey, did you hear about that fairground man getting shot?'

I put on my best "yes I did and no, I haven't any gossip for you" face before answering. 'Terrible, wasn't it?'

Doris leans across the counter. When someone does that, you have to mimic them—not to would be the equivalent of refusing a handshake. 'He was in 'ere that day,' she whispers. 'Couldn't have been more than an hour or two before. I remember because they were taking up a table at 5pm when we were busy with the teatime rush. They only had a coffee apiece—didn't even order cake.'

'They?' I whisper back—because it seems impolite not to mirror.

'The chap that got shot and another fella. I knew the fairground man because he'd been in before, but his friend was a stranger.'

When we're seated, I keep my voice low so Doris won't hear. 'Did you catch what Doris told me about why she opens on Sundays?'

Daisy shakes her head, more interested in a chocolate eclair headed for her mouth with the navigational accuracy of a stinger missile.

So I tell her, finishing with: 'Poor old soul—do you suppose we'll ever get like that?'

Daisy's answer takes me aback. 'We already are—think about it, Sam. *Our* lives revolve around the detective agency—and the hotel, of course.'

'Yes, but...'

With a shock, I realise she's right. Here's me feeling sorry for Doris—yet I wouldn't have my own life any other way. Which, of course, reminds me of Davy. Maybe it *isn't* such a bad thing if we split up...?

Except, was Davy my last chance for domestic bliss? But do I even *want* domestic bliss?

'Penny for 'em,' Daisy chirps, and I wave her off. 'Nothing—hey, look who that is.'

The famous "Kat"—or *in*famous, more like—is on her way in.

Daisy waits until Doris makes Kat's coffee, then calls: 'Kaa-aat. Over here.'

To me she says, sotto voce: 'This should be interesting.'

Kat flounces over and parks herself opposite. 'Hello, girls. I'm just waiting for Em. What are you doing?'

'The same,' Daisy tells her. 'My boyfriend's upstairs getting Mr M's advice about something, and we're meeting him after.'

'It's nice getting a chance to chat with the two of you. Em's always talking about Sam and Daisy—think he sees himself as something of a father figure.'

She giggles. 'Makes me quite jealous.'

'Are you going to be staying long?' I try.

'Possibly. Em's thinking of bringing me into the business—I'm a solicitor too, you see. Poor Em isn't getting any younger—doesn't have the stamina he once had.'

Kat winks and Daisy's jaw drops—she's thinking back to what I said earlier and putting the same spin on Kat's words. Except, from Kat's salacious wink, hers hardly *need* spun.

Recovering quickly, Daisy says: 'So you're thinking of moving here permanently? Won't that mean giving up an awful lot? I mean, you've already got a high-powered job in London.'

Kat's eyebrows arch. 'Why, Daisy—have you been checking up on me?'

Daisy doesn't react, but *my* cheeks burn. 'Mr M mentioned it,' I put in (lie) quickly.

'Does it bother you?' Daisy asks brazenly. 'What you just said about Mr M being so much older.'

I cringe, but Kat doesn't bat an eyelash—and believe me, you'd know straight away if one of *them* moved. 'Oh no,' she says, acting guileless—and making the "acting" part obvious. 'In my experience, mentor and pupil situations make for wonderful partnerships. Well... I *am* rather more than a pupil, of course. What I'm trying to say is, *his* savoir-faire and *my* vigor are a perfect combination.

I daren't meet Daisy's eyes

Fortuitously, Paul and Mr M arrive then. Saved by the bell.

Kat bounces up. 'Emmy, darling.'

She throws her arms around his neck and I have to say, he doesn't look *too* unhappy—definitely embarrassed, though.

'Come on, Em,' Kat croons gaily, seizing his arm. 'You won't believe what I've cooked for dinner—it's taken me all afternoon.'

Mr M waves weakly before Kat pulls him out the door. Paul chuckles. 'He must be some smooth operator—that chick's barely half his age.'

Oh-oh

Daisy drops her eclair on its plate. 'Chick?' she grates. 'What does that make me—a duckling?'

'Sorry,' Paul says immediately, and Daisy shrugs.

'Forget it.'

Wow. It HAS to be love—or maybe she's going easy on him because of Tina?

'Any joy?' I ask.

'Yes and no,' Paul replies morosely. 'Mr M reckons the fair's net asset value at around 130k and it astonished me when he put the business as a whole, sold as a going concern, somewhere the right side of 200k. Trouble is... oh, you don't know. The kidnappers have been in touch—they're giving me another chance to pay, but the price has gone up to 150k in retaliation for today's shenanigans. Even if Dobson paid me full whack, I'm still well short after losing that first hundred.'

Daisy holds up a finger and makes him wait while she crams the last piece of eclair into her mouth. Then chews it, slowly, holding his gaze with sparkling eyes. Finally, she swallows. 'No, you aren't. We got the original ransom back from Pete—it's in the hotel safe and before you ask, Sam's changed the access code.'

Paul's face couldn't light up more if we plugged him into the mains. 'Wow. That's fantastic news—how'd you manage that?'

'Long story—tell you later.'

'Oh, okay. Well, that means I only need another fifty. Dobson will go to that—I'm sure of it.'

'What're the new arrangements for delivering the ransom?'

'Same place as before, tomorrow at noon. But listen, Daisy—I have to go by myself. The kidnappers insist on it and made clear this is my last chance.'

'Does that leave time to get more cash from Dobson?' I ask.

'It'll have to,' he replies grimly, getting up. 'I'll go outside and phone him right now.'

After the door closes behind Paul, Daisy scowls. 'Don't you think it's dodgy how this Dobson character can produce sizeable sums of cash at short notice?'

'Yes, I do—but there again, fairgrounds are still cash businesses and Dobson has several.'

'S'pose. Something bothers me about his involvement, though—handing over a hundred grand in cash like he did. He's obviously very keen to get his sticky hands on Paul's fair—and it's terribly convenient he had the right amount to hand, at the right time, and in used notes.'

'I think you're reading too deep, Dais'. It's no secret how much he wants the fair, and we've just said he has access to lots of cash. To suggest he might be behind Tina's kidnap—I take it that's where you're going with this? —is an enormous leap.'

'Is it, though? Dobson's got motive—always a biggie. But he has means and opportunity too. Dobson can afford to hire thugs and has an intimate knowledge of the fairground business—especially, it seems, Paul's. We need a closer look at this guy.'

Mm… when she puts it like that…

Paul slouches back in and collapses on the chair beside Daisy. She studies him for a moment. 'Dobson wouldn't go for it?'

'It's not that—he's getting another 50 grand ready for me to pick up tomorrow morning. But in return, wants me to sign a contract saying the fair is his soon as I'm able to transfer it. Which means Dobson's paying over 50 grand below market value—and I'll be left with nowt.'

'Heck of a discount,' I agree.

'It is,' Paul says sadly, 'but what choice is there? It's the only way I can raise that much cash.'

'How well do you know Dobson?' Daisy probes.

'Not very—it was always Dad he dealt with. Why?'

'Oh, nothing. Listen, how about Sam and I drive you to Dobson's in the morning? Where do you have to go, anyway? One of Dobson's fairgrounds?'

'No, Dobson doesn't get his hands dirty any more. He runs everything from an office in Aberdeen—I'm picking the cash up there at nine, which gives me plenty time to be back for the drop. But I can drive myself.'

'Paul, you're a nervous wreck. It's one thing taking a spin in the country to deliver the ransom, but Aberdeen's busy. Suppose you have an accident—where does that leave Tina? No, let us take you—just to be on the safe side.'

'Oh, maybe you're right… and to be honest, I *would* appreciate the company. Look, I'd better go make sure everything's alright at the fair. Then I really should get to bed early—today's drained me.'

'Do you want to stay at the hotel again?' I offer.

Paul shakes his head. 'No—no need. If the kidnappers were going to play that game, they'd have done it last night. I'll be fine in my caravan and the money's safe with you—but will you pick me up about eight tomorrow? Just in case of holdups on the road?'

Daisy assures him we will and Paul leaves, looking shattered and older than his years.

His cheeks have sunk, he's dragging his feet— from a distance, anybody who didn't know him would wonder where his Zimmer is.

When Paul's gone, I ask: 'Are you really worried he isn't fit to drive to Aberdeen tomorrow?'

'Course I am—and also, I want a proper look at this Mr Dobson.'

'But when we get there, Paul will go in to see Dobson on his own—won't he?'

She smirks. 'That's probably what Paul thinks, too…'

20

Miss Dobie's cottage is similar in design to ours, but at the opposite end of Cairncroft. A major difference is Miss Dobie's being one of six, all neatly lined up and backed by a wasteland of meadow broken only by the distant horizon. Presumably, in times gone by, these were farm cottages.

Since there's nothing more we can do for Tina until tomorrow, Daisy suggested we make our surprise visit to Mr M's loyal secretary—a little over eight hours later than originally planned.

We both jump when the door opens while my finger's still an inch shy of its bellpush. Daisy automatically reaches out a hand to steady me while Miss Dobie scrutinises us curiously. 'Hello, girls. This is a pleasant surprise—if unexpected. Do come in.'

Miss Dobie leads the way through her hall and into a cosy sitting room. From what I can see, the internal layout is pretty much a match with ours. We turn, politely awaiting an invitation to sit on her flowered suite, and find she's gone. 'I'll just make some tea,' drifts back from the hall and we take that as permission to plonk ourselves on the sofa.

It can't be over two minutes before Miss Dobie wheels in a tea trolley. Daisy's eyes bulge at the contents—home-made jam sponge, a small mountain of freshly baked scones, and oodles of chocolate biscuits. 'I'm so sorry,' Miss Dobie whines. 'I should have asked—would you prefer coffee?'

'Tea's lovely,' I assure her. Daisy's already piling goodies on her plate—I doubt she even heard.

HOW does she stay so thin?

'I'll be mother,' Miss Dobie trills, picking up a silver teapot and pouring delicately into bone china cups. After we've done the "do you take milk?" and "how many sugars?" routine, she delivers our drinks and withdraws to a massive armchair. Not saying she's wee, but it practically swallows her whole.

'Now, girls. What can I do for you?'

Mm... there goes any chance of leading up to this gradually. Luckily, Daisy's mouth is full, giving me an opportunity to employ the tact she wouldn't. 'I do hope we're not imposing, Miss

Dobie, but Daisy and I are a little concerned about your boss. I presume you know about his, um… new friend?'

'Kat?'

Miss Dobie leans forward to set her cup and saucer on the trolley. 'Yes,' she montones—and waits.

I'm not getting a good feeling about this

'Well, Kat is an awful lot younger than Mr M and we're afraid…'

'*What* are you afraid about, dear?' Said with a quizzical intonation that makes clear where this conversation is headed.

Uh-oh—Daisy just swallowed the last of her sponge cake. 'We're worried Kat's a gold-digger intent on taking Mr M to the cleaners,' she interjects—in a helpful tone.

Miss Dobie simply stares for a long moment. Then she inhales, doing an excellent impression of Alanna with a bottle feed. 'I appreciate you have Mr MacLachlan's best interests at heart, but he really is most capable and to suggest what you did then is not only an underestimation of his capabilities—it is, frankly, rather rude.'

Grabbing the biscuit plate, I thrust it at Daisy. Satisfied her mouth's fully occupied, I turn back to

Miss Dobie. 'Daisy's just worried—as am I. Surely you agree, Miss Dobie, that it's an... unusual development.'

She sniffs. 'I suppose it must appear so. But I have a duty of discretion on any matters relating to my employer. Please rest assured, however, Mr MacLachlan is entirely capable of protecting his own interests.'

'Is he, though?' I press. 'Are you really sure about that?'

Her mouth puckers. 'I must concede he is not addressing the current situation with his usual aplomb. I have every expectation, however, that it will resolve equitably.'

Daisy's lips move soundlessly as she plays that back in her head, but basically what Miss Dobie's saying is: 'I've no intention of interfering—or helping you to.' So I stand and smile. 'Thank you for your time, Miss Dobie—and the tea.'

'And the cake—it's brill,' Daisy adds. 'Did you make it yourself?'

Miss Dobie's face lightens. 'I did—would you like a piece away?'

'Deffo.'

'Daisy means she very much would,' I translate, and Miss Dobie transports into the kitchen. (I mean, we saw her rise and depart, but she still seemed to disappear in the sort of swoosh you associate with Scotty and the Starship Enterprise.)

Driving off in the Panda, I ask: 'Did we get anything from that?'

Daisy lowers the napkin-wrapped slab of cake Miss Dobie pressed on her and chews as she speaks. (It's one of her superpowers.) 'Absolutely zilch. I was hoping she'd want to join forces for Mr M's sake, but the old bird's too mired down in misguided loyalty.'

'Guess it's up to us, then,' I conclude glumly, before remembering. 'And Jodie, of course.'

'Yeah—let's have a word with her next. She'll be waiting to hear what happened with the ransom drop, anyway—and probably throw a strop when we tell her. Oh, and I need to find Rebecca while we're there—want a wee chat about something.'

Me too—but without you

⁂

AT THE HOTEL, AFTER A RIDE TO THE SECOND FLOOR THAT brings back memories of the "Pirate Ship", Daisy suggests I go ahead while she pops down the corridor to Rebecca's room.

I can't really protest, since I plan to pull a similar wangle on the way out. But before she disappears, I need to check something. 'I hope you aren't planning on making Rebecca sit outside Paul's caravan again tonight.'

She holds up her palms. 'Absolutely not. Paul's right—if the kidnappers were going to heist the ransom, they'd have done it last night. Naw, this is another thing... see you in five.'

I'm surprised when it isn't Jodie who comes to the door. 'Rosemary—are you Jodie's nanny now?'

Rosemary's grin couldn't be wider if she'd won the lottery. 'Yep, isn't it great? She even got me a room in the staff corridor—I mean, mum's lovely and all, but I was needing an excuse to move out into my own space.'

'You haven't set a date yet, then?' (Rosemary's engaged to her boyfriend, who we thought for a while was the Bus Stop Killer before he turned out to be a helpless pawn in Lena's game.)

'No, and it'll be awhile before we can—got a lot of saving up to do. What about you?'

Ouch—left myself wide open there

'Oh, lots of things still to do before we nail it down—you know how it is. So, is Alanna behaving herself for you?'

'She's sooo gorgeous. Here, what am I thinking? Come away in.'

I follow her into the living room, where Jodie looks a lot more relaxed than last time I saw her. Rosemary lifts Alanna from her mum's arms. 'I'll give her a bath now, shall I—get in practice for the nights you're late back?'

Jodie's eyes fill with angst, but she keeps her voice level. 'Yes, good idea Rosie—but bring her to me for her bottle afterwards.'

When Rosemary's gone, I smile my sympathy. 'It's what you wanted, yet isn't really, eh?'

Jodie nods. 'I'm *so* looking forward to tomorrow, but the thought of leaving her…'

'You'll soon get into a routine that's the best of both worlds—for you *and* her.'

'I suppose—thanks, by the way. Rosie's absolutely brilliant with Alanna.'

'You didn't waste any time.'

'Didn't have it to waste. Come on, then—what happened today with your ransom drop? Did you find Caron? And is Tina safely back?'

I've been dreading this conversation—trust Daisy to land it in my lap. I wonder if she REALLY needs to see Rebecca about anything...

'Not exactly.'

Jodie's face gets grimmer as I relate the gory details. 'Sam, we can't keep this from CID any longer. Surely you see that.'

'I don't, Jodie—because how is anything different from when we spoke earlier? Daisy tried something and it didn't work—now the kidnappers are giving us a second chance to play it their way. Last time we spoke, you agreed to that.'

She huffs. 'Yes, but... oh, I suppose. This is *it*, though—if you don't tell Inspector Wilson what's going on by tomorrow teatime, *I* will. And don't forget—I knew nothing about it until five minutes before you speak to him.'

'Absolutely—and thanks, Jodie. We'll let you know what happens soon as we hear from Paul, after he makes the drop.'

'Make sure you do—anyway, where's your shadow?'

'Oh, she's down the corridor asking Rebecca something. We've just been to see Miss Dobie.'

Jodie chuckles. 'Bet that went well.'

'Did it ever.'

I give her a summary, and she laughs some more. 'I could have told you that—Miss Dobie worships the ground he walks on and thinks it only rains when his roses need watering. She'd never accept he could fall foul of...' she lowers her voice to a whisper '... base desires.'

'So what are we going to do?'

A shrug. 'Mac's a big boy—don't see what we *can* do. Maybe it *is* true love...'

She trails off. '... yeah, okay. But it's looking as though he'll have to find out the hard way. See, if we do something... scratch that, if *Daisy* does something to scare Kat off, we'll be the bad ones. It's kind of a no-win situation.'

'We either watch the old fool being taken for a ride,' I summarise, 'or risk him falling out with us.'

'*Nope*...' comes from the doorway. Daisy pads in and drops on the sofa beside Jodie, reminding me I'm still standing and prompting my grateful flop into an armchair. '... there's always a third way.'

'Love to hear what that is,' I say, not even trying to keep the sarcasm from my voice.

'Simple—we scare Kat off by letting her find something out that would only send her packing if she really *is* a gold-digger, but the trick is not to let Mr M know we had anything to do with it.'

Jodie sits up straight. 'Sounds good—what's your plan?'

Daisy flushes. 'Um—that's as far as I've got. It's a work in progress...'

Rosemary comes in with Alanna, giving Daisy an opportunity to scrabble out of the hole she dug herself. While she makes funny faces at the baby, I reluctantly pull myself out of what turned out to be a very comfortable armchair. 'Daisy, if you're happy playing with Alanna, I'll head back to the cottage and start something for tea. See you there?'

Her answer's muffled because Alanna has a grip on her nose ring, but I think it was in the affirmative. I don't wait to confirm my impression though, and once I'm out of Jodie's flat it isn't the lift or stairs I head for—rather, I turn left towards the staff corridor and Rebecca's room. This is *my* chance for a wee private word.

21

Rebecca opens the door and Hector peeps between her legs—then, seeing it's me, strolls forward and wraps himself around my ankle.

Funny how he always seems to know which is the real one

'Hi, Sam. You got my text, then?'

Yes, I did—it's been eating away at me ever since

Rebecca has her coat on. 'Sorry—were you off out?'

She flaps a set of red talons my way—I think they're longer than Hector's. 'Just popping over to see Graham the gardener about something. But there's no rush—and you need to hear this.'

She beckons me inside. Hector leaps onto the bed and stretches lazily but I stay standing—there isn't a lot of space for entertaining in the staff bedrooms and I know how hard their single rattan chair is. Normally we'd sit on the bed, but with Hector fully extended… 'Quick work,' I congratulate her, because it was. And possibly to put off hearing what she's about to tell me for a few seconds longer.

I decided earlier it was pretty stupid to own (a share in) a detective agency and worry about what my boyfriend is up to. So, I gave Rebecca a new assignment—to find out if Davy's cheating on me.

'I was giving Liz a lift to Donstable anyway—you won't believe this, but she asked me to drop her at Caron's. Seems to think she can just waltz back into her old room now her and Pete have fallen out.'

'Hah. She might be in for a shock there.'

'I didn't hang around to find out. But being in the area, I decided to drive past Davy's on the off chance of seeing any strange cars parked outside.'

'And were there?' Rebecca held back on details in her text—saying only she had something to tell me.

'No—but I saw Davy getting into *his* car.'

'Did he see you?' I ask, alarmed. Davy lives in the middle of nowhere and couldn't miss another vehicle on the track—it's a straight stretch, ending at his house.

'No. I left the car on the main road and hoofed it down—just in case he was about. Then I hid behind a bush until he'd put his suitcase in the boot, and...'

'Suitcase?'

'Right. So, I watched until he turned at the top of the road, then dashed back to the Audi and floored it. Caught up with him and tailed the blighter to the Donstable Arms.'

'The Donstable Arms?'

Rebecca must be wondering about the echo in here

'Luckily it was busy, so I was able to get parked without being spotted. Davy got out of his car, unloaded the suitcase, and went inside.'

'I can't think why...?'

'No, there's more. I followed him in—again, I was lucky because there were a few people milling about. Plus, I had my raincoat on—that was a good idea of yours, by the way.'

Tinted windows on the car—raincoats—could she not just dress properly while she's working?

'Then I saw him checking in...'

'CHECKING IN?' My blood's beginning to boil as I see where this is going.

'... well, they gave him a key, so I presume... Next thing, this... um... kind of nice-looking lassie comes rushing out of the bar and they... em, hug. Then the two of them went upstairs...'

Either Logan's running an unscheduled fire drill or my ears are ringing. Something at the very core of me turns to ice as I say: 'Well—that's pretty conclusive.'

'I'm so sorry, Sam.'

Rebecca can barely look at me, and suddenly a tear runs down her cheek. I slip an arm around her. 'There, there. It's alright.'

I'm comforting you?

'But it *isn't*. You don't deserve this, Sam—it's horrible.'

Can't argue

Slowly I take my arm back and, a little unsteadily, start moving towards the door. 'Thanks, Rebecca. Yes, this is a shock—but it's always better to know.'

Is it?

'You did great—really, you're a full-fledged detective now.'

It all catches up, and my voice breaks. 'Got to go—sorry—thanks. Bye.'

POOR DAISY'S IN FOR A DISAPPOINTMENT WHEN SHE OPENS the cottage door and tries to sniff out what we're having for tea.

Carryout, probably. If she can be bothered going to Donstable for it—although some places *have* started delivering to Cairncroft now. Oh, wait a minute—I'm *in* Donstable. So *I'll* pick up Chinese on my way back.

I went straight to the Panda after leaving Rebecca and, like Daisy at her best (or is that worst?), came shooting over to the Donstable Arms with no plan beyond getting here.

Maybe I just need to see this for myself

Now I'm sitting in the car park, belatedly deciding how to proceed. Davy's car is two rows in front of mine—the first confirmation of Rebecca's account. Forcing down a sob in my throat, I get out and march around to the main door.

It only then occurs that if they've come up for air and gone down for a drink, I don't want them seeing me—not until I've decided whether to have a public slanging match or keep my powder dry for a private execution. So I stop off at the reception desk—good, the girl on duty isn't anyone I know—and casually say: 'I'm thinking of going into the bar, but not if it's crowded. *Is* it busy tonight?'

She shakes her head. 'Not yet—but it will be soon. We're expecting a bunch of local workies who meet here once a month. They *can* get quite rowdy…'

'Okay—tell you what, I'll have a peek in and check it out.'

Having effectively obtained authorisation to stop at the bar entrance and keek around with one eye—from the only person who'll see me doing it—I do just that.

It's a big lounge, which also does bar meals. Their fish and chips has the most delectable batter—though nothing could entice Daisy from her own favourite, the "Monster Burger". Tonight, it's practically empty—this must be a sweet spot between teatime and the evening revelries. There's only a few people scattered about—including Davy and Leslie, sitting together on a two-seater, chatting gaily.

So they have come up for air

I want to march in there and tip Davy's pint over his head. Leslie, I might dream up something more painful for...

That would be stupid, though—they're in the wrong, but it'd be me who'd end up in a cell for the night if I cause a disturbance. No—I'm in no fit state to confront them. I need to calm down—and anyway, who cares? The fact of the matter is, Davy and I are over—what I say to him isn't important, and won't change anything.

The receptionist gives me a puzzled look as I pass by again. 'There's hardly anybody in there just now.'

'Um. Yeah, but what you said about it getting wild later—I don't want to be here when that kicks off.'

She nods understanding and goes back to whatever she's doing. If only she knew—I was *this* far off creating a bigger ruckus than the workies will. But I'm quite proud of myself, I realise, strolling around to the car park. For acting like a sensible adult. Instead of lashing out mindlessly, I'm being civilised about this... and preserving my dignity at the same time.

Then I see Davy's car—and something snaps. Stooping over a rear wheel, I dip into my bag for a pencil with one hand while unscrewing his valve cap with the other.

Then I let the cheating slimeball's tyre down.

22

'Where have you been?'

Who needs Davy anyway? Living with Daisy is close enough to being married. 'Out.'

I say it in a manner that brooks no truck with further enquiries. *But*—this is Daisy. 'Ah—take it you went to see Davy?'

I turn away and start arranging cartons of Chinese takeout on the kitchen table. A clear signal if ever there was one.

'It didn't go well, then?'

Oh, I give up

So, over Singapore noodles, I tell her all. She listens carefully and at the end says: 'D'you want me to sort out a duffing up for him?'

'NO. Anyhow, who do you know that would...'

'Loads of guys in the Cairncroft Cowboys would do it for a night's free pass at the bar. Some of them are massive, especially the farmhands.'

'DAISY. I am not having my fiancé "duffed up". What good would that do?'

'Make you feel better?'

Mm... it would...

'NO. Absolutely not.'

Daisy gets distracted then but after coming out from under the table, having retrieved her chopsticks and wiped them on a sleeve, she asks: 'Did you key his paintwork, too?'

'"Key his paintwork?" Daisy, don't be ridiculous—of course I didn't.'

'Why not? You let his tyres down.'

'Only one... and that was a moment of madness. No, our separation will be amicable and civilised.'

'What're you going to say to him?'

'Nothing—I don't intend speaking to the cretin ever again. Daisy, you're doing my head in with those chopsticks. Would you *please* just use a fork?'

Huffing, she slouches over to the kitchen drawer for a cutlery upgrade. 'D'you think they do web courses on using chopsticks?'

'Not on the dark web,' I retort cattily. 'Maybe if you could bring yourself to slum it on Google... Anyway, I can see you're bursting to tell me something—if we've finished talking about my failed love life, that is.'

'Aw, don't be like that, Sam. I really feel for you—listen, are you sure there isn't some way you've read this "Leslie" thing wrong?'

'Positive.'

'Guess that's that, then. Yeah, I had Paul on the phone while you were out...'

Her endless empathy never fails to astonish me

'... he's in a right state. I would have gone over, but he wants to be on his own for a while.'

Half my mind is still on Davy and his treachery, but she's piqued my interest. 'Did the kidnappers contact him again?'

'Naw, it was the police. They've done a PM on his dad and it turns out he was poisoned.'

'But I thought he was shot?'

'Yeah, he was—talk about making sure, eh? Toxicology says there was a poison in his system that would have killed him about an hour after he ingested it.'

'But that doesn't make any sense.'

'Only if there were two murderers. Murderer number one slips him poison, then before it has time to work, somebody else shoots him.'

'That's a bit improbable—isn't it?'

'Agreed.'

We're silent for a moment, and I push away my barely touched carton of noodles. Daisy does the same—except hers is empty.

'Let's go through to the sitting room. You need a drink, Sam.'

I do wonder if Daisy and I are starting to overuse alcohol—this is how it starts, as a crutch in desperate times. Next thing, you're pouring it on your cornflakes. I've got enough problems without becoming dependent on alcohol.

Sod it—she's right. I DO need a drink

FOR ALL MY WORRYING, I DISCOVER A LITTLE-KNOWN FACT. When you actually *try* to get drunk, that's when the stuff stops having any effect. Halfway through the first bottle of wine, I give up. 'Want a coffee?'

Daisy goggles at me. 'Okay, yeah—I was being careful anyway, with tomorrow coming up. But I really thought you would...'

'No, it's only making me feel worse.'

After fetching two double-shot macchiatos, I return to the subject of Paul's dad—hoping it isn't overkill.

Ouch—not one of my best. I must be in a bad way

'What's going on, Dais'? How does somebody slipping Paul's dad poison make sense with him being shot before it has time to work?'

'Either the guy was *really* unpopular, or... how about this for a theory? What if... it was the poison that killed him? Then someone else finds him dead and fires a bullet into his corpse to frame Tina's husband, Ivor. That cuts down on the coincidence factor cos', as Rev Margaret might say, the poisoning begat the shooting. Course, we're still left with a kidnap just happening to come out of the blue that same night.'

'So you're saying it *wasn't* the kidnappers who shot Paul's dad?'

'Can't see it. Whoever did the shooting framed Ivor, and we've already established the kidnappers wouldn't do that because it was guaranteed to get the flatfeet involved.'

'Always assuming you're right about Ivor being framed... okay, who else, then?'

'Somebody who happened on the corpse, assumed a heart attack, had access to Ivor's gun, and saw their chance to frame him.'

My head hurts

'Who?'

'Hah—answer that and you've solved Wilson's case for him. Basically, anybody who had it in for Ivor—ironically, Tina springs to mind.'

'Tina?'

'Yeah—considering how Ivor treats her, she's got motive aplenty to want him out of her life. But we can think about that later— after Tina's safely back. What I'm really struggling with is the idea of Paul's dad being poisoned and his daughter kidnapped, both on the same night, without the two being connected.'

'Too big a coincidence, isn't it?'

'Deffo. Somehow, the two are linked—they have to be. But blow me if I can see how.'

'Daisy—what's Paul's dad's name? We can't keep calling him "Paul's dad".'

'Mr McNab—Roy.'

'I've just remembered something. I don't know how relevant this is, but Doris told me Paul's dad—I mean Mr McNab—was with someone in The Cuppa Tea at five on Friday.'

'What? Why are you only telling me now?'

'I didn't think it was important—is it?'

'Sam, it's crucial—assuming there's anything to my theory. What if that was the poisoner? If Paul's dad—sorry, Mr McNab—was poisoned in The Cuppa Tea at five o'clock, he'd have been dead by six. Likely leaving plenty of time for somebody to find him and set Ivor up before the kidnappers arrived. Unfortunately, we've no idea of the various timelines—the police weren't considerate enough to mention what their pathologist put time of death at, and we don't know *when* exactly Tina was kidnapped. Okay, the jackpot question—did Doris say *who* Mr McNab was with?'

'She'd never seen him before.'

'Description?'

I shake my head sadly. 'Didn't think to ask...'

'We'll pop in first chance and quiz Doris properly.' 'We also need to question the fairground folk—try and find out when Mr McNab and Tina were last seen.'

She's getting carried away. 'Um—kidnap?' I remind her gently.

She nods reluctantly. 'Yeah, that'll all have to wait until Tina's back, but I'm looking forward to pole-vaulting ahead of Wilson when we get time to investigate properly.'

'The visit to Miss Dobie didn't go well,' I say, as much to distract her before she comes up with any more mind-bending conjectures.

'Didn't, did it? Miss Dobie makes a nice bit of cake—shame that's all we came away with.'

'I was worried that would happen—Jodie says she's fiercely loyal to Mr M.'

'Which is precisely *why* she should be eager to help—I mean, it's obvious Kat sees him as a sugar daddy.'

'But Kat's a high-flying solicitor in London,' I remind Daisy.

'Yeah, and from what she said earlier, has her sights set on taking over Mr M's business. And don't forget Kat's conveniently disposed of two husbands to date.'

'I think you're getting neurotic about those dead husbands. No way is Kat a female bluebeard—but I do wonder why she'd want to leave the glamour of London and move to Cairncroft?'

Daisy smiles enigmatically. (Which I didn't know she could.) 'I can think of two clichés straight off—"Big fish in a little pond" and "Better to reign in

Hell than serve in Heaven". That last's Milton,' she adds, trying to sound offhand.

Even after all these years, she can still gobsmack me

'Okay—so are you any further on with your "concept" for getting rid of Kat? Though I have to admit the whole idea worries me—what if we're wrong and they simply met and fell in love?'

Shades of my old maths teacher—even he never gave me a look quite like that

Then she grins. 'Fair enough, but my plan's got a built-in safeguard for true love. We agree Kat's likeliest motivation for taking up with Mr M is his money—or the law practice? Maybe both? Well, let's convince her he's about to go broke—lose everything. Money, practice, the lot. If it really is a Mills and Boon job, she'll stick by him. But my money's on her disappearing quicker than Graham the gardener after tramping his muddy boots over Sadie's clean carpet.'

'Have you thought spreading that kind of rumour really *could* ruin Mr M?'

'I'm still working on the details, but somehow we'll make sure only Kat gets to hear it.'

'Then she'll go straight to Mr M, and he'll put her right.'

'Kat'd expect him to deny it—doesn't mean she'll believe him.'

Typical Daisy—the perfect plan, but half-baked. To be fair, it rarely takes her long to sand off the rough edges.

My brain's overloaded and I need to turn in for the night, but—there's something else I want to ask. 'What were you seeing Rebecca about earlier? Something to do with Tina's case?'

'Sam,' she cries, jumping up. 'You look utterly exhausted—listen, get yourself to bed. That's where I'm going—we've got a lot on tomorrow, remember?'

And just like that, she's gone. Must have been taking lessons from Miss Dobie.

Listening to her clump up the stairs, I half-close my eyes and take a deep breath.

What's she up to now?

23

Next morning, I don't feel like cooking breakfast and suggest we call into the hotel for a fry up before picking Paul up.

'The restaurant doesn't start serving until eight,' Daisy reminds me.

'They start preparation at seven,' I counter. 'It shouldn't be any problem to throw something on for us.'

She grins. 'Well, if it's *you* asking, they can hardly refuse... suits me, because I'm going over there anyway. Need another quick word with Rebecca.'

'She won't thank you for knocking her up this early.'

Daisy winks. 'Rebecca'll be up, don't worry.'

She scurries off, promising to meet up in the restaurant and leaving me again with a clear sense of *something* brewing—but without a scooby what it is.

As usual.

I'm about to push open the hotel's main door when Jodie comes charging through it. A quick glance at my watch confirms it's five past seven. Of course—this is her first day back. 'What time do you start, Jodie?'

She bites her lip. 'Eight, but I want to be in early.'

'You managed to tear yourself away, then?'

'Sam, I felt dreadful leaving her—it was such a wrench. I'm starting to wonder...'

'Aw, Jodie.'

I reach out and grab her shoulder. 'It'll be fine. This time next week you'll both have settled into the new situation—and with Rosemary taking care of Alanna, you don't need to worry about her.'

A little smile creeps onto her lips. 'Rosie's a natural—she's *so* good with Alanna. You're right—and I *am* looking forward to getting back. It's kind of like being *me* again, if that makes sense.'

'Course it does. That job's also your vocation—it *is* part of you.'

'You aren't forgetting this kidnapping has to be reported by tonight at the latest?'

'Absolutely not. Straight after the ransom drop—regardless of outcome.'

'Okay.'

She pivots to leave, then hesitates—turns back. She pivots to leave, then hesitates—turns back. 'Sam, about the Kat thing—I know Daisy means well, but please don't let her do anything stupid.'

'Course not. Jodie, Daisy thinks Mr M's the best thing since they invented motorbikes—that's why she's so concerned. But for the same reason, she'd never do anything that could rebound on him.'

'Okay. It's just, Daisy *can* get carried away...'

'I know—and promise to keep an eye on her. Now—go arrest somebody.'

She smirks, waves, and trots down the steps towards her car.

Ten minutes later, Daisy comes into the hotel restaurant looking pleased with herself and goes to sit opposite—then freezes. She looks down at the table in disbelief. 'Cornflakes? And toast—where's the bacon?'

'Ah—Louis has a very rigid routine and claims turning on the burners before 7.45 is detrimental to the oil.'

'What a load of twaddle. Anyway, you're the owner—well, part-owner.'

'Yeah—and Louis's *Louis*. We were lucky to get the toast, Dais'. Better make the most of it—so, what were you seeing Rebecca about so early?'

She goes to tap her nose ring, then thinks better of it and snags a slice of toast instead—the last one. 'Tell you later,' she says—infuriatingly. 'Any jam...? Oh, and don't rush—I phoned Paul and told him to come over rather than us running back and forth to the fairground.'

'Aren't you worried about giving him extra driving—in his state?'

'Naw—he'll be fine.'

WE SPEND OUR TRIP TO ABERDEEN IN AN ATMOSPHERE better suited to the undertaker's waiting room, despite Daisy's best efforts to chivvy Paul out of his gloom. 'What if they don't let her go?' he says, for the third time.

'*That's* why we should involve the police,' I snap—finally losing patience.

'But they'd want to stake out the drop site—and the kidnappers' drone would spot them.'

'Look, we're here,' Daisy says—sounding not a little relieved. 'One thing about early appointments—there are plenty parking spaces, even in town.'

As we get out of the car, I nudge her. 'Have you been here before? Only, there's nothing to say this is Dobson's office.' The street we're in has stone-built villas on both sides and while some have brass plates outside, this one doesn't.

'Only on Google Street View,' Daisy explains. 'Wanted to see what kind of setup it was—always do that when I'm going somewhere new. Sorry, Sam—but Paul says Dobson's office is on the first floor.'

My mouth forms an involuntary grimace as I follow them to a marbled entrance. Daisy knows I'm feeling my leg achy today and could do without hauling it up a flight of stairs.

Paul stops at the outer door and turns, obviously wondering why we aren't waiting in the car. 'Em… you don't need to come in.'

'Oh, I think we should,' Daisy pipes up. 'You'll be bringing out a lot of money—safety in numbers and all that.'

'Okay, but you can wait down here. I'm not likely to get mugged on the stairs.'

Daisy shakes her head. 'Down and outs sleep in closes—that stairway could be more dangerous than the street.'

I glance around—at affluence practically oozing everywhere I look—and keep it firmly zipped.

'Daisy, I really think...'

She steps past him and pushes open the outside door. 'Besides, I'm looking forward to getting a look at Mr Dobson after all you've told me about him. Coming?'

By the time Paul's gathered himself, Daisy's halfway up the stairs. He grunts, then follows—and with a sigh, I start my own ascent.

It's immediately apparent Dobson's office is plainly utilitarian—the chairs in his reception area look less comfortable than Donstable police station's. Dobson's decorator obviously gets a good deal on whitewash, and a carpet that's either patterned or fading unevenly was probably around when the Kennedy's ruled America.

Dobson hears us and appears in the doorway to his inner sanctum. 'Come in, Paul... who's this?'

The term "sleazy" was invented for men like Dobson, whose best feature is a full head of red hair—despite his looking to be on the verge of a sixtieth decade. But as for the rest of him...

His face makes me think "rat". Paradoxically, underneath is better described as "stocky." His interior designer must have taken him clothes-shopping as part of the package—overall, you'd never guess this was a successful businessman. Easier to imagine him standing on a dodgem's bumper, one hand gripping the rear pole while the other steers it into the side ready for a new wave of punters.

Paul introduces us and Dobson looks decidedly unamused. The big square room we follow him into has a desk and chair that look like they're marking time until Council collection day. As do two visitor seats against the far wall, beside a bank of battered filing cabinets. Dobson definitely doesn't believe in spending money on his business premises.

Paul makes for yet another canvas holdall, waiting on the desk, but Dobson slaps a hand on it. 'Not so fast, me old son. Need you to sign the contract first.'

He points to a thick sheaf of papers lying beside the bag. Daisy sidles up to Paul. 'You should get Mr M to look that over—*before* signing it.'

Paul waves her off. 'There isn't time.'

Then he looks at Dobson. 'It's as we agreed, yes? £50,000 cash, and I'm signing the fair over to you.'

Dobson nods. 'Exactly.'

'Why so many pages?' I ask. 'You could fit what Paul just said on one sheet.'

Dobson folds his arms and glowers. 'Paul doesn't have control of the fair yet, which complicates matters legally—but I assure you, the contract simply clarifies terms we already agreed.'

'I'd feel better taking a quick skim through it.'

Paul turns with his face on fire. 'Sam, leave it,' he hisses. 'All I care about is getting the cash for Tina.'

He grabs the pen Dobson holds out and scribbles his name. 'There—can I have the money now?'

'Of course, my boy—and good luck with rescuing your sister from those blaggards.'

Blaggard? I'm sure that's Irish slang—yeah, you've got to concentrate not to miss it, but he hasn't completely lost the accent. 'Em—doesn't Paul get a copy of that contract he just signed?'

I have a bad feeling about this

'I don't have a copy,' Dobson says wearily. 'There was barely time to produce the original—I'll post one out to you, Paul.'

Paul obviously couldn't care less and makes no protest when Dobson hustles us out. With Paul and I back on the landing, Dobson jerks around. 'Where's the other...?'

He breaks off when Daisy comes staggering through the outer office, clutching her stomach. 'Sorry, guys—came over all queasy.'

She glares at me. 'I *told* you that bacon at breakfast smelt off.'

'Hurry up—I have other things to attend to.'

Dobson goes to close the door behind her, but relents at the last moment. 'If you need one, there's a public toilet downstairs.'

Then he slams the door.

Daisy yelps 'Quick,' her gastroenteritis forgotten as she takes the steps two at a time. Exchanging puzzled glances, Paul and I follow. Outside, she insists we hurry into the car.

While pulling on my seat belt, I see Dobson appear at the main door. He's crimson-faced and shouting something. Paul, who's in the back, sees him too and goes to open his door.

From the front passenger seat, Daisy rears up and twists around to smack Paul's hand as it closes around the handle. 'Ouch.'

'Sam, drive,' Daisy cries, and not being inexperienced in "Daisy-situations" (which can arise anywhere, anytime) I comply instantly.

Roaring along in second gear, I watch in my rear-view mirror as Dobson jumps up and down in the middle of the road and shakes his fist. Daisy looks back and chuckles.

'Okay—just *what* was all that about?'

She grins and lifts the front of her T-shirt, then turns and hands Paul the contract he signed. 'Reckoned it was better you get that checked first...'

24

This time, to everyone's relief, the first 100 grand is still in the hotel safe.

In the detective agency, we add it to the 50 grand Dobson was kind enough to supply. Strangely, Rebecca's nowhere to be seen. 'Must be out looking for Liam,' Daisy dismissed when we found the door locked.

Before we picked up the original ransom, Daisy stopped off in the Last Chance Saloon and snagged a carton of crisps from its store cupboard. Yes, a *carton*—that's *30* bags of salt and vinegar crinkle-cuts. Paul's too nervous to eat and I'm only halfway through my first bag, so the mess of empty packets currently overflowing her waste basket is undeniably down to Daisy. 'I missed breakfast,' she explains sadly.

It's getting near time for Paul to make the drop, but he has other worries besides. 'What if Dobson comes looking for that contract?' he wheedles.

Paul was *not* over-pleased with Daisy for swiping it back.

Daisy tuts. 'Then he'll go to the fair, dummy. Dobson knows nothing about Sam and me—well, other than we're a right pair of hotties. You're going straight from here to make the drop—after that, it doesn't matter.'

'It does, though. Dobson's... dodgy. I wouldn't fancy the idea of getting on his wrong side—there's been stories of people doing that and ending up in hospital.'

Now he tells us

Rather than worried, Daisy looks fascinated. Of course—she hasn't ruled out Dobson as a suspect in the kidnapping and this is feeding that theory. 'What *kind* of "dodgy" stuff is he into?'

'I don't know specifics—just that he has a reputation. Honestly, Daisy, I wish you'd asked me before...'

'Oh, stop fretting.'

In an aside to me: 'Wonder if Dobson knew Jack the sack? They sound like soulmates.'

Paul screws up his face. 'Who?'

'Never mind. Look, after you've got Tina back we'll sort Dobson out—if you still decide to hand over the fair, that'll get him off your case. But wait until Mr M's checked that contract, just in case there's anything dodgy in it.'

Paul stiffens. 'The deal is, Dobson's buying the fair for 150 grand in cash—simple as that.'

'So let's make sure that's what he gets—regardless of what his contract *actually* says. Listen, time's going on…'

Daisy gives Paul a hug before he climbs into the jeep. 'Good luck, mate—you'll be fine.'

He replies only with a tight smile, and we wave him off.

'Bit of a baby, isn't he?' Daisy mutters.

'Last I heard, he was your boyfriend.'

'Yeah—I'm going off him fast. You can't really know somebody until their sister gets kidnapped. Okay—let's go.'

'Where are we going?'

'Well, first, over there—to your Panda. Then, after Paul—should arrive just about when the drop's happening.'

I feel my eyes pop. 'Daisy, he'll throw a wobbly if we turn up. Anyway, what's the point? There's nothing we can do.'

'Oh yes there is. C'mon, Sam—I'll explain in the car.'

ON DAISY'S INSTRUCTIONS, I STOP WELL BEFORE THE DROP site and reverse into a convenient copse. 'This is perfect,' she trills. 'Paul will come out this way—I just want to be sure he's safe.'

She gets her phone out. 'Alpha two, this is Alpha 1. Status?'

She's got the phone on speaker and Rebecca's voice answers. 'Alpha 1, this is Alpha 2 receiving and in position. Camouflage in place. Nothing happening here. Over. Oh, and out. Did I do that right...?'

Daisy clicks the red button. Shakes her head, then makes a second call. 'Alpha 3, this is Alpha 1. Status?'

'Ee, y'mean am I here? Aye, I am. Here. In the middle o' some muckle bushes. Nae sign o' onybody yet. Unless ye count thae sheep.'

Huffing exaggeratedly, Daisy cuts him off and mutters: 'Hope I won't regret drafting Graham.'

'You already explained that on our way here— there *wasn't* anybody else.'

She frowns at me. 'Davy would have been better, but I was scared to ask *him.* Not with what's going on between you... I have to say, Sam, this was a terribly inconvenient time to fall out with your fiancé.'

'Sorry to put you out, Daisy—and I haven't fallen out with him. Not yet—you'll hear it when I do. In fact, they'll hear it all the way to Aberdeen…'

'Yeah, exactly. Anyway, Graham'll be fine—maybe I should have asked him to bring Sadie for extra muscle.'

Sadie's Graham's wife and Daisy's only half-joking. Sadie is a… formidable woman. 'So—you said last time there's only three roads in and out of the drop spot? And it's so isolated out here, traffic's practically non-existent?'

'Yep. Rebecca and Graham are watching the other two roads and they're to assume the first car that goes past belongs to our kidnappers.'

'Okay—got all that. But Daisy—if these roads are so empty, won't the kidnappers twig they've got a tail? Not to mention they have that drone looking for stakeouts.'

'Alpha 2 and Alpha 3 came early—long before the drone would be up. And you heard them—they're both well hidden. As for following the kidnappers, there's something I haven't told you… oh, listen.'

Sure enough, through the open window, I hear engine noise—getting steadily louder. There's something familiar about it…

Then Paul's jeep shoots by, heading back the way we came.

'Okay,' Daisy croons gaily. 'The game's afoot. The kidnappers should also head for home any time now.'

'Yeah, about that... as I was saying, on an otherwise deserted road, whoever goes after them will be spotted straight away. What if the kidnappers turn around and chase *them*? And have you thought these guys might have guns...?'

Before she can answer, her phone chirrups. 'Alpha 1. Oh, alright Graham, let's forget the call signs. Grey Escort—aha. What's the registration? Is it really? Yes, I do know who that is. Is Digby in place? Great—thanks, Graham. Love to Sadie.'

She must have switched off the speaker, so I'm left trying to decipher all that with only her side to go by. 'Who the blazes is Digby?'

'Shh—give me a minute.'

It's more like two when she breathes a sigh of sheer pleasure and tilts her phone to let me see the screen. It's an aerial view—far below, I can just make out a green car trundling along narrow country roads. Then, of course, it clicks. 'Digby's another drone? Following the kidnappers?'

She nods happily. 'Following Liam, to be precise—which we now know is the same thing. I had two drones delivered by overnight courier. Digby and Donna. Cost a fortune, but that doesn't matter because they're going on Paul's bill. Gave one each to Alpha… um, to Graham and Rebecca, whose first job when they arrived was to place a drone on flat ground far enough from the road so it wouldn't be seen going up. Then, when Graham phoned, I launched Digby.'

'What about the kidnappers' own drone? Won't it spot yours?'

She shrugs. 'I'm assuming when it landed with the ransom, they—or rather, Liam—chucked it in the boot.'

'Daisy, that's brilliant.'

'Yep—my only worry was some stupid birdwatcher might choose the wrong moment to drive past our watchers, which is why I was so relieved when Graham rattled off Liam's registration number. Now we know for sure it's the kidnappers Digby's following—and that Liam's one of them. Okay, start the engine.'

'Why?'

'Because we're going to shadow Liam back to wherever Tina's being held—then rescue her.'

25

'Shouldn't we call the police now?'

'Mm.'

'I said...'

'Yeah, I heard. Do you realise we're headed back towards Cairncroft?'

'Really? What—you think the kidnappers are based in Cairncroft?'

'Can't be sure yet, but—course, a big worry is if Liam isn't taking the ransom to wherever they're holding Tina. That's why I'd prefer not to involve the police at this stage—we might still have to rely on the kidnappers releasing Tina, now they've got their dough.'

'You don't think Liam could be working alone, then?'

'From what Keisha told us about Liam, he doesn't sound capable of crossing the road by himself—same as Ivor. Naw, I'd guess Liam was a plant to milk some inside information from Tina that helped the real kidnappers plan the snatch.

And a workhorse to offload donkey work on, like collecting the ransom.'

She jerks her phone closer and stares at its screen. 'Hey—you won't believe this.'

'What?'

'Liam just turned onto the track that leads to Struthers' holiday chalet.'

Now THAT brings back memories—none of them pleasant

A few years ago, old Struthers built a log cabin outside Cairncroft, in a desolate spot, intending to start a holiday letting business. Strangely, the business never took off… but he gets *some* bookings from ornithologists, writers seeking seclusion, more recently a psychotic mass murderer (actually, Lena wasn't a booking—she broke in) and now, it seems, kidnappers.

'That's good, Sam.'

'How is it "good"?'

Having to go back THERE is BAD in my book

She huffs with a show of exasperation. 'First, it's a pretty safe bet that's where they're holding Tina. Second, we know our way around Struthers' chalet.'

'Third, so does the Donstable police force.'

'True, but... we can't be *absolutely* sure Tina's there. And I promised Paul not to interfere while there was a chance the kidnappers would keep their end of the bargain.'

I take my hand off the wheel for a second to gesture at her phone and Digby the drone's control app. '*That* isn't interfering?'

'So long as the kidnappers don't know about it, we aren't interfering,' she states positively, then yips with delight. 'Yes, confirmed. He's stopped outside the chalet. Okay, I'll land Digby somewhere out of the way—we don't need him any more. Remind me to pick him up later.'

The tracks are becoming familiar—and bringing back bad memories. 'We're nearly at the entrance road—what d'you want me to do? Drive up and hide the car where we stashed it last time?'

'No—too risky. Carry on past the turnoff—then look for a way into the woodland. We'll leave the car there and walk up.'

I do as she says, wondering how my leg will cope with rambling through a jungle of untamed countryside—especially at the speed Daisy goes. Although it's the flashbacks this place is resurrecting that really unsettle me—my pulse is already rattling like a Salvation Army tambourine.

In fact, Daisy sets a sedate pace during what turns out to be a fifteen-minute hike. Not, I discover, so much through consideration for her poor disabled friend, as because she wants time to think.

'What are you thinking *about*?'

'Weighing up the pros and cons of giving Jodie and her flatfoots a shout. Assuming Tina's in there, getting caught when we *could* have sent in an army of coppers would be a definite "con". Equally, though, Tina's kidnappers might panic and do something stupid if they see the approach road turn into a blue-light disco. It's hard deciding what to do for the best.'

'Well, you'd better make your mind up because we're nearly there.'

Her lips set. 'Let's go with our gut and do what we did last time—sneak up for a keek through the windows.'

OUR gut?

She leads me into the woods where we "Davy Crockett" it until, suddenly, Struthers' chalet comes into view just as we run out of trees.

The chalet's frighteningly close now—about ten feet away. Ten feet is a lot when you want to cross it unseen. With a shock I realise this is the same spot we ended up in April, just before launching our operation to rescue Rosemary.

Three months on, however, the clearing is a sea of tall grass—at least a foot high. Maybe we could wriggle through it—soldiers do that all the time in war movies.

Yeah, right... I can see *me* doing a Private Ryan, with *my* left leg—*not*.

Maybe Daisy could, though... does she *really* need me along.?

Oh bother, she does—it's my job to give her a leg-up to the window.

Then an elbow embeds itself in my ribs, so abruptly it's all I can do to suppress a cry of alarm. 'Look, Sam,' she hisses, and I follow her finger. It's old Struthers, walking up the balcony steps.

'I don't believe it—Struthers? A kidnapper?'

Daisy shakes her head. 'Naw, it'll be to do with the property—probably checking they aren't trashing the place. What a stroke of luck, though—now everybody inside is focused on the front door. Meaning we can nip around back.'

Two sharp raps echo into the clearing as Struthers announces his presence, which is Daisy's cue to take off at a sprint.

My throat constricts—*here we go again*—and with a sigh, I hobble after her.

No shouts of alarm ring out (or worse, gunshots—my imagination is working overtime) and very quickly we arrive at the chalet's back wall. Daisy nudges me and points at huge sliding doors only a few feet from where we're standing, then flattens herself against wooden cladding and edges towards them. She keeks around with one eye—then beckons to me.

Heart in mouth, I follow.

Daisy carefully slides open the nearest door, just enough to permit access. Before I reach her, she slips inside and I hurry to catch up.

This is obviously the main living area. A cavernous space with an American-style open-plan kitchen at its far end. The furniture's all teak and ornamental cushions, typical holiday-home fare, and a faux-stone mock chimney has an enormous pot of artificial flowers in its redundant fireplace. An assortment of "homely" bits and bobs are littered about—from colourful "popular" prints on the walls to pottery ladies and animal carvings scattered indiscriminately on various surfaces. On the coffee table, a four-inch solid sphere of rainbow-coloured glass rests on its mahogany cradle—I remember seeing a tray of those in the window of a shop called "Arty Artefacts" on Donstable Main Street.

Daisy diverts to scoop up the sphere—either she sees it as a weapon, or we're diversifying into burglary—then makes for the hall door with me trailing behind.

The door's closed and Daisy very slowly, very carefully, turns its handle. When it's open a crack, we hear old Struthers' voice. 'If you're sure? You won't get fresher meat and veg anywhere.'

Ah, that explains it—Struthers is only trying to drum up extra business for his farm shop. (Which he's kept control of, despite handing over the farm itself to his son.) A younger, rougher voice answers. 'No, we're well stocked up, but thanks anyway.'

After a final flurry along the lines of "good of you to ask" and "if you change your mind" we hear Struthers leave. Daisy pulls me to the hinge-side of the door and flattens herself against its adjoining wall, motioning I'm to do the same.

Seconds later, the door swings open and my stomach clenches when the rougher voice's owner walks in—he looks rather like a young

Leonardo DiCaprio. If this is Liam, no wonder he's so popular with the ladies.

I'm thinking his peripheral vision isn't that great, since he doesn't seem to notice Daisy skipping towards him—or maybe it's because she's moving so fast. Either way, he won't be noticing anything for a while because that sickening crunch was Daisy clocking him one with the glass globe. He goes down like his strings have been cut, collapsing onto the (unfortunately for him) laminate floor.

26

I'm keeking out between my fingers, horrified. 'You've killed him.'

Daisy kneels beside the corpse. 'No, still breathing—have a right old headache when he wakes up, but I was careful. I've read up on this.'

'What's the book called? "How to knock people out without killing them?"'

She doesn't laugh. 'Yeah, that's about the size of it—cor, Liam's heavier than he looks.'

'What are you doing to him now? And how can you be sure this is Liam?'

'Putting him in the recovery position in case he's sick—don't want the poor sod choking. And I know it's Liam because of the photo Keisha gave us—remember?'

'It wasn't a very good photo,' is the best defence I can muster—also, it wasn't.

Daisy holds up a driving licence. 'Plus, his name's on this.'

We're speaking in whispers—and it's time to address the reason. 'Do you think there's more of them?'

'Definitely—we've already decided Liam's an unlikely criminal mastermind. Even the name's wrong...'

She pads to the doorway and carefully looks out. Then beckons. 'C'mon—and keep quiet.'

After establishing both toilet and hall cupboard are empty, Daisy makes for a timber stairway at the rear. This hallway is etched in my memory because, last time we were here, it's where all the action took place.

Tall floor-to-ceiling windows look out on the side balcony and I recall how gloomy it was in here, back in April. Today, though, a summer glow throttles April's shadows at birth.

'Step on the sides,' Daisy instructs in a hoarse whisper, pointing at the first step. 'Stops any creaking.'

Then she glides up, like a cat.

As if I don't have enough trouble walking up stairs with a partial prosthetic, she wants me to "step on the sides"? Needless to say, by the time I get there, Daisy's already investigated the entire upper floor. 'Anything?' I ask fearfully.

She frowns. 'Two bedrooms and a bathroom. Bedrooms are empty, and somebody's taking a shower in the bathroom. Talk about being laid back...'

'So where's Tina?'

'Dunno—weird thing is, the bedroom doors don't have locks. My guess is they tied Tina's doorhandle to the one opposite so she couldn't get out.'

She isn't here now, though—if she ever was. Just whoever's in the shower

Listening hard, I hear water running... then it stops. Daisy flits back to the bathroom door and I say, softly but urgently: 'You still got that glass globe?'

She holds up her hand—and it's holding a taser.

I almost forget to whisper. 'Why didn't you use that on Liam? Instead of braining him with...'

'Needs a minute to charge up when I switch it on—remember? Liam would have heard the whine. Don't worry—it's set to go now.'

We wait and listen to the kind of sounds you expect from someone who's just had a shower. When the door opens, Daisy draws back her taser ready to strike...

… and a woman walks out, wearing two towels, one wrapped around her hair. When she sees us, her eyes pop. Then she screams.

Daisy says: 'Tina? Almost didn't recognise you with no clothes on.'

This is Tina?

After leaning sideways to check the bathroom's empty, Daisy puts her taser away. Tina has a death grip on her towel. 'Who are you—how did you get in? Wait a minute… you're Paul's new girlfriend. Aren't you?'

She looks at me. 'Who're you?'

'She's in shock,' Daisy says, sotto voce. Then to Tina: 'We've come to rescue you. Liam's downstairs, but he's out cold and nobody else seems to be around—you're safe, but we'd best leave in a hurry.'

Tina breathes in quick gasps. 'I see—wow, that's incredible. Can I just put something on…?'

Daisy grabs Tina's arm and yanks her into the nearest bedroom. 'Are those yours?' she demands, pointing at clothes discarded over the bed.

'Yes.'

'Okay—make it fast.'

While Tina drags a T-shirt over her now towel-less head, Daisy wanders across to the window. She bends, straightens, then turns around with a huge grin plastered on her face and holds up a canvas holdall. 'Guess what I've found—Liam must have left it here when Struthers knocked.'

Right now, I couldn't care less about the ransom money—and more about getting away before the other kidnappers arrive. 'How many of them are there?' I ask Tina, dreading her answer.

She yanks a pair of jogging bottoms up and ties their drawstring. 'Three—big guys, too.'

'Where'd they go?' Daisy asks, opening the top drawer in a chest against the back wall. 'Hey, what's all this?'

I crane to see. The drawer's full of ladies' underwear—and not the sort of stuff *I* would wear. Rebecca, maybe...

Tina bats a hand. 'They must have bought it—probably got a job lot online, but at least I had clean knickers. As to where the other kidnappers went—no idea.'

'Right, time we were out of here,' Daisy announces, and Tina's face falls. 'But my hair—it's still wet.'

'Definitely in shock,' Daisy mutters, taking Tina's arm. 'Sorry—no time for that. It'll soon dry in the sun. Now, listen—keep quiet, and follow me. Sam, you bring up the rear. Let's get out of here.'

Starry-eyed, Tina obeys—and Daisy leads us down the stairs. 'Stay here,' she says, and runs into the living room.

She re-appears a moment later, looking puzzled. 'Is he alright?' I ask.

Daisy shrugs. 'Thought I'd better check on him, but yeah—he's *definitely* alright. Beggar's legged it.'

I don't know whether to be relieved she didn't seriously injure him, or annoyed because he's escaped. Tina says: 'You're talking about Liam?'

I nod and Daisy curses. 'Should have tied him up,' she growls.

We go out by the front door and down the balcony steps. That puts us on the track that leads out—and in. 'Daisy,' I hiss. 'If the others come back, we'll walk straight into them.'

'I know—but they'll be in a car, so we'll hear them. Keep to the verge and if necessary, we can nip into the woods.'

Knowing more kidnappers could appear any moment makes the trek seem endless, but eventually we make it to the main (=slightly less track-like) road. It only takes another couple of minutes to reach the Panda and I dive into its driving seat, feeling almost light-headed with relief. 'We made it,' I breathe.

    Once Tina's safely settled next to me, Daisy opens a rear door and tosses the holdall on Panda's rear seat. Jumping in beside it, she barks: 'Okay, Sam—get us out of here. And don't stop for anything.'

27

Daisy phones Paul from the car and puts it on speaker. 'Where are you?'

'In my caravan, back at the fair. There's been no word from the kidnappers.'

Daisy winks at Tina and points the phone her way. 'Got somebody here wants to say hello.'

'Paul, it's me. Daisy and her friend rescued me.'

'TINA. You're safe? Oh, Daisy—this is incredible. I can never thank you enough. But how...?'

'Paul,' Daisy interrupts. 'We'll be there in five minutes, so save the questions for then.'

Paul stutters more thanks and after Daisy ends the call I reach over to give Tina's hand a squeeze. 'It must have been horrible,' I sympathise.

She nods, then looks at her knees. 'Don't know which was worse—being kidnapped, or watching my scum of a husband shoot Dad. Did they arrest Ivor yet?'

Daisy's head shoots through the gap between our seats. 'Yes, they did, but... you *saw* Ivor shoot your dad?'

Tina swallows a sob. 'They'd been arguing over money—Ivor wanted some and Dad wouldn't give him any. Then Ivor took out his gun and...'

This time, her sob makes it all the way out. Daisy says slowly: 'So you're saying it really *was* Ivor shot Mr McNab?'

'Then...' Tina gets out with obvious effort, ignoring Daisy, '... Ivor ran off and next thing these men wearing hoods barged in and grabbed me. They threw me in the back of a van and took me to that chalet.'

'But what about the poison?'

'What poison?'

'Oh, you don't know—the postmortem showed your dad had also been poisoned.'

Tina looks poleaxed. 'But why would anybody poison him?'

'That's what we'd like to know. Tina, what time were you kidnapped?'

'I don't really know. Maybe around eight... or nine? It's all very hazy...'

'That's understandable. Did they hurt you?'

Without waiting for an answer, Daisy leans between the seats and keeks around. 'You looked a bit knocked about in the photo they sent— mind, that black eye's healed quick.'

I can't help myself—did I mention being a former optician? 'Black eyes generally take around two weeks to fade.'

Tina shakes her head. 'It wasn't a black eye—the kidnappers used greasepaint to make it look like one for the photo. They actually treated me alright.'

'Even let you shower,' I observe.

'Yes, I was allowed to shower once a day, but apart from that they kept me locked up in a bedroom. Oh, and the food they brought... yeeuch.'

'There weren't any locks on the bedroom doors,' Daisy points out, and Tina squints at her.

'Well, I don't know—the door wouldn't open, though. I spent enough time pulling at it.'

'Must be what I said. They'll have attached your room's doorhandle to the one opposite. Funny the rope wasn't lying about—thought they'd have kept it handy.'

'Those sorts of details aren't important,' I interject. Daisy has a habit of tying herself in knots over minutiae. 'Did you get a good look at any of the kidnappers? Good enough to give the police a description?'

'In particular,' Daisy cuts in, 'was Dobson one of them?'

Tina rounds on her. '*Dobson?* No, of course not... why would you think *he* was involved?'

Daisy tuts. 'Are you saying he isn't?'

'Of course Dobson wasn't involved—oh, I suppose Paul's been repeating those rumours about him. That's all they are—rumours. I've known Dobson for years, and there's no way he'd get mixed up in something like this. But no, I didn't see any of them apart from Liam—the other men kept their hoods on whenever they came near me, which wasn't often. I think they gave Liam the job of minding me because I already knew him.'

'It's lucky Liam's a minor cog in the operation,' Daisy muses. 'Otherwise they might have topped you, so you couldn't ID him to the police. Mind, they might have planned to do away with you after...'

Tina does a theatrical flinch and I shoot Daisy daggers through the mirror. 'Have a care, wilya?'

'Mm... oh, yeah. Sorry—anyway, they didn't. What about their motors—you said they took you in a van? Did you get a good look at it? Or better still, its registration number?'

'No, the first thing they did was blindfold me. I didn't see anything that would help.'

'Never mind,' I tell her. 'You're safe now—which is all that matters.'

Daisy pats the bag of money. 'And we got Dobson's cash back—which is quite the bonus. Paul won't have to sell Dobson the fair after all.'

Tina laughs. 'If Dobson gave Paul all that cash, you can bet he tied him up in an unbreakable contract first. The man's no criminal, but *is* a cutthroat when it comes to business. No, the fair's gone...'

Her gaze jerks sideways when I burst out laughing. 'No Tina, it isn't. The Artful Dodger back there lifted Dobson's contract after Paul signed it.'

Then an unsettling thought occurs. 'Course, we don't know what Dobson had him sign to get the first load of cash...'

'Oh beggar.' Daisy looks horrified. 'D'you think the contract I nicked was just an update because of the extra cash—and that Paul already committed to giving Dobson the fair?'

Tina sniffs. 'Anybody who knows Dobson wouldn't need to ask that question—he doesn't part with a penny before wrapping it up in an iron-clad contract. Take it from me, Dobson's finally got the fair—and to be honest, it might not be a bad thing. Now Paul and I can start afresh. No fairground—no Ivor—and don't get me wrong, I loved my dad, but there was never any chance of making normal lives for ourselves while he was alive. That fair's been in our family for generations and Dad would never have let us leave—I did, and he guilt-tripped me into coming back.'

Sounds like Tina feels everything's worked out just peachy

'You seemed—glad? —your husband's under arrest,' I observe. 'Things must have been very bad between you.'

She laughs, in a way that reminds me of Cruella de Ville. 'Bad—oh, *darling*. You don't know the half of it. That man's an animal—I'm *delighted* to hear they've arrested him. I hope they throw away the key.'

Okay—even more peachy

'What shall we do about the police?' Daisy asks. 'I'm thinking you could probably use some quiet time before we bring them in.'

'Police?' Tina blurts. 'Why do we have to involve the police?'

Daisy goggles. 'Because you were kidnapped?'

'No—there's really no need. Um—won't you two get into trouble? Surely you should have sent the police instead of storming in yourselves.'

'Hmpf. We'll try and remember that next time.'

Tina throws Daisy an apologetic glance. 'I didn't mean to sound ungrateful. I just don't want the police giving you any hassle. Do we have to tell them? After all, is there any proof I even *was* kidnapped?'

'She's got a point,' Daisy muses. 'Make that *two* points—Wilson's going to hit the roof when he hears about this.'
Then she sighs. 'But after telling us you witnessed a murder... we can't keep quiet about that.'

Tina pulls a face. 'I suppose not,' she says, sulkily. 'But you are right—I'm *not* ready to face the police yet.'

'What do you think?' I ask, catching Daisy's eye in the mirror. 'Would Jodie be okay with leaving off reporting this until morning?'

Daisy shrugs. 'We can ask—don't see why not, though.'

Arriving at the fairground, I turn into Struthers' countryside version of NCP. 'I'm not driving over to Paul's caravan,' I declare, and clarify with: 'My suspension's suffered enough over the last couple of days.'

'I thought he had appendicitis,' Daisy mutters, as we get out of the car and somebody wearing a peaked cap bears down on us.

'Stanley did,' I tell her—and as the parking attendant draws closer, add: 'but that's Struthers. He must be filling in while Stanley's out of action.'

Sure enough, clad in a hi-vis jacket that's too small for him and holding his receipt book at the ready, old Struthers struts up. When he sees Tina, his face falls. 'Ah, you have a fairground person with you. Hmm... they're *supposed* to get complimentary use of the parking facilities.'

He eyes us hopefully, as though hoping we'll waive such a silly rule.

Daisy claps him on the back. 'Cheers, mate.'

Then we head off to Paul's caravan, before old Struthers bursts into tears.

As we pass between the Waltzers and that *horrible* Pirate Ship ride, Tina pauses. 'Uh, Sam. You own a hotel, don't you?'

'With someone else... but, yes.'

Tina nods at the bag swinging from Daisy's hand. 'Neither Paul nor I will be up to going into the bank with that, not today, so I was wondering... do you have a safe it could spend the night in?'

'Sure—no problem. It's already been there—well, not all of it at once.'

'Oh, wonderful. Can I ask another favour?'

Knock yourself out

'Of course.'

'Could I get a room there tonight? After being snatched from here, I'd feel safer...'

'Certainly.'

I should have thought to suggest that myself. 'In fact, if you'd rather, why not come and stay in our cottage?'

'Thank you *so* much, but can you understand I'd like to be alone—only somewhere safe? While I come to terms with everything that's happened.'

'Of course—listen, go spend some time with Paul, then get him to bring you over—tell him to text me so I know you're coming and I'll have the room all ready. On the house.'

'Oh, you don't have to do that...'

'My pleasure, really. The least I can do after what you've been through.'

I catch Daisy's eye. 'Shall we let Paul have Tina to himself?' I ask, inclining my head towards the car park.

'Good idea, Sam. Besides...' she holds up the holdall '... sooner we get this locked up, the happier I'll be.'

On the way out, I remind Daisy that Jodie will be waiting to hear what happened today. 'I hadn't forgotten—let's go and see her later when she's back from work. With any luck, she'll agree to leaving off the red tape until morning. By then, Tina should be up to giving the police a statement.'

'Yeah—Jodie should be alright with that.'

Although—I'd rather not be the one to tell her

28

Paul drops Tina off at teatime and I meet her in reception. She's effusively grateful and refuses my offer of a dinner reservation, claiming to have eaten earlier with Paul, but accepts a drink in the residents lounge. After that, I show her the room before leaving the poor lass in peace.

Daisy's gone to fill Rebecca in on what happened—and Graham, if he's still around. I'm meeting her in the resident's lounge at seven, then we'll go speak to Jodie.

That should give our favourite CID sergeant time to make it home, play with Alanna, and have something to eat. Hopefully, in other words, put her in an amenable frame of mind for our request to leave off making Tina's kidnap "official" until tomorrow.

I've plonked myself in an armchair just inside the residents lounge where I'm trying to figure out how to sneak a private confab with Rebecca when the lady in question strolls through reception. Jumping up, I catch her at the lift. 'Rebecca—need a word. Fancy a drink?'

'Ooh, you bet.'

She holds up a plastic carrier. 'Okay if I bring Hector?'

'So long as he stays in his box—Louis would have a fit if Hector invaded his kitchen.'

'He does know it wasn't Hector nicked his steak that time?'

This was several months ago, when Daisy needed a steak to introduce herself to Jack the sack's guard dog—which steak unfortunately turned out to be earmarked for Mr Entwhistle. When he found it missing, Louis assumed it was "dat cat". 'Well, I told him, but he looked dubious—though why Louis would think I'd cover up for Hector by daubing Daisy in is beyond me. He isn't the most... *rational* of people, but when you cook the way Louis does, it excuses a lot.'

'Oh, I know,' she purrs, batting at her hair. Rebecca really should consider growing it longer if she's going to wear translucent blouses, especially considering her aversion to bras.

Translucent? More like transparent. As for those shorts—put it this way, it's a relief to see she's shaved her bikini line.

'I was so disappointed today,' she moans. 'Lucky old Graham—wish I'd had his post.'

'You didn't miss much—Graham phoned it in and that was him finished.'

'But it's the sense of *achievement*—being instrumental in rescuing that poor girl.'

'Everybody played their part,' I assure her. 'And yours was vital.'

She titters modestly. (That's what Rebecca does— "titters". Somehow, it works for her—in a "Blackpool-postcard" sort of way.) Looking down at the cat carrier, I comment: 'He's quiet.'

'Hector's either in the huff, thinking he's missing something—or sleeping. Both equally likely. Anyway, what did you want to ask? As if I couldn't guess...'

'Did you get it?'

She nods. 'Wasn't hard—we already knew she was in the Donstable Arms. Room 7. That's hers.'

'Well done—how did you find out?'

'There's a lad works behind the bar in there and he keeps asking me out—I might have given the impression that doing this little favour would improve his chances.'

Grinning, I ask: 'And has it?'

'Oh, no—he's a ghastly youth. Still got teenage acne, so no—I'm more into mature men. Like Alan.'

Jake wasn't mature

I let that go. 'Cheers, Rebecca—I think that's a wrap on the assignment.'

I pass her an envelope and she peeks inside. 'Oh, I *couldn't*—the agency pays me.'

'You weren't working for the agency, so it's only right I pay for your time.'

'But everything I did for you was in agency time.'

I wink. (Well, I try to, but from Rebecca's reaction it looks as though I haven't quite mastered the art yet.) 'I won't tell if you don't...'

PARKING BEHIND THE DONSTABLE ARMS, I REFLECT ON OUR current state of affairs. (Daisy's and mine—not *Davy's*.)

The kidnapping case is solved—it's only been three days, but feels much longer.

We still have the problem of Mr M and his gold-mining friend—I can't wait to see what Daisy's got planned for poor Kat. Apart from that, we're back to our normal workload—leaving me some time for personal business.

I *had* intended to confront Davy, throw his ring at him, and that would be that. However, it isn't fair this Leslie harlot should get off scot-free—she might be an old flame, but must have known she was coming between an engaged couple. Besides—I want a proper look at her. Whether it's because I'm a nosy bitch, or a need to know what she's got that I haven't...

It's the same girl as before on reception. 'Oh, hello. You're in luck—the bar's quiet tonight. Didn't half kick-off last night, though. Those workies are a wild bunch.'

I smile sweetly. 'Actually, I'm going upstairs to see one of your guests.'

I don't add: *If you think things kicked-off last night—you ain't seen nuthin' yet.*

The Donstable Arms has two floors with four rooms on each—surprises me they have full-time receptionist cover, but there's probably a lot of multi-tasking involved with the kitchen and bar. No lift, though—sometimes I wonder if the

Cairncroft would be better off without *its* lift, but after climbing two flights of stairs with my leg protesting even more than it did at Dobson's this morning—trekking through wild woodland tends to upset it—I suddenly feel kindly disposed to our very own thrill-ride.

I give myself a moment to recover—then, when the fiery ache shows no sign of easing, limp along to room 7 and knock on the door.

My heart sinks when she opens it. Up close, Leslie's even more gorgeous than I realised. It isn't only the looks—you can tell straight away they're only a prop for her effervescent personality. She's the kind of person who's comfortable in any situation and must have men eating out of her hand with one flutter of those lashes (they can't be real—no way) together with a quick flash of the little dimple in her right cheek.

Well, madam-prepare to be made UNcomfortable
'Hello', she trills, as though delighted to see me.
'You Leslie?' I grate, channelling my inner Daisy.
'I am, yes. Have we met?'
She makes you want to smile along with her—it's like hypnosis
'I'm Sam—Samantha.'

She puts the tip of a finger to her lips. Then shakes her head. 'Sorry...'

'Davy's fiancé.'

'Oohhh.'

She sounds so pleased? 'You're *her?* Oh, how lovely. Want to come in...?' she takes a step back '... or would you rather go down for a drink? I'm so looking forward to chatting with you.'

You are?

'Leslie, you're stealing my fiancé away—I don't want to have a drink with you.'

For the first time, she looks worried. Her chin dips. 'I'm awfully sorry—you must be furious with me.'

I was starting to think (hope?) this was all a misunderstanding—which it plainly isn't. 'Of course I am. How can you live with yourself?'

She pouts. 'Samantha—Davy's a big boy. It's his decision...'

'Don't you feel any... shame?'

'Of course not—why should I?'

Now she looks irritated—and I'm getting mad. In fact...

I hold out my hand as though to shake and she takes it automatically, as people do—auto-suggestion, which I suppose is another form of hypnosis—then sinks to her knees, squealing like a stuck pig. I put my face right up against hers. 'You just should,' I growl, wishing I could come up with something less lame.

Then I release the leverage on her finger joints and walk away. (Trying not to hobble, because it would spoil the effect.)

Behind me, Leslie's lost her smug assurance. 'You're a horrible woman.'

Hah—she's no better at smart comebacks than I am

Descending two flights of stairs that suddenly seem indistinguishable from Everest's north face, I'm glad Daisy explained that very basic aikido hold so clearly.

One down—I'll tackle Davy tomorrow.

I wonder if Daisy would lend me her taser…?

29

'You alright?'

Walking into the residents lounge I find Daisy already there, wearing a quizzical expression. I drop into the chair beside her, still shaking. 'Fine—why?'

'Oh, nothing—apart from you looking like when we came off the Pirate Ship on Saturday.'

So I tell all—and watch her mouth drop open. 'Cor, you did *that*? I'm proud of you, Sam—bet you need a drink now.'

Too right

She brings me a huge vodka & tonic and sets it down next to her pint of best. 'What about Jodie?' I remind her.

'Aw, she'll wait. And a little dutch courage won't hurt—I'm expecting her to be narked about Tina wanting to put off reporting the kidnap until tomorrow.'

I take a long swig and feel instantly better. Obviously, the secret is not to *try* and get drunk, but rather let it happen naturally... 'Probably,' I agree. 'But hearing Tina's an eyewitness to Mr McNab's murder might soften Jodie up—even though I've a feeling you don't believe her.'

'I don't. But right now, I want to hear more about you beating up that slag.'

'*Which* slag has *who* beaten up?'

It's unfortunate Daisy took a slurp of beer right at that moment—and even more unfortunate when she chokes on it. Jodie helpfully slaps her back.

'Ouch—gerroff.'

Grinning, Jodie pulls over a chair and sits facing us across the low table. 'Well?'

Recovered, Daisy asks: 'Where did you come from?'

'Alanna's having a nap and Rosemary's still there, so I decided to take a wander and look for you two—I presume you've reported that small matter of a kidnap since I got off duty?'

'We were on our way up to discuss that,' Daisy protests.

'So I see—mine's half a cider, by the way. I've a lot of catching up to do now Alanna's on bottle feeds.'

Daisy goes to fetch Jodie's drink and I try to butter her up. 'How was your first day, Jodie?'

'Fine—what's this about somebody being beaten up?'

'Oh, alright—I expect it'll be public knowledge soon enough.'

After I've filled her in on my shameful behaviour, Jodie sits back and shakes her head. 'Well, knock me down with a feather duster—I didn't see that coming.'

'Me neither. I had no idea he was capable of such deception.'

'No, I'm talking about you doing a "Daisy" on Davy's girlfriend. Sam, she could have called my lot and had you charged with assault.'

Jodie grins. 'But... sounds as though there weren't any witnesses and I don't see the Donny Arms having CCTV, so it's her word against yours.'

She winks. 'Nice one—about time you stopped being such a wimp.'

Wimp...?

Luckily, Daisy comes back with Jodie's drink then—I'm not really inclined to discuss that last comment further.

'Have you told her?' Daisy demands.

'She has,' Jodie says. 'Who'd have believed Minnie Mouse over there would give her fiancé's bird a going-over?'

'It was NOT...'

Daisy cuts in. 'I mean about Tina.'

'Crumbs.' Jodie laughs shortly. 'Forgot about her—alright, let's have it.'

Daisy gives her the story (I'm still in the huff) and when she finishes Jodie takes a long swig of cider. 'Ahh—needed that. Well, as you rightly surmised, Tina's idea about sweeping it under the carpet isn't on. Not after telling you she witnessed her father's murder.'

'We know that,' Daisy says. 'What I thought was, let Tina have tonight to get over what can't have been a very nice couple of days—then bring her in to the nick tomorrow morning?'

We brace for Jodie's reaction, but she surprises us. 'Great—suits me. Make it around eleven—gives me time to soften up Inspector Wilson because he *will* do you for obstruction if the notion takes him. You need to give him the full story—unedited. Getting an eyewitness to his murder case should calm him down, though.'

'We were kind of hoping it would be you who...'

'I'll take statements from the four of you—oh yes, bring Paul in too—but then it *has* to be passed onto Wilson. I'll try and present everything in the least damaging way—but can't skimp on the actual facts.'

'Maybe he'll be in a good mood,' I quip.

Jodie makes a face. 'He's *never* in a good mood... actually, that's unfair. The old so-and-so's bark is worse than his bite, and he likes you...' she glances at me '... so that'll help.'

'Doesn't he like me?' Daisy asks with a show of innocence.

Jodie just raises her eyebrows. Then gulps the last of her cider and slams the glass down. 'Right, better get back. See you tomorrow.'

When Jodie's gone, I catch Daisy's eye. 'You don't think Wilson *will* charge us with obstruction—do you?'

Daisy stares into her pint. 'Dunno—hope not. Don't think so... he acts it a bit, but Wilson's a reasonable enough bloke deep down.'

'Those smug quotes you keep giving the Donstable Gazette won't help.'

'His are just as bad,' she retorts, looking indignant. 'All that rubbish about having "reservations over civilians involving themselves in police business." I was only responding...'

She looks at my empty glass. 'I'll get you a refill,' she says. 'One way and another, I reckon you could use it.'

You wouldn't be wrong

While she's away, my phone rings—again. It's Davy—that's four times in the last half-hour his name's appeared on my screen.

I'm not ready to speak to him—don't know when I will be—so decline the call. Moments later, a beep signals an incoming text from—guess who?—and I throw a quick glance at the bar. Daisy's still talking to Colin, so I open the text.

Sam—I've had Leslie crying down the phone at me. WHAT are you playing at?

No kisses?

What am *I* playing at? That's rich. I've had enough of this—mauling my way through the on-screen controls, I block him.

'Who was that—or need I ask?'

I didn't hear her coming back, and just nod. She frowns. 'You'll have to speak to him sooner or later.'

'It'll be later—I've blocked him.'

'Mm. Don't you think...?'

'No, I don't. We're over, and I can't see the point in extended postmortems. Now, *leave it*.'

She gapes, and I feel a little thrill—I'm not used to being assertive. It feels good—and proves Jodie wrong.

Wimp? Where did that come from? (Leslie doesn't think I'm a wimp)

In a conciliatory tone (because being assertive is all very well, but I've never been one for conflict), I quickly change the subject. 'So, what about Tina's claim she saw Ivor shoot her dad?'

'Yeah—and I'm the tooth fairy.'

'Take it you're sceptical, then?'

Daisy shakes her head. 'Of course I am—she's at the top of our "who framed Ivor" list. Tina had means and opportunity—hardly surprising she'd take things a stage further and lie about seeing it happen. Otherwise, we're back to Mr McNab having half of Cairncroft trying to kill him on Friday night.'

'S'pose so. Take it we're moving on to investigating the murder now Tina's back safe?'

'You bet—we'll go after Tina's kidnappers as well, but I'm itching to get at the murder case. The publicity we get from solving those is more valuable than any paid advertising—plus, they're fun. After we've smoothed things over with Wilson, I want to question all the fair folk.'

'Wilson will already have done that.'

'Yeah, but Wilson thinks Ivor did it—despite the PM results, he seems to have a blind spot about the poison. Which reminds me, we need a chat with Doris at the Cuppa Tea before anything else. Because she might well have seen the poisoner.'

'Does Tina saying they took her between eight and nine help?'

'If her dad *was* poisoned in the Cuppa Tea, which would have him dead by six, it pretty much proves she's lying. Even if old McNab belted back home and dived straight into a fight with Ivor, it leaves Tina sitting on her tush for two or three hours looking at his body instead of calling the police. Or even an ambulance, just in case...'

'Mm... I see that. But of course, we don't *know* yet Mr McNab was poisoned in the Cuppa Tea— or even if he was poisoned at all. Hey—won't the PM say what actually killed him?'

'Quite probably not—the poison works by inducing cardiac arrest, so it depends how much of his heart was left to examine after somebody put a bullet through it. And he had two heart attacks last year—so there'd be scarring from those, to confuse the issue further.'

'Any idea who the poisoner could have been?'

'Haven't the foggiest—and I'm not wasting brainpower speculating when Doris might put us straight on to him. I'm hoping when we find out who he or she is, their connection to the kidnap will come clear—because I still say there has to be one.'

On that note, our brains pack up—so we decide to go home and hit the sack. It's been quite a day—and tomorrow doesn't look any better. We can only hope Inspector Wilson has such a wonderful evening, his good mood carries over…

30

Next morning, we're in reception before nine to meet Paul and hand over his cash. Predictably, he's already there—on his second cup of coffee.

'I'll come with you to the bank,' Daisy tells him. 'Just in case.'

Paul's face falls. 'In case of what?'

'That's a good idea,' I put in. 'It *is* a lot of money. Not that anyone will know you're carrying it, but still... I'll come too, then we'll all go into the police station together.' Daisy phoned Paul last night and warned him about our upcoming encounter with Inspector Wilson.

'We aren't due there until eleven,' Daisy reminds me, 'but we can slob out in a café until then. A few double shots might be a good idea before we tackle Wilson.'

'How's Tina this morning?' Paul asks, with more than a hint of anxiety.

Daisy shrugs, looks at me, and I repeat the gesture. 'She isn't having breakfast in the dining room—I was through there not long ago. Unless she came early—but it's more likely the poor lass is having a lie in. You'd better go up and fetch her, Paul—wait and I'll get you the cash out, though.'

Hazel shifts over and I stoop to unlock the safe.

Daisy laughs. 'Remember last time we did this? You opened the safe and it was empty—well, apart from Liz's envelope.'

'Remember?' Paul puts in. 'I'm still having nightmares about that.'

Hesitantly, Hazel asks: 'Anything wrong, Sam?'

I straighten, then hold up both arms. 'The money isn't there.'

LIGHTNING CAN STRIKE TWICE, IT SEEMS

After an understandable period of behaving like sheep looking for their feed buckets, rationality filters back in. 'Somebody's taken it,' Paul asserts—not very helpfully and prompting an eyeroll from Daisy.

'*Obviously*. Sam, who all knows the access code?'

'Me, Logan, Hazel... actually, that's it, because I changed the code after our last incident. Nobody else has the updated version yet.'

'Are the bar takings still there?' Daisy asks, and I nod.

'They are.'

'That's something, but this still has to be another "Caron" scenario—LOGAN,' she yells, and it's clear poor Logan wishes he'd stayed in the lift.

Visibly gathering himself, Logan tries to saunter over. Unfortunately, it looks as though he's undergoing one of those sobriety tests you see American cops inflicting on suspect motorists. (If you watch the sort of programs Daisy insists on making me suffer through.)

Good job it's not that—he'd fail.

'Yes, Daisy?' Logan says, pulling himself straight in ongoing pursuit of his lost dignity. 'What can I do for you?'

'Did you...' she glances at Hazel '... or *you*, put anything into the safe last night?'

Hazel shakes her head but Logan says: 'The bar takings, of course. Oh, and a package for the lady in room 6—Tina Patterson.'

He looks at Paul. 'That's your sister—isn't it?'

The lift doors haven't closed—Daisy tears across and leaps inside. As they slide closed, we hear her say: 'This is *not* a good time to mess with me.'

A few minutes later, the lift's back and Daisy storms out. 'Tina's gone—she's nicked her own bloomin' ransom money.'

'Is her package still in there?' Hazel asks—the only one of us thinking straight. I stoop again, and yes... there it is. When I bring it out, Daisy snatches the neatly wrapped parcel and rips its paper off.

Then she groans and holds up a Gideon bible. 'From the bedside cabinet in her room. And that paper's pretty tatty—she probably got *it* out of the bins. Tina did a "Caron" on Logan—and the silly idiot fell for it. Again.'

Paul's voice is shaking. 'But why—I mean, it's her own money. Well, hers and mine.'

Daisy reaches up to grip Paul's shoulder. 'Don't you see, Paul? Tina was never kidnapped—it was all a scam. Because the money *wasn't* yours and hers—it was just yours. Your dad left *you* the fair in his will—and Tina diddly-squat. Looks like she wasn't too happy about that.'

LOGAN'S TAKEN PAUL INTO THE RESIDENTS LOUNGE WITH instructions to pour some very sweet tea down him. Poor bloke appears on the verge of collapse. After three days of worrying what the kidnappers might do to his sister, he's struggling to cope with the distinct possibility Tina orchestrated her own "kidnapping".

'It's obvious now,' Daisy says, as we ride up in the lift. 'This clinches our theory about Tina framing Ivor—and fills in the gaps. When she found her dad dead, Tina also decided she was entitled to a share of his legacy—and being honest, I see her point after putting so much into the business. So Tina pushes grief to one side and forces herself to fire a bullet from Ivor's gun into her dad's corpse. Then she writes the ransom note, pushes it under Paul's door, and calls the new boyfriend—loopy Liam—to spirit her away, when no doubt the allure of Tina *and* all that cash sent Keisha and their wains straight to the bottom of Liam's priority list. There *were* no kidnappers— the thugs Tina "never saw properly" didn't exist.'

I nod. 'No locks on the doors—no rope lying about to tie them shut—and she was having a *shower.* Yeah—hindsight's a wonderful thing.'

The lift stops and we exit. I pause to look back, wondering if it's blown a fuse. Daisy sees what I'm thinking. 'Jodie told me where to kick it—so I did, first time I went up.'

She glances down at my left leg. 'Wouldn't work for you, Sam—sorry. Hey, look on the bright side. At least the bar takings are still there.'

'Yeah—why d'you think she left *them*?'

'Way she reckons it, Tina's entitled to the ransom money. She doesn't see it as stealing—and knows anyway Paul would never press charges. Taking *hotel* money, though—that'd be outright theft. If she ever got caught, *you* might press charges.'

'Mm—makes sense.'

Following her to Tina's room, something else occurs. 'But if Tina arranged her own kidnap on the spur of the moment, how'd she get ahold of a drone so fast? It isn't the sort of thing most people have lying around.'

'Ordered it special delivery on her phone. Same as I did—well, I used my laptop—there's a specialist place in Aberdeen would have bussed it over for the right price. Same as they did for me.'

She throws open the door and stomps in. 'What are we looking for?' I ask, as Daisy upends the mattress.

'Dunno—anything she left that might give us a lead on where the besom went.'

Five minutes is all it takes to search a hotel room pretty thoroughly. 'Nothing,' I say.

Daisy slumps on the mattress-less bed. 'She was hardly going to leave a handwritten travel itinerary, but I just hoped...'

'So what now? Hand it over to the police?'

'S'pose, for all the good that'll do, but I don't like to think Tina got one over on us. Wait a minute... it's not so much *where* she's gone as *how* she went. Taxi... bus... that's where we start.'

I shake my head. 'If the kidnap *was* a scam, surely she'd get Liam to pick her up?'

Daisy's look is sheer adoration. 'Sam, you're brilliant. Yes, of course she would.'

'Why does that make you happy?'

'Because Tina doesn't have a phone here. Obviously had one in the cabin, with a fancy voice-changer app for calling Paul—but those jogging bottoms didn't have pockets, so she couldn't have brought it with her. *How* then did she contact Liam to arrange a pickup?'

Ah—now I get it. 'The room phone,' I blurt, spinning to look at it, sitting on a bedside cabinet.

'Yes, and Liam left *his* mobile at Keisha's. So unless he's got a burner, we're talking landline. Maybe where he's staying...?'

Daisy grabs the handset and pushes buttons. 'Last number called,' she mutters by way of explanation, then holds it up so I can see. 'And there it is—an outgoing call at six this morning.'

She pushes the green button. Puts the handset to her ear.

I hear the muted sound of ringing, then a muffled voice. Daisy hangs up and leans towards me. 'You're never going to believe this...'

31

Paul, Daisy and I are sat in front of a wobbly, battle-scarred wooden table. We're waiting for Inspector Wilson after deciding it prudent to keep our appointment at the police station before going after Tina and Liam.

We *have* told Jodie about Tina doing a runner with the ransom cash. (Omitting the fact we know where she went.)

She already knew Tina claims to have witnessed Mr Mcnab's murder, but we decided not to mention Daisy doesn't believe her—no point in complicating things at this stage. Especially when the promise of eyewitness testimony in his murder case is likely to soothe Wilson's fevered brow.

The door opens and Inspector Wilson marches in, followed closely by a tight-lipped Jodie. After all our past dealings, you'd think Wilson would be an old friend—but his expression suggests otherwise.

He throws a pile of papers on the table (our statements, presumably, as taken by Jodie) and lowers himself onto a seat opposite. Jodie remains standing in front of the door.

Wilson's gaze fastens on Daisy. '*You*, I expect this of.'

He switches his aim to me. '*You*, Miss Chessington, I am *extremely* disappointed in.'

Finally, Paul's in the spotlight. 'And *you*. What were you thinking of, putting your sister's life—as you thought—in the hands of these clowns?'

Paul doesn't look intimidated—he *is* a fairground worker, after all. 'Listen mate, that's not how it was at all. The note I got said Tina would die if I went to your lot—which is why I *had* to go it alone. *After* I'd made that decision, Daisy and Sam agreed to provide some backup—but all along, they've been on at me to involve the police. So don't blame the girls for helping me—or keeping my secret when I'd sworn them to silence.'

The defence rests

Wilson picks up the statements Jodie crafted so laboriously on our behalf and flicks through them, then laughs shortly. 'Does your sister have suicidal tendencies, Mr McNab? Just trying to understand how she was "at risk" from her "kidnapper".'

'We can't be sure that's what...' Paul starts, but Wilson cuts him off.

'You might not be, but from where I'm sitting it's pretty plain what happened. Ivor Patterson—who we already know wasn't on good terms with his father-in-law—lets temper get the better of him and shoots Mr McNab senior. Then your precious sister seizes the chance to take what she sees as due to her.'

Ignoring Paul's angry insistence that he "doesn't know that", Wilson shifts his laser-stare back to Daisy and me. 'I *should* charge you both with obstruction—and have seriously considered doing so. Even if this wasn't a kidnapping, you still withheld information pertinent to a murder inquiry. Especially now Tina Patterson claims she saw her father being shot.'

He glares at Jodie. 'Is that BOLO out yet?'

Jodie snaps to attention. 'Yessir.'

Daisy leans in and whispers: 'Be on the lookout. It's the same as an APB. Presumably on Tina...'

Wilson thumps the table. 'Stop whispering, will you? I still can't believe you managed to lose my eyewitness.'

Daisy raises her hand. 'Um... which you wouldn't even know she was, if it weren't for us.'

'Mm. I suppose you've got a point.'

He whips off his reading glasses. 'Because of that, I've decided not to charge you with obstruction. That, and the fact my sergeant has made a powerful appeal on your behalf. But let me make something clear, ladies—this is your *last* "get out of jail free" card. With that in mind, have you anything else to tell me?'

Daisy's head swings from side to side, her expression solemn. Mine too.

Wilson huffs. 'Alright—hop it. Oh, wait...' he points at Paul '... do you want to make a complaint regarding this money your sister's run off with?'

Paul's eyes widen. 'Of course not.'

Wilson looks disappointed. 'In that case, it appears she'll get off scot-free. She didn't waste police time because the "kidnap" wasn't reported—and playing a practical joke on her brother, however distasteful, isn't a crime. As a material witness, of course, she *has* withheld evidence—but any competent brief will insist on immunity before she testifies.'

He points a rigid finger at us. (Actually, I think it's pointed at Daisy.) 'Remember what I said—last warning.'

Wilson stomps out and Jodie winks. 'I'll show you out,' she says, in her best "police officer" tone.

At the front entrance, Jodie places a hand on the door handle but doesn't turn it. She keeps her voice low. 'If you have any idea where Tina is and don't tell Wilson, he really will blow.'

Daisy looks innocence personified. 'Jodie, how could we possibly know that?'

'Hmpf.'

She pulls open the door. 'I'll be home between five and six—come and see me after you catch up with her. Probably best if I break it to him...'

WE CAME IN SEPARATE CARS SINCE PAUL'S GOING BACK TO the fair, then has another appointment with Mr M to check over Dobson's contract and find out where he stands.

Once we're safely in the Panda and headed east, I glance sideways at Daisy. 'You heard

Jodie—Wilson would go spare if he thought we knew where Tina was and didn't tell him.'

'He'd have no right. You heard Paul—he isn't making a complaint. As for Tina being an eyewitness—well, they've already got Ivor in a cell. What's the rush—his trial's months away?'

'*Wilson* won't see it that way—and when we bring Tina back, it'll be obvious we lied to him.'

'No, it won't. For a start, I'm not interested in bringing *Tina* back—just the cash. Paul's our client—not Wilson. If old grumpy-boots wants Tina, he can go fetch her himself. Anyway, we worked out where she'd gone *after* speaking to him—and Wilson can't prove otherwise.'

'But he'll say we should have told him straight away, instead of going after her ourselves.'

'We were worried she would vamoose again—there wasn't a moment to spare. You worry too much, Sam.'

I still think this would be a good time to binge-watch "Bad Girls"—get some tips on surviving prison life

'Who'd believe it?' I say, still struggling to get my head around our destination. Because when Daisy dialled the "last number called" on Tina's room phone, a cheery female voice said: 'Excelsior Hotel, how may I help you?'

Daisy grins. 'I'm just hoping we run into Pete again—two for the price of one.'

'Shouldn't we be in disguise—after last time?'

'Unless you're an actual expert—which neither of us is—disguises are more likely to make you stand out. We've got our sunglasses—they won't be out of place in the Excelsior—and I'm planning to pick up a couple of floppy hats somewhere. That should do it—eyes and hair colour are two of the major identifying features.'

'What about elevator shoes?' I suggest, admittedly tongue in cheek. The frosty silence makes me wish I hadn't.

It's half-past twelve when we get into Aberdeen, where it isn't hard to find a "touristy" shop selling straw sunhats with wide, undulating rims. From there, we proceed to the Excelsior Hotel and I zero in on a space near the front entrance.

'No, go into that one over there.'

'Where—and why?'

She points, making a terrible job of trying not to smile. 'The one next to Rebecca's Audi—see, she's standing beside it, waving.'

'What's Rebecca doing here?'

'Waiting for us—thought she might be useful. The reception staff haven't seen *her* before, have they?'

'You could have told me.'

'Yeah, but I enjoy seeing you gobsmacked.'

There's no answer to that—or not one I'm quick enough to come up with while easing the Panda in beside Rebecca's car.

REBECCA JOINS US, SLIPPING INTO THE PANDA'S BACK SEAT. 'How'd it go with Inspector Wilson?'

Daisy grins. 'Well, he obviously didn't lock us up.'

'He was thinking about it,' I add, darkly.

Daisy flaps her fingers. 'Anyway, down to business. We need Rebecca to front this because you and me, Sam, are persona non grata in there.'

'Actually, it's only you they...'

'That maid saw us together, though, so they might have figured it out. Naw, safer bringing in a fresh face. Rebecca, have you checked in yet?'

Rebecca nods. 'You wouldn't believe the prices they're charging.'

Oh, I would

'I booked in as Tina Patterson, like you said,' Rebecca goes on.

Daisy gives her an approving thumbs up. 'Good. Now we need to find out which room they're in, so you can ask for a replacement keycard. And if the clerk happens to remember booking in a Tina Patterson who wasn't you, they'll soon discover there are two guests with that name.'

'What if he remembers the other Tina's room number?' Rebecca asks, with a frown.

'Then he can get a better-paying job playing memory man in one of Paul's sideshows,' Daisy dismisses.

'How will we find out which room Tina's in?' I ask.

'With our sunglasses and these hats, I think you and me can get away with sitting at the back of whichever bar Tina and Liam are in. Rebecca can fetch us some nice, cold orange juice. I'm betting that pair won't want to go out and leave the cash, but they'll be in celebratory mood—which is why I expect to find them in a bar. When Liam goes up for refills, Rebecca can buttonhole him and ask what his room number is.'

'And you think he'll tell her? Just like that?'

'He will—it's all in the way she asks. Rebecca's great advantage is men are too busy gawking to question anything she says.'

She's not going to be happy, but I see a flaw. 'This scheme hangs on Rebecca having registered as Tina Patterson—won't the room be in Liam's name? He was here first.'

'Don't see it. We had the bag of money—Liam couldn't have afforded this place. It must have been pre-booked—and that would be Tina. Somewhere to de-stress after scamming her brother—the Spa for Tina and plenty bars for Liam.'

The Excelsior has three bars, but Tina and Liam aren't in any of them. Instead, they've settled themselves in a mocked-up "conservatory" area forming part of the football field that comprises this place's foyer.

I didn't say anything but, like Paul, it's been niggling at me that Tina might *really* have been kidnapped, then been unable to resist snaffling the ransom money when her chance arose. Bad enough, but not nearly so cold and calculating as orchestrating a fake kidnapping. Liam's presence, however, puts the kybosh on that.

Keeping other patrons between us and them, Daisy and I settle in wicker seats that put our backs to the terrible twosome. Rebecca sits opposite, across a bamboo and glass table—we'll have to rely on her to be our eyes on Tina and Liam.

Or so I thought—until Daisy brings out a compact and starts dabbing at her cheeks. 'Daisy,' I hiss. 'When did you start wearing blusher?'

She huffs and points at the compact's lid. Oh, right—she's watching Tina and Liam through the mirror. I can see from her expression Daisy's unhappy. 'Where's the bar?' she mutters.

'There isn't one—it's table service out here.' I incline my head at a smartly dressed server coming our way and Daisy closes her compact with a snap.

'Beggar,' she exclaims.

After we've ordered a round of orange juice, Daisy's fingers are still drumming on her armrest. 'The idea was Rebecca would get talking to Liam when he went up to the bar, and find out his room number—you know, something along the lines of "Are you on the fourth floor too? Oh, the second?—my friend's on the second. Which room are *you* in? No, that's nowhere near her—bye."'

Rebecca has hero worship in her eyes. 'I can do that.'

'No, you can't—because there's no ruddy bar. Hmm... I suppose you could follow Tina into the ladies and strike up a conversation, but we don't know anything about her bladder capacity—might wait all day for it to go critical. Hang on—got it. Somebody dropped a twenty-pound note outside the door next to yours, and you *think* it was them—but could they confirm their room number? Just for your peace of mind.'

'Oohh, brilliant,' Rebecca exclaims. 'Shall I do it now?'

'Unless you've got other plans,' Daisy says wearily, and Rebecca leaps up. As she trots towards Tina and Liam, several pairs of eyes—predominantly male—follow her. Today's outfit is white leggings under a halter top consisting mainly of its straps. The guys watching must be wondering if they took a wrong turning and ended up in downtown L.A.

I daren't look for fear of being spotted, but Rebecca returns in no time. 'Did it work?' Daisy whispers.

Rebecca beams. 'Did it ever. Room 351.'

'Well done. Sit down, then.'

'No, I haven't finished yet. Um... do either of you have a twenty-pound note...?'

Once Tina and Liam have been paid off (another used note for their collection) and Rebecca returns (again), Daisy gets up. 'Back in five.'

'Where are you going?'

'To arrange a little surprise for Liam—Sam, if you're getting more orange juice in, ask if they've any crisps. Salt and vinegar, preferably. Rebecca, go see if you can con reception into handing out a replacement keycard for Tina Patterson's room.'

She winks 'Make sure they get your room number right—there might be more than one of you.'

Daisy takes a step towards the lifts. She pauses, then walks backwards until Rebecca's in front of her. 'Rebecca, suss out first if the guy you dealt with before is still on—if so, leave it until he goes for a break.'

Rebecca looks puzzled. 'But you said the clerk wouldn't remember which room he gave me?'

Daisy's gaze sweeps her up and down. 'Yeah, but on second thoughts... he might.'

32

When Daisy comes reappears, Rebecca has a big grin on her face. 'I got the keycard,' she crows, albeit in a whisper. Daisy nods approvingly. 'Well done.'

'Do you want to go get the money now? I can watch Tina and Liam—and ring you if they look like going up.'

'No, not yet. They'll have hidden the cash away, so I might have to tear their room apart—and if I don't find it before they head up, it'll be obvious somebody's been looking. Then we'd lose our chance—no, I've set something up that kills two birds with one stone.'

She obviously doesn't intend letting us in on her plan, but something occurs to me. 'Daisy, when *we* had it—*we* put the money in our safe. What if Tina's done the same here?'

'Thought about that, but I don't think so—she'd be worried in case the hotel staff realised it was cash. Too much chance of them either pilfering some, or calling the police. No, it'll be in their room—but as I say, well squirreled away.'

I feel myself fidgeting. 'How long before this diversion you've arranged kicks off? They won't stay down here forever.'

'Relax, Sam. Those two don't seem in any hurry—most they're likely to do is move bars.'

Rebecca raises her eyebrows—not a powerful mode of expression in someone who plucks them practically into non-existence. 'You said they'd be in a mood for celebrating. If that was me, I'd be taking a bottle of Champagne up to the room.'

Daisy rolls her eyes. 'Luckily, they aren't you... Sam, any luck with the crisps?'

How can she think about her stomach at a time like this? (Anyway, I forgot)

Before I have to confess what Daisy will see as a hanging offence, all thought of bar snacks is rudely driven from my mind. I grab Daisy's arm. 'Don't look now, but Pete just came in.'

Of course, she does... fortunately, Pete doesn't seem to notice. From his Logan-like walk, *he's* been celebrating—or more likely, drowning his sorrows.

The server who brought our orange juice casts an uneasy glance at Pete as he sways around a potted palm. A middle-aged business-type in a suit, carrying a drink in each hand and making for an already seated platinum blonde, swears loudly when Pete barrels into him. Luckily, this is the breed of punter who orders cocktail concoctions that come in half-filled glasses, as opposed to the brimming pint pots you'd see in the Last Chance Saloon.

Pete accepts all blame gracefully, brushing off the man's lapels and offering to replace his drinks. The guy waves him away—he's more interested in getting back to his, uh, companion.

Pete peers around as though confused, then changes direction—putting him on a direct course for Tina and Liam's table. Looks as though he's going to walk into *it* next.

Liam jumps up and places a restraining hand against Pete's chest. We barely catch Tina's annoyed mutter: 'You don't expect this kind of riff-raff in *here*.'

Liam seems to be holding Pete up—those sorrows, it appears, weren't so much drowned as swept away in a tsunami of booze.

Then Pete appears to come aware of his surroundings—he detaches himself from Liam with a flurry of apologies and apparently finds a second wind which propels him towards the lifts in a reasonably straight line. I see the server, who's been watching throughout, breathe an enormous sigh of relief. 'Pete's the worse for wear,' I comment to no one in particular.

'Some people just can't hold their booze,' Daisy agrees, then jumps up and waves both hands.

'What are you doing?' I hiss, aghast at this sudden deviation from all our efforts to blend in. At least she's keeping her back to Tina and Liam… then I see who Daisy's waving *to*.

A pair of large Aberdeen bobbies, in full stab-vest and utility-belt regalia, are walking our way in response to Daisy's summons. I look questioningly at Rebecca, who makes a face that says: "Not a scooby".

Daisy strolls over to her new friends and they all go into a huddle. Then Daisy returns to our table, and both policemen stride over to the businessman Pete collided with. After a whispered conversation, the businessman slaps at his jacket—suddenly frantic.

The policemen confer briefly in low voices, then stroll over to Liam and Tina. After another hushed exchange, Liam stands—wearing an outraged expression.

The policeman doing the talking persists, softly but insistently. I catch a few words as his voice rises ever so slightly. '... can do it at the station if you'd prefer?'

With an angry headshake, Liam empties his pockets. Then stops and looks blankly at whatever's in his hand. One police officer snatches it and marches back to the businessman, who nods excitedly. Policeman one signals policeman two, who produces a pair of handcuffs and fastens them around Liam's wrists.

A buzz of conversation that only moments ago filled the foyer becomes a pregnant silence. All eyes are on the police officers as they march Liam towards the doors, with Tina trailing behind. Discreetly, we get up and follow.

When Tina turns towards the lifts, Liam's head whirls and he shouts: 'Tina—where are you going?'

Tina glances around. 'This is your mess, not mine. Good luck.'

Spying a lift with open doors, Tina speeds up while his captors manhandle a struggling Liam out of the hotel.

Tina stops dead in front of the lift, spins, and stalks back to the reception desk. She faces a bemused clerk and throws out a hand at the now closing glass doors. '*He* had our key,' she declares. 'Can I have another one? Patterson, room 351.'

The clerk (who I suddenly recognise as young Valerie from Sunday) goes to operate her keycard machine, then hesitates. She turns to work a keyboard, watching the screen intently. Beside us, Rebecca shrinks visibly.

Valerie peers suspiciously at Tina, then at her screen again—and laughs. 'Oh, you must be the *other* Ms Patterson. What a coincidence. I just had a Ms Patterson...'

'For goodness' sake,' Tina explodes. 'Give me my key.'

'Sorry...' Valerie programs a new magnetic keycard in record time and Tina snatches it, then turns on her heel.

Daisy hisses with frustration. 'I thought she'd go with him to the copshop.'

'How did you...?' I start, but Daisy's staring at the wall behind me. Turning, all I see is a fire extinguisher mounted on its bracket alongside the usual red alarm box.

Daisy squints over her shoulder at Tina (who has her finger on the lift's call button) then, after a brief scan around, skips past and jabs an elbow at the glass-fronted alarm box.

Instantly, screaming sirens batter the eardrums of already disorientated staff and guests. We can't hear Tina's curses, but her expression speaks louder than words as she storms towards the glass doors where a scrum of bodies with similar intent sweep her away.

Daisy disappears through a stairway door.

33

'They'll have you on CCTV—setting off that fire alarm.'

In the Panda's passenger seat, Daisy scoffs. 'They don't know who I am—and with the hat and sunglasses, it won't be easy to ID me. Anyhow, I doubt Interpol's going to be interested in a little prank...'

'Prank? The place was in chaos when we left.'

By the time Daisy joined us in the car park (or rather, the fire evacuation assembly point) it was full of glassy-eyed guests wandering about, some still with drinks in their hands. Mission accomplished, though. 'What took you so long?'

'Besom *had* hidden it—I was beginning to think she'd put it in the hotel safe, after all.'

'So where was it?'

'She'd knotted a belt from one of those complimentary bathrobes to a tieback behind the curtain and hung the bag of cash out the window. Their room's at the side,' she adds. 'Nothing down there, so nobody to look up and clock it.'

'How did you figure out where it was?'

She shrugs. 'Lateral thinking—if it wasn't *inside* the room, it had to be *outside.* Course, I was thinking more of the hotel safe. Until I looked at the window, and thought... aha.'

'Nice work. Listen, why that big performance with the police? There must have been a simpler way to keep Tina and Liam out of their room for a while?'

'You're forgetting about our other client. Keisha needs to know where Liam is so she can serve him with maintenance orders—the clink's ideal for that.'

'And just *how* did you set that up?'

'Phoned the local rozzers and said I'd seen a tea leaf lift some poor guy's wallet. Told them I played a lot of bridge tournaments with people who cheat, so had a good eye for that kind of thing—thought that'd be a typical persona for anybody staying in the Excelsior.'

'So what about Pete? How come he helped us?'

'Oh, Pete's on his downers. I found him in his room with a half-empty bottle of Scotch—that performance he put on wasn't *entirely* faked—and offered him three hundred quid out of the bag. He jumped at it—that was the other reason I took so long. Had to find Pete in the car park and pay him.'

'Actually, I caught a glimpse of Pete on our way out. He was limping, and looked kind of dishevelled...'

'Yeah,' she says distractedly. 'He tried to take the whole bag off me.'

Poor Pete

But Daisy's mind is off somewhere else. 'Now we can finally get on with solving Paul's dad's... Mr McNab's murder.'

'And if you're right, poor Ivor's still locked up for something he didn't do.'

'I'm not so sure it's *poor* Ivor. If Tina was telling the truth about him abusing her—and from what Paul's said, she likely was—Ivor stewing in jail for a few days doesn't bother me. Right, our first stop's the Cuppa Tea—if Mr McNab *was* slipped the poison in there, it gives us a timeline to base our investigation on. Not to mention Doris might solve it straight off if the dopey old mare can remember enough to ID the guy with him.'

'Daisy—Dora's lovely.'

'I know she is—but a bit spaced out sometimes, you have to admit. We'd best go see her on the way back—she's probably losing memory cells by the minute.'

'Don't be so rotten—oh, and I think we'd better stash that lot first.' I jerk my head back.

Daisy wheels to the bag of money behind us. 'You're right—forgot about that. Oh, and when you change the code this time, don't tell anybody what the new one is. *Especially* Logan. We'll go from there to the Cuppa Tea… I fancy a snack, anyway… then call in at Paul's and update him on his psycho sister. Wonder how he got on with Mr M earlier? Surely, if Paul gives him all the cash back, Dobson won't have any claim on the fair?'

'Depends what Paul already signed.'

'Hmpf—didn't care for that Dobson character. There was something off about him, whatever Tina says—not that anything she said is worth tuppence now.'

'Why does Dobson want Paul's dad's—well, it's Paul's now—why does he *want* the fair so much?'

'Paul reckons because of the pitches they've got dibs on—like the one in Cairncroft. His dad wasn't exploiting them properly, but Dobson would bring in a load of new rides and spend tons of money on marketing—seems those locations could be gold mines with the right backing and savvy.'

'Don't forget, Jodie wants to know what happened with Tina.'

'Yeah, yeah—we'll get to Jodie. If Doris comes through, we might be able to drop the murderer right in her lap tonight. That'll shut Wilson up—and give Jodie some kudos on her first week back. Hey, maybe she'll get a promotion and replace Wilson...'

It's a relief to walk into the Cairncroft Hotel again. ("Murder Hotel" that *should* be—I'm as bad as the locals.) Impressive though the Excelsior was, I prefer our homely atmosphere.

After I've stowed the money safely away *and* changed the code one last time, we drive down to the Cuppa Tea. While Doris is ringing up Daisy's selection of cream cakes and pastries, I ask: 'Doris, remember you were telling me about the fairground man being in here—the same night he was murdered?'

She hits the wrong key, tuts, and corrects her total. 'Oh my, yes. Did they get anybody for that?'

'No, not yet,' Daisy tells her through a mouthful of apple turnover. (She might at least wait until we get to a table.) 'The guy he was with—d'you remember what he looked like?'

Doris frowns. 'Well, we were busy at the time… but I did think he sounded Irish. Just a wee bit—wasn't obvious. Oh, and he had red hair.'

Doris moves on to the next customer and, a little dazedly, we transport Daisy's haul of snacks to the nearest table. 'Dobson,' Daisy hisses when we're seated. 'Irish—red hair—has to be him. I knew that guy was a villain.'

'But why would Dobson want to murder Mr McNab?'

'Because he thought Paul, unlike his dad, could be persuaded to sell him the fair.'

'Are you going to tell Paul?'

'No—not yet. I'm thinking we should head back to the hotel. Remember Jodie said she would be home between five and six? I reckon the sooner Donstable CID hears about Mr Dobson, the better. Not to mention it'll sweeten Wilson up after he finds out we went after Tina.'

I check my watch—4.30. 'We can stake out reception from the residents lounge to catch Jodie going by—don't know about you, but I could do with a drink while we're waiting.'

She grimaces. 'I couldn't half—but maybe not. I still feel obliged to whip over later on and tell Paul what's happened…'

Then she stuffs the last bit of scone in her mouth and stands. 'On second thoughts, I'm finishing with Paul anyway and it's too late to bank the cash today—I'll tell him on the phone. C'mon—I can almost taste that pint.'

On our way out, we nearly collide with old Struthers and his wife. Mrs Struthers chirps a friendly: 'Hello, dears,' while her husband pretends not to notice us.

'Quick word, Mr Struthers?' Daisy says, and Struthers turns scarlet.

He puts a hand on his wife's back. 'You carry on, dear. I'll be along in a moment.'

Mrs Struthers seems perfectly happy to "carry on" towards Doris's cake display while Mr Struthers glowers. 'What is it now?'

Daisy raises a palm. 'Only take a sec—just want you to confirm it was a Tina Patterson who rented your chalet last.'

Old Struthers looks at us curiously, then shakes his head. 'No, not even close. Oh, if you must know, it was a Mr Dobson who phoned on Saturday morning—all very last minute, but it just so happened the chalet was vacant. Now—will you *please* leave me alone?'

34

In the Cairncroft residents lounge, Daisy attacks her pint with gusto while I toy with a glass of white wine. 'Right,' she announces, using her sleeve as a napkin. 'That puts a whole new light on things—again. Struthers says it was Dobson who rented the chalet—which means Dobson must have been in on the kidnap scheme. Tina was covering for him when she gave us that character reference.'

My head's buzzing. 'But wouldn't that also mean Tina was in on her dad's murder?'

'Mm... seems likely. Anyway, not our problem any more—far as I'm concerned, we've solved it. Soon as Jodie arrives, she can have the whole mess for CID. Oh, that was Paul who rang while you were fetching drinks. Mr M said the new contract did refer back to a previous version—promising the fair to Dobson for the net worth of its rides, less Dobson's "deposit" of 100 grand. The one I swiped was only an update, saying the extra 50 grand made up the balance and no further payment was due.'

'Thing is though, if Dobson was involved in the kidnap, proceeds of crime rules will apply—and Dobson's contract will become null and void. Did you tell Paul what we've found out?'

'Naw—figured it was better to wait until the police tie everything up. Plus, I wanted time to enjoy my pint in peace before Jodie gets here.'

I lean sideways to peer through at reception, and my heart skips a beat. 'No sign of Jodie yet,' I mutter, 'but speak of the devil—Dobson just walked in.'

'What?'

Daisy wriggles around in time to see Dobson stroll under the archway, flanked by a gorilla-like character who's not nearly so big as Jack the sack's Tiny—but looks pretty formidable all the same. The thug (because that's obviously what he is) stops in front of the opening, blocking our view of reception—and theirs of us. Dobson keeps walking, looking decidedly unhurried, past Daisy and behind my armchair. Before I can turn to check what he's up to, his almost-Irish accent whispers in my ear.

Halfway to her feet, Daisy freezes at the same moment cold metal touches the back of my head. 'Just stay where you are, little lady. And Miss Chessington—in case you can't tell, that's a gun-barrel you feel.'

Daisy straightens slowly and asks: 'What do you want?'

The pressure on my skull increases as Dobson drills his gun into bone, making me squeal. 'My money. Here's what we're going to do. Miss Chessington and I will take a stroll out to the car park. Meanwhile you, little missy, will fetch my cash and bring it out. Then you can have your mate back and everybody'll be happy. Get up, please, Miss Chessington—but slowly.'

The gun withdraws from my head and, shakily, I haul myself up. Dobson steps forward and takes my arm with his left hand, pulling me sideways against him. I feel the gun again, pressing against my ribs this time. 'I will shoot you, Miss Chessington—you're looking at a desperate man who has nothing to lose. Now—start walking.'

Hazel's going to wonder about my being scrunched up against Dobson, but the gun won't be visible and there isn't anything she could do anyway. As we reach the archway, Dobson's thug moves aside.

'Sam—what's the code?'

I stop, and Dobson grinds the gun into my side. Quickly, I explain: 'She can't get your cash without the safe's access code—and I'm the only one who knows it.'

Dobson breathes out noisily. 'Well—tell her what it is, then.'

'6197,' I call back to Daisy and she nods. Then Dobson tugs at my arm and we carry on towards the front entrance.

'Sam—everything alright?'

Darn—Hazel doesn't think this looks right. While I'm searching desperately for something convincing to shut her down, I hear Daisy's voice say: 'S'alright, Hazel. Just Uncle Dobbin.'

The thug snickers, then swallows it when "Dobbin" glares at him. Next thing, we're out front and Dobson drags me over to his ubiquitous white van.

Why do killers always have white vans? Ironically, that thought's prompted by Rosemary's fiancé, Eric, having one—but he turned out to be nothing more sinister than a delivery man.

Dobson, however, *is* a killer—I see it in his eyes.

He holds out a hand. 'Phone.'

I drop it in his palm and the thug yanks open a rear door. Dobson pushes me against the back bumper. 'Get in,' he snaps.

'Why?' I ask, surprised, and he slaps me. Cheek stinging, I make an honest attempt to hoist my left leg onto the van's lip—but fail. 'Part of my left leg's artificial,' I tell Dobson, hating the whine in my voice.

Dobson grunts, then: 'Mickey.'

The thug—Mickey—strides over and throws an arm around my waist, then hoists me into the dark interior. (Did I mention he's over six feet tall?) 'There's a bench along the side,' Dobson growls. 'Sit on it.'

I'm glad to—my mind's swimming and it feels like I might pass out. This'll be over in a moment, I tell myself. Soon as Daisy brings him his cash, they'll let me out and leave.

'Here.' Daisy's voice—presumably handing over the money.

'Thanks,' Dobson says, sounding cheerier. 'Now give me your phone, then climb in beside your mate.'

'Why?'

The question I asked—and it gets the same response. When the crack of palm on flesh rings out, I half expect it to be followed by a thump of Irishman on tarmac. But all I hear is Daisy's trainers whacking the van's floor as she springs in. Well, not entirely—Daisy's mumbling angrily under her breath. 'Beggar knows what he's doing. Kept the gun at his hip when he smacked me—otherwise, I'd have had 'im.'

The bag of money sails past her, the door slams, and a moment later the van's engine roars to life.

Daisy rushes to sit before the sudden movement throws her off balance. I try to keep my voice steady—and fail. 'Daisy—where are they taking us?'

She breathes in, then lets it out in a long whoosh. 'No idea—and I don't want to worry you, Sam, but this isn't looking good.'

35

It's more than half an hour before the van finally slows. From the way we're being shoogled about, it's turned onto an off-road track. My imagination is running riot—is this what the Mafia calls being "taken for a ride"?

Daisy sucks at a broken nail. She spent her time trying to open the rear doors—unsuccessfully.

The off-road journey doesn't last long, only a few minutes, before we judder to a halt. Then nothing happens for about ten minutes. 'Do you think they've just left us here?' I ask Daisy.

'Naw—they're getting something set up, I reckon.'

'What?'

'No idea... listen. They're back.'

What little light we have comes via a roof vent because the cargo area has no windows—when its doors fly open, we both throw a protective arm over our eyes.

When they adjust, I peek over my sleeve and see Mickey clamber in. Seems to be his turn for holding the gun. 'Word is you're some kind of kung fu expert,' he tells Daisy. 'Fair warning. One wrong move and...' he waves the gun '... I *will* use this. Okay, out—both of you.'

'Nice to be famous,' Daisy drawls as she jumps from the tailgate, then helps me down.

Mickey laughs. 'Jack the sack and my boss were tight—so we know exactly what you're capable of.'

I've no idea where we are, but catch a definite tang of sea air. We're standing on concrete in some kind of yard. A high wall surrounds it and glancing back I see the van's parked in front of a rectangular, pre-fab type building. The rest of the yard is filled with fairground rides, some in bits.

Dobson comes up behind Daisy while Mickey keeps the pistol level with her chest. 'Just going to check for things like tasers,' Dobson explains, patting her down. 'Heard you're rather handy with one.'

All he finds is a half-eaten chocolate bar, which gets tossed to the ground. 'Littering's illegal, you know,' Daisy murmurs, but nobody laughs.

I get frisked too and even through terror so stark it knots my insides, I *am* mildly insulted that Mickey doesn't feel it necessary to point the gun *my* way while Dobson's searching *me*...

Daisy lifts her arms, palms up. 'Why?' she asks. 'You've got the money back—what's all this about?'

Dobson actually looks regretful, if only for a moment. 'It's complicated,' he mutters, and Daisy laughs coldly.

'We're not going anywhere.'

'It started with Tina—she had me over a barrel, you see.'

He pauses, looking thoughtful. 'If only the stupid mare hadn't pulled that stunt with Ivor's gun. Chances were everyone would have assumed old McNab had a heart attack—Tina did—and the police would never have gotten involved. He already had two last year… everybody knew the poor bloke was on borrowed time. After you told her the old man was poisoned, Tina twigged I did it and wasn't chuffed—think she almost turned me in, but glass houses and all that. Anyway, a chance of getting the money back more than trumped her uncharacteristic attack of sentimentality. Now you've been kind enough to return said money, I'll pass it on to Tina—who intends disappearing, which of course suits me fine.'

Daisy frowns. 'I still don't understand why you didn't just take the money—what's your problem with us?'

'The money *was* all I came after, but that changed when you pair got too clever for your own good. Bad enough you discovered I was involved in Tina's "kidnap" —if that comes out, it nixes the contract I have with Paul. But you've also cottoned on it was me who poisoned old McNab.'

'How could you know all that?' I gasp.

'After Tina phoned from the Excelsior demanding I get her money back, we staked out your hotel. When you appeared, but went straight out again, we followed. I parked across from the café and saw you chatting up the woman who works there, which is when I got worried and sent Mickey in to earwig. Good thing I did—whichever one of you said "sooner CID hears about Dobson, the better" sealed your fate. I *am* sorry—there's nothing personal in this—but while I can buy Tina off, there's no other way to silence you.'

I've thought of something he seems to have overlooked. 'You're forgetting Paul knows about the "kidnap that wasn't". More importantly,' I add, gaining steam, 'so do the police.'

Dobson laughs. 'Yes, but they don't know I had anything to do with it.'

I'm not finished yet

'If *we* could find out you met Mr McNab an hour before he died, so will the police.'

Which gets me another of those looks that take me right back to "O" level calculus

'So? I had good reason to meet him, being in the process of buying his business—borne out by my honouring our deal with his son. And now they've Ivor bang to rights, courtesy of Tina, the police aren't looking for anyone else. My meeting McNab in the café is only a problem if certain ladies not far from me start blabbing.'

'But the police know Mr McNab was poisoned,' I persist.

Dobson shrugs. 'They'll probably think that was Ivor too—he's daft enough to do both.'

'*Why* poison Paul's dad?' Daisy asks. 'I see the rest—cooking up this kidnap plan with Tina so you'd get Paul's fair in return for her ending up with the cash. But what was the point...?'

'You didn't know McNab. He was old-school carny—I wasn't sure he'd give up his family business, even for Tina. But I've waited a long time to get ahold of that fairground, put a lot into this scheme—and I knew *Paul* would pay up if he thought his sister's life depended on it.'

I'm horrified. 'You killed Mr McNab—just to guarantee getting his fairground?'

'From where I'm standing, it was a pretty good reason. Unfortunately, it gave Tina the idea to frame her feckless husband, which caused chaos. The "kidnap" was supposed to happen yesterday—not Friday. Tina even had her room booked at the Excelsior—planned on spending her time "kidnapped" in style—but then she went and brought it all forward on a whim *and* involved that idiot Liam. Joke is, Tina had nothing to gain from setting Ivor up—she was leaving him anyway, so it was pure malice. Didn't even have the guts to do her own dirty work—she made Liam do fire the gun. Then—they woke me up at six on Saturday morning in a panic. "Where will we go, Mr Dobson?" The Excelsior was full, you see—but I managed to get them old Struthers' white elephant of a holiday chalet. Of course, you already know that from blabbermouth Struthers himself. Enough already—much as I'm enjoying our little chat, better get a move on. Start walking please, ladies.'

'Where is this?' I ask, as we follow Dobson—Mickey bringing up the rear with his gun pointing at our backs.

'Stonehaven—it's a service and repair depot for my rides.'

He stops beside a tall tower made of girders woven in a pattern that reminds me of Blackpool Tower. (Though nowhere near as high, and square-shaped—roughly ten-foot square.) It rises from a wide circular base which has steps built-in that give access to a ring of seats around the tower, each fitted with a padded pull-down harness. 'This one, for example—do you know it?'

Daisy answers, sounding puzzled. 'It's a Vertical Drop.'

'Well done, but then I already know you're into the thrill stuff, like bungee jumping… amazing what a bit of snooping on social media throws up. I don't see anybody finding it hard to believe you broke in here for a private go on this baby, dragging your mate along…' he chuckles '… for *the ride*.'

'Nobody who knows us would…'

Dobson interrupts. 'It's what the procurator fiscal decides that matters. To him, it'll be obvious what happened.'

'What *is* going to happen?' Daisy demands.

Dobson scratches his nose. 'Well, you know how the Vertical Drop works? Punters get strapped into those seats, then the—we call it the "doughnut", that circle of seats—carries them up to the top. 60 feet, if you're interested—that's the equivalent of three two-storey houses. It stays there a few minutes to let them enjoy the view, then they plunge into free fall. Trick is, as the doughnut drops, it drives attached pistons down tubes inside the tower and they create a cushion of compressed air—which brings you to a soft landing.'

He pauses, with a stupid grin on his face. 'With me so far?'

Daisy looks bored. 'Knew all that—get to the point.'

'Well, the reason this one's in dry dock is to have its pistons replaced—we do that at specified intervals to comply with safety regulations. Now—the boys have taken its old pistons out—and tomorrow, they'll fit the new ones.'

He pauses, no doubt for dramatic effect. I nudge Daisy. 'What does all that mean?'

'I think he's saying they're going to strap us into what he calls the "doughnut" and start the ride.

The doughnut'll go up as normal. But coming down, it'll hit the ground at full speed...'

My vision blurs and acid rises in my throat. I try to concentrate on what Daisy's asking Dobson. 'Does it all happen automatically after you throw the "on" switch, or will somebody have to trigger the drop itself from that control panel?'

Dobson claps his hands. 'Oh, well done—you *are* a smart one. Yes, this is a manual model.'

Daisy frowns. She's pointing at a waist-high control panel rising from the platform's edge. 'It looks like your maintenance people didn't bother erecting the usual cabin around that. When we come flying down and crash, the "doughnut" will break up—there's going to be a lot of metal shrapnel whizzing about. Whoever's standing there, I don't give much for *his* chances.'

Reaching into his coat, making a dramatic gesture of the movement, Dobson produces a... TV remote control? 'Which is why...' he burbles happily '... I have clamped a little electric pulley on the control panel. A cable runs between it and the ride control lever. So—I'll push the lever up, and you'll go... up. Then I'll walk way over there...' he points '... and press the red button on this remote. That activates the electric pulley unit, which will pull the lever back down and you'll both get the thrill of your lives—for a few seconds. Afterwards, I'll remove the pulley so it's obvious whoever was with you, the person who operated the ride, survived the shrapnel shower and legged it. A tragic accident, brought about by your own stupidity.'

Dobson puts the remote back in his pocket and Mickey gestures with the gun. 'Move—over there.'

Numbly, I follow Daisy up four steps to the platform, and then over to the circle of seats—or "doughnut"—encircling the tower. Daisy sits down, but I stand and stare at the seat next to her. I can't make myself...

I feel myself seized and spun around, then Dobson shoves me into the seat and lowers the padded harness over my shoulders until it clicks. He sidesteps to Daisy and goes to secure *her* harness.

Daisy reaches up, grasps both Dobson's jacket lapels, and yanks hard. Dobson's head jerks down and his nose flattens against Daisy's forehead. He staggers back, clutching his face. 'My dose,' he screams.

Mickey raises his gun, but Dobson waves his arms. 'Doh,' he shrieks, blood bubbling from both nostrils. 'Dickey, dongt. That's what she wands. Have you got a haderchief?'

Mickey produces a not-very-fresh tissue and Dobson grimaces before holding it over his nose. 'Is it broken, boss?'

'I don't know—not a flamin' doctor, am I?'

Well—he's pronouncing his "n"s again, so I reckon not. Pity…

He takes a step towards Daisy, then stops. 'Do it yourself,' he grates. 'Now—or I *will* let him shoot you.'

With a sneer, Daisy pulls her harness into place and Dobson stomps over to the control box. He looks at Daisy with a mix of hatred and satisfaction, then pushes a lever all the way up.

Immediately, we start rising. I can't stand heights at the best of times, and my stomach is threatening to give Dobson and his thug an unpleasant surprise. Except, he's already moving away—him and his gun-toting henchman. I turn to Daisy. 'I think I'm going to be sick.'

'Please don't,' she snaps—a tad unsympathetically, I thought. After swallowing and taking a couple of deep breaths, the moment passes. I hear a "snap", then feel Daisy fumbling at my waist. 'What're you doing?'

A second "snap". 'Fastening our lap belts—Dobson forgot about them.'

I've got my eyes tightly shut. When I force them open, my mouth drops in horror. We're already halfway up—according to Dobson, three storeys high.

Then it's like something shifts in my head—maybe a realisation that there's nothing either of us can do to stop this, and the only sensible thing is accept it. A Zen master would treasure every second he had left—I remember a story, a sort of parable, about a Zen master. A tiger has just chased him over a cliff and he's clinging to a bush halfway down. The tiger's looking down at him and another waits at the bottom. The bush is uprooting under his weight and has a big juicy berry growing on one of its branches.

The question—what does the Zen master do next?

Answer—he eats the berry with enjoyment and relish.

Only problem—I'm not a Zen master

But—suddenly, I understand the point of that story as never before.

I fix on Daisy—doing my best to ignore the increasingly map-like panorama laid out below. (So FAR below.) She tilts her head. 'What?'

'I'm trying not to look down,' I explain.

She tuts. 'Well, don't then. On second thoughts, *do*—there's something you should see.'

Then the besom grabs my chin and twists, forcing my gaze towards the void and—a string of blue lights tearing along the road to Dobson's facility. 'Is that...?'

'Yep—the cavalry's on its way.' As she speaks, the first faint whine of sirens reaches my ears.

'How'd you manage that?'

She shrugs. 'Weren't me.'

Who cares—we're going to be saved

Daisy shouts down to Dobson. 'Listen—they're coming for you. I'd start running now.'

Dobson and Mickey are moving their heads from side to side—they hear the sirens, too. And then, the "doughnut" jolts to a stop and I realise with a shock we've reached the top of the tower. Every bit of me shakes and my throat's so tight I can barely breathe. Dobson's voice floats up. 'Get the van started, Mickey—we'll go out the back way. After I've finished this.'

To my horror, he reaches inside his jacket—for the remote control. 'He's still going to do it—the police won't arrive in time,' I hear myself whimper. Daisy grips my wrist. 'Sam—SAM. Look at me.'

My head weighs a ton, but somehow I turn it. She's waving something under my nose and I take a moment to focus on whatever it is.

Then I gasp. 'Is that... Dobson's?'

She nods, a huge grin breaking out on her face—and Dobson's remote control in her hand. 'Yep—lifted it when I butted him. What—you didn't think I was grandstanding just for the sake of it?'

I force myself to look down again—urgh—and see Dobson waving his fist at us, then wrench my gaze further afield and—wonder of wonders—the blue lights are nearly here. Dobson must realise they're getting close because he pelts back to his van. Moments later there's a screech of rubber and it rockets off in the opposite direction from what looks and sounds to be a flotilla of "blues and twos". No doubt intending to escape via the "back way" Dobson mentioned.

I close my eyes again—the police will have us down in no time.

We aren't going to die after all

The sirens reach a crescendo, and we hear car doors being thrown open.

Voices—running footsteps—strange how the acoustics work up here. It's so quiet and still all around—yet the clamor below is amplified, like an echo.

Daisy hasn't let go my wrist and I'm grateful for the comfort of her warm flesh.

I'm not alone in my little closed-eye world.

Then her fingers tighten and she draws a sharp breath. 'What's wrong?' I blurt, still not daring to look.

She doesn't answer. Instead, she yells:
'Oi. DON'T TOUCH THAT LEVER...'

36

We've been waiting up here for twenty minutes, but it feels more like that many hours. The constable intent on finding which lever would bring us back down thankfully stopped when Daisy yelled at him. Then followed a long, shouted discourse.

'Why?'

'He's rigged the ride to crash when it comes down.'

'What...? I can't hear you...'

'HE'S RIGGED...'

And so it went on...

When the police finally grasped the gravity of our situation (ouch) they formed a huddle, presumably trying to come up with a solution. Two cars eventually took off after Dobson, but by the time Daisy had convinced them to leave the control panel alone *and* explained about Dobson, I doubt they'll catch him.

The huddle seemed to go on forever—I dread to think what ideas they bandied about, but my imagination cooked up a few possibilities.

(Anybody good with heights? Alright, where can we get a ladder? One that long? No, you're right—what about mountain rescue?)

Finally, somebody thought of the obvious, helped by Daisy and me screaming it down at them—and called the fire brigade.

That was ages ago—where are they? 'Might be at a fire,' Daisy suggests.

If they take much longer, my head's going to split open...

Then, mercifully, another siren cuts through the uneasy silence and a fresh set of emergency lights speeds along the access road. The fire engine barrels between police cars with inches to spare and screeches to a stop just short of the ride platform. Helmeted figures leap out, and moments later the hydraulic ladder rises.

With a sigh of relief, I see there's one of those "rescue buckets" mounted on it. I was dreading being carried down a ladder.

It's crazy, but with the end to our ordeal imminent my panic hits a new crescendo. Daisy glances sideways, her face tight with concern when my teeth chatter and—bless her—wraps a comforting arm around me.

Whoever's controlling the "bucket" is incredibly accurate—it stops dead level with us and mere inches away. A cheery fireman waves and calls: 'Fancy meeting you here.'

Then he looks properly at me and his expression tightens. 'Better take her first?' he mutters to Daisy, who nods.

Leaning out, the fireman fixes a harness around me. A line attaching it to the bucket is awfully thin, but I suppose they know what they're doing...?

Then, to my relief—I was imagining being dragged over the metal lip—he unlatches a door at the front and swings it open. (It opens inwards, folding against an interior wall.) Finally, a loud click signals the release of my padded restraint and simultaneously Daisy leans in to unclip the lap belt.

The gap between my seat and the "bucket's" floor is only inches wide—no more than the space between platform and carriage when you board a train—and big, powerful fireman hands haul me across before I've time to think. Daisy already warned him about my prosthetic, so he's careful to steady me at the back of the bucket before turning around—and yelling: 'Hey. What d'you think you're doing?'

Daisy has her restraints off and she's skipping nimbly into the bucket. The fireman looks apoplectic. 'You should have waited till I got your safety line on.'

He gets "the look" and like countless men before chooses the path of least resistance. In this case, busying himself with unfolding the door and latching it (I hope) securely.

The ride down is agonising. Strange, you'd think I could relax now, knowing we're safe—but we aren't *yet*, so I sink to the floor and bury my head between shoogly knees while Daisy chats to our rescuer about bungee jumping—turns out he's a fellow enthusiast.

Then the "bucket" jerks, making a metallic bang. Even as my mind plays the opening titles of a horror movie that ends with shrieks of buckling metal as we collide with Dobson's concrete-floored yard, I hear words that fill me with joy. 'Right, that's us. Let's get you out.'

My left leg being what it is, getting me down from the fire engine turns out to be technically more difficult than the transfer from "Vertical

Drop" to "bucket". Eventually, they figure it out—a solution that involves the combined efforts of four firemen with strong arms.

I inhale until my lungs fill, then a little more. Solid ground under my feet—the sky back where it's supposed to be—little fireballs of relief explode inside me.

Daisy gives me a quick squeeze—she's been my rock. But when she draws a breath and opens her mouth, I can guess what's coming. Daisy is going to confess she was scared too, despite keeping a brave face throughout.

'Woooo—that was fun.'

I *MUST* BE CLOAKED IN BONHOMIE AFTER THE MOST frightening experience of my life—when Davy runs up, I actually smile at him. 'Sam, are you alright? I've been beside myself.'

Jodie appears at his shoulder. 'He has,' she confirms. 'And now might not be the time, but we were stuck in a car together for getting on an hour and he told me about your misunderstanding over this Leslie woman. Trust me, Sam—it isn't what you think.'

My life—*and* my fiancé—both restored to me? Things are definitely looking up.

But as Jodie says, now's not the time—whatever Davy's explanation *is*, though, it better be good. Unfortunately, I can't imagine it being good *enough*.

Forcing my mind into the here and now, I ask the obvious. 'How did you two get here?'

Davy passes a hand over his brow. 'I wanted to see you so we could talk about… you know? And decided to come unannounced, so you couldn't say no. I was parked outside the hotel trying to get my courage up when you and Daisy came out and got into the back of that van. I was at the opposite end of the car park and didn't realise what was happening until they closed the doors, but that's when I glimpsed a gun in that stocky guy's hand. Before I could do anything, the van went tearing off down the drive.'

Jodie breaks in. 'I was just coming home when it whipped past me with inches to spare, so I stopped to note down the beggar's registration number. Next thing, Davy's car shoots by…' she turns a baleful eye on Davy '… and takes my wing mirror with it. Of course, I turned around and went after him. Luckily, I was in my "company car" with blues and twos—I switched them on and pulled him over. Davy told me what was happening, and I called it in. An ANPR camera picked you up on the A90, by which time there was a helicopter up and it shadowed you here—then passed the location to every available patrol car in the area. Including us. We'd have been here quicker, but it's a blind turnoff amongst a mess of "B" roads and took a bit of finding.'

'Did they get Dobson?' Daisy asks.

Jodie shakes her head. 'No, he's long gone. Won't get far, though—there's nowhere for him to go. We'll be watching all his business premises and freezing his bank cards, so it's only a matter of time…'

Daisy coughs. 'Um, maybe not—see, he's got a bag of money with him. 150 grand in used notes…'

37

It's after nine o'clock when we get back to the hotel. Jodie makes straight for the lift, desperate to see Alanna. As the doors close, her voice rises above their usual clatter. 'Do NOT test me tonight...'

Hazel rushes out from behind the desk and hugs first me, then Daisy. 'I *knew* something was wrong. Thank goodness you're both alright.'

Daisy looks askew at her. 'How do *you* know about it?'

'Jodie phoned Logan from her car—it's Rosemary's night off, so he had to take over upstairs.'

'Who's minding the bar, then?' I ask, unable to help myself.

Its manager, Jeff, staffs the Last Chance Saloon along with his assistant, a young lass called Clara—but this is also Jeff's night off. On Tuesdays, Clara depends on Logan "being around" to handle the more rambunctious cowboys. Which makes him sound like a bouncer, something he's anything but. Logan's trump card is the authority to ban troublemakers—nothing scares a Cairncroft Cowboy more than the threat of losing his spurs.

Hazel holds up a reassuring palm. 'Colin went to help Clara—and I'm keeping an eye on the residents bar from here. Being a Tuesday, it's quiet.'

'I'll go through and see they're okay,' Daisy says. 'Quite fancy a chill-out with the boys after tonight.'

The look she throws me, which slides first over Davy, tells me Daisy's also being tactful.

Davy watches her leave and I explain as we wander through to the residents lounge. 'Daisy used to run the Last Chance Saloon in its early days.'

Davy missed that period in the hotel's development; he spent much of it in hospital, recovering from horrendous injuries after my turncoat boyfriend-at-the-time caused Davy to crash his motorbike.

'Plus,' I add, 'she can let her hair down in there... Pint?'

Davy says he'd love one, and I slip behind the residents bar to pour his lager—and a *very* large vodka and tonic. I'm about to lift them when Colin rushes in. 'You sit down, Miss Chessington—I'll carry those over for you.'

'Thanks, Colin—put them on my tab.'

Despite there only being two other guests in here tonight, Davy's chosen the furthest away table. It appears we're going to have "the talk". I'm tempted to insist on postponing hearing whatever explanation he's cobbled together—after looking death in the eye (or *down into* its eye, that should be) I could do with sipping my drink and zoning out. But another part of me wants to hear what he's got to say.

Then I can send him packing—and zone out.

Once Colin's back behind the bar, Davy raises his glass. 'Cheers—how are you feeling?'

'How d'you think I'm feeling after spending half an hour 60 feet in the air on a faulty carnival ride? Davy, just get to it, eh? I'm not in the mood for beating about any bushes.'

He nods, slowly. 'Alright. Sam, what was that about with Leslie? She was going to the police until I talked her out of it. And was it you let the air out of my tyre?'

'Hmpf.'

I remember what Jodie said. 'The police couldn't have done anything—no witnesses, you see. It'd be her word against mine. Oh, and the tyre—yes, that was me.'

Davy looks shocked.

Hypocrite—after what he's done. 'Look, I'm not interested in *poor Leslie*—or your tyre. Let's hear whatever story you've cooked up.'

He breathes out in a long sigh. 'Sam, there's nothing going on...'

I raise a palm. 'Can I stop you there? Am I supposed to believe you went up to her room for a game of Scrabble? Because Rebecca saw you on Sunday...'

'I never went to her room...'

'Oh, so Rebecca was lying? I wonder why she'd do that?'

'SAM. Will you just listen—I went up to my OWN room. I booked it a week ago, in case they ran out...'

'The Donstable Arms—run out of rooms?'

'They always do when the local builders' association throws one of their shindigs—none of that lot are designated driver material, and the local taxi firm's blacklisted them. I'm a building contractor, Sam—these are the guys I work with. I *have* to attend their monthly booze-ups.'

'Monthly, you say? Yet you've never mentioned it before?'

Davy's shoulders fall and his gaze drops. 'Look, everybody gets plastered at those bashes—including me. I wasn't sure how you'd feel about that—given you can be a bit straightlaced sometimes. That's why I've never told you about them.'

Me—straightlaced? Does this man know me at all? Nobody would ever say I was… but let's not complicate things with tangential spats. I'm still far from convinced. 'So it was just work? Only problem with that, Davy—*Leslie* isn't a builder. Is she?'

'No—but she's head of HR for one. A big company in Glasgow—so big, even a few guys around here do piece-work for them. Which is why Leslie's well-known locally. Since she was in the hotel anyway, Leslie joined us for a while. Then went back to her room—alone.'

'Davy, I'm confused. I don't understand what all that has to do with anything. I know what I heard from the horse's mouth, though. After I accused Leslie of stealing you away, she didn't say: "what are you talking about?" No, she apologised. Then the brazen hussy came out with: "Davy's a big boy. It's his decision."'

Davy lifts his pint and takes a long swig. Then leans closer and looks me in the eye. 'She was talking about the job her company's offered me.'

'Job? What job?'

'Look, it's true Leslie and I were an item at uni, but that was over and done with years ago. We stayed friends—and last month, she got in touch because her company has a vacancy. For a project manager. She thought I might be interested—which I am.'

'But... you work for yourself.'

'And I do alright—but this is a real step up. High-roller salary, stock options—Sam, it's a once in a lifetime opportunity.'

'Okayyy,' I say—slowly, while I try to fit my head around this ever-changing situation.

He slumps back in his chair. 'If I take the job, it means moving to Glasgow. I really want this job, Sam—but I know you're settled here. Which is why I haven't said anything—had to decide first what I'd do if you refused to come. Leslie thought you'd found out and were mad at her for offering me it.'

'Oh.'

So, okay. It looks as though Davy hasn't been unfaithful after all—but he's still a conniving sleazeball for keeping schtum about this

My poor, beleaguered mind tries to process the deluge of new facts. He wants me to go with him—to Glasgow? Not *so* far away... come on, who am I trying to kid? It's a *long* way away—and I belong *here*. And yet... 'So—what will you do if I refuse to go?'

He looks down at his feet. 'I'll turn the job down.'

Oh—okay

'Davy, this is a lot to take in—especially after the night I've had. First thoughts—I *can't* stop you from accepting Leslie's offer, because you want this job and my nixing it would drive a wedge between us. But—neither can I see me moving from Cairncroft. This is my home. The home—the life—I dreamt of for so long.'

He goes to speak, but I raise both hands. 'No, please. Really, I'm not up to discussing it further tonight. I know we have to, but please, please— give me a little time to take all this in and mull it over. I'm sorry Davy, but right now I need to be on my own. Look—this is Tuesday. How about we go out for dinner on Thursday and talk about it then?'

His eyes twinkle. 'Shall I book that French restaurant you like?'

Despite myself, I'm laughing. 'Absolutely not—Chinese or nothing. And no tampering with the fortune cookies.'

He's laughing too. 'Okay—Sam, we'll sort this. I promise. I'm just so glad you and Daisy are alright—again. Listen, I can see you're wilting—and no wonder. I'm off—text you to finalise something for Thursday?'

I nod, and he leans over to give me a chaste kiss. Which ends up being not quite so chaste as I intended. 'Go,' I say, pushing him.

He grins and gets up, looks at me for a long moment, then spins around and lopes off.

But pauses at the archway, turns, waves—then he really *is* gone.

I feel every muscle in my body loosen—at last. I'm alive and, though Davy's opened up a whole new Pandora's box, at least he's not the cheating scumbag I believed. My world is coming back into focus.

And my glass is empty—no sooner does that thought enter my head than Daisy slams a refill on the table. She looks at me over the top of her pint mug. 'Cor—turn up for the books, eh? Sounds a neat job, though.'

My mouth falls open. 'You heard—how? Have you got the residents lounge bugged?'

She smirks and points at the wall above me. 'You're sitting under a vent, bang up against the stairwell lobby—which the Last Chance Saloon's connecting door opens into. Didn't you know somebody standing underneath that grill can hear everything anybody says at this table?'

'No, I did not—Daisy, that's low. Spying on us…'

'I wasn't—it's quiet through there and Clara's coping fine, so I came back to see how you were doing. Total accident it was—I didn't *try* to listen. Well, not at first…'

'I thought we kept that door locked, to segregate the public bar from through here.'

'We do—but I've got a key. So—what will you do? You aren't going with him—are you?'

When did we move on from the blatant eavesdropping?

'Oh, I'm not sure, Daisy. I can't imagine leaving Cairncroft—but Davy's my fiancé. Honestly—I know this affects you too, but my brain's too tired for thinking any more tonight. Any moment now, I'm going to pass out.'

'Can't blame you—it's been quite a night. Listen—Clara's managing fine. How about we head back to the cottage with a bottle or two of wine and order in a Chinese? Then hit the hay early.'

'Daisy,' I say, and it's heartfelt. 'I can think of nothing I'd like more.'

As we get up, she pauses. 'Oh, just remembered. We'd better make it an *Indian* takeaway. Seeing as you're going for Chinese with Davy on Thursday...'

38

Mid-morning on Wednesday, Daisy phones Keisha to tell her Liam is being held at Her Majesty's pleasure. I'm chatting to Hazel in reception when she comes dancing in to gloat about having yet another satisfied client.

It's the first I've seen of her today because, when I came downstairs after a well-deserved long lie, all that awaited me was a fast-fading smell of bacon. Breadcrumbs on the work surface around an opened packet of rolls confirmed her choice of breakfast—I'm getting quite good at this detective lark.

'Trouble is,' Daisy goes on, 'Keisha doesn't quite understand how it all works. I had to explain she needs to get the house put in her name and contact Child Maintenance to serve an order on Liam—not hire a couple of heavies to "have a word", as she thought.'

'But you've got her straightened out now?'

'Not really—Keisha's clueless. At least there's no rush—Liam isn't going anywhere. Wilson's been on to Aberdeen and got his bogus pickpocketing charge upgraded to desecrating a corpse—they picked up Tina, and she's dumped that on Liam. He'll probably get done for aiding and abetting Tina, too. I was wondering about dropping in on Mr M to see how he'd feel about having a pro bono chat with Keisha. What she needs is somebody to run through it all properly—maybe even give her a cheat sheet.'

'Citizen's Advice would do that.'

'Yeah, but the nearest one's in Aberdeen. Which means bus fares, finding a babysitter—or if she takes the kids along, more bus fares, not to mention...'

Both my palms go up. 'I get the picture. Plus, it gives us an excuse to have a chat with Mr M on his own?'

Daisy puts a forefinger to her lips and sucks. 'Cor,' she says. 'Never thought of that...'

Hazel tries to stifle a chuckle and I nod sagely. 'Of *course* you didn't. I presume you want me to come with?'

'Yeah. You're better at this kind of thing.'

'What—cadging free legal advice or trying to counsel somebody we suspect is being taken for a ride by his younger girlfriend?'

'Both—and if that doesn't work, you can be good cop. Guess which I bags?'

Poor Mr M has no idea how his day is about to disintegrate. 'Alright, no time like the present. We'll try and catch him between appointments.'

The sun's shining, which in Scotland is no small event, so we walk down to Cairncroft and, after dragging Daisy away from the Cuppa Tea's window display, mount the stairs to Mr M's office.

As the entrance door swings shut behind us, Daisy's gaze lingers on now-mirrored black letters stencilled on its glass panel.

"Dougall and MacLachlan." 'Who IS Dougall,' Daisy asks, as though noticing it for the first time.

'Wasn't that your drone? The one that crashed?'

'Ha flippin' ha. No, really—Mr M doesn't *have* a partner. Does he?'

'I asked Jodie about that a while back. Seems Mr M started the practice with this Dougall fella, who died soon after. For some reason, he kept the name.'

'Oh. That's a shame...'

For all her tough guy act, Daisy's a softy at heart

'... cos if Dougall was still around, bet *he'd* have talked some sense into Mr M by now. Saving *us* all this hassle.'

Mentally binning my shattered preconceptions, I glance around. 'That's funny—we've been here at least 10 seconds and Miss Dobie hasn't materialised.'

Miss Dobie has an uncanny ability to appear like a genie from its bottle—leading us to conclude she has a buzzer in her office, activated by the door opening. Either that, or psychic powers are yet another of her talents. Daisy looks puzzled, too. 'Yeah, I wonder...'

The great reveal of whatever Daisy wondered is forever lost to humanity as a cheery voice rings out. 'Hey, guys. What can we do for you?'

Kat appears at the other end of Mr M's hallway-like waiting area—I'm guessing from Miss Dobie's inner sanctum. (We've never been past Mr M's office door, hence the guesswork.) Daisy glances sideways and speaks sotto voce. 'What's *she* doing here?'

Either Kat's got better hearing than Walt Disney's Dumbo or Miss Dobie's loaned out her psychic powers. 'I'm filling in for Miss Dobie—her sister's in Aberdeen Royal Infirmary, and she's gone to visit.'

'Nothing serious, I hope?' This is the first we've heard of Miss Dobie *having* any family—when it comes to her private life, she makes undercover MI6 agents seem like amateurs.

'No—just an ingrowing toenail,' Kat informs us cheerily.

Daisy throws her a querying glance. 'Bit of a comedown this, is it not? The high-flying London solicitor filling in for a secretary.'

Kat laughs lightly. In different circumstances, I could quite take to her. 'I forgot you'd done a background check on me. It's only for today—if I end up working here, it *won't* be as a secretary.'

There's a mischievous tone to her voice—she knows exactly what we think and doesn't give a hoot. 'We came to see Mr M,' I cut in quickly.

'You're in luck—he's between appointments. On the phone right now, though. Take a seat—he won't be long.'

Daisy makes no move towards the old-fashioned armchairs either side of a table covered with magazines. In the past they were all golf publications, but today I'm noticing copies of Cosmopolitan and Tatler amongst them—is Kat putting her mark on the office already? Then Daisy says: 'How *is* Mr M these days? Any nearer to recovery?'

I gape sideways and Kat frowns. 'Recovery?'

'Yes, you know? After losing all that money last year. Poor guy came within a whisker of bankruptcy—beats me how he managed to keep this place open on a shoestring budget. Tragic, it was.'

Kat's mesmerised. 'What happened?'

Daisy flicks her fingers. 'Oh, if he hasn't told you the details, it isn't for me to... but you've come along at just the right time. There wasn't any money left to bring someone in so he could convalesce properly, like the doctor advised, but with you taking the load off his shoulders poor old Mr M can finally start taking it easy.'

Kat looks floored. 'I didn't know anything about...'

Daisy lowers her voice, making Kat come a step closer. 'Just between us, my first thought when I saw you pair together was: "Wily old devil. He's finally found somebody who'll work for free..."'

She breaks off when Mr M appears at Kat's shoulder. He must have been taking that call in Miss Dobie's whatever-she-has-back-there—and from his expression, it isn't soundproofed. 'My office—now,' he snaps, glaring at Daisy and striding past Kat.

'Bummer,' Daisy mutters as we follow, leaving Kat wearing a dazed look.

Mr M slams his office door and storms around the desk. His old captain's chair wheezes resentfully when he throws himself at it, while Daisy and I obediently sit in the visitor chairs he points at. 'Now. What *on earth* was all that about?'

I don't ever remember seeing Mr M ruffled, but his face is pink and all five fingers are drumming—tap-tap-tap—on a rare space amongst the usual clutter of files on his desk.

Daisy swallows. 'Okay—cards on the table. We've seen how besotted you are with that gold-digger out there and I was trying to scare her off before she fleeces you.'

That's right, Dais'—lead up to it gently

For a moment, I think our formerly amiable adopted uncle is going to explode. His eyes narrow, both cheeks blow out, and pink turns to red.

Then he slumps in his chair, to the accompaniment of an ominous creak, and gazes ceiling-ward. Slowly, he rotates to face the window behind. I remember him doing this the first time we were here—he was searching then for a kind way to tell me the hotel I'd inherited was about to go bust.

The chair turns again, completing its 360 degree excursion, and Mr M's colour is back to normal. The anger in his expression is gone, replaced by a weariness that makes him suddenly look very old and tired. He coughs, then leans forward and plants both elbows on his desk. 'Kat was right. I should have come clean from the beginning. She thinks this is a jolly jape and has been taking great delight in playing it to the hilt, but enough is enough.'

Daisy scoffs. 'You haven't exactly tried to hide what's "going on".'

'Oh, but I have. Let's cut to the chase—Kat's my daughter.'

Motormouth beside me charges on. 'Yes, that's the whole point, she's young enough to be your... what did you say?'

'A long time ago, I had a partner—Michael Dougall—a dear friend who died suddenly in a terrible accident. I felt bound to comfort his widow—spent too much time with her—and, well, something happened that never should have.

Joyce had already made arrangements to move away, nearer her family, so we agreed never to speak of it again. I... had no idea she was pregnant, and she chose not to tell me. Joyce was also friends with Alanna—my late wife. Joyce would have been mortified if Alanna had found out—as would I—and I believe part of the reason she kept silent was to protect Alanna and myself. Our marriage.'

He looks so sad, but at the same time seems to relax somewhat. Confession, they say, is good for the soul—I can't help feeling Mr M's relieved to, finally, get this off his chest. 'When did you find out?' I ask.

'A few months ago. Joyce was dying—and decided taking her secret to the grave would be wrong. So she confessed all—prompting Kat to seek out her biological father. Forgive me, girls—I should have been open about this from the start, but I come from another era. In my day, we had different attitudes to such things—and I am a product of my past. At first, I saw no reason for anyone around here to know. After the initial shock passed, it was a delight to discover I had such a fine, personable daughter. A blessing I never expected so late in life. Kat lives in

London—so I thought we would keep in touch, and that would be that. Kat, however, has other ideas. She has no other family now, you see. The poor girl was married twice—and lost both husbands under tragic circumstances, all in the last five years.'

'So she *didn't* off them, then?' Daisy cuts in, and at least has the grace to look ashamed.

'Pardon?'

Mr M squints, then seems to decide he misheard. 'I'm all Kat has now and will be overjoyed if she moves here—albeit, I have counselled her at length regarding what she's giving up in London. The only grey cloud on my new horizon was the thought of disappointing those around me—who think Mr MacLachlan to be someone he patently is not. Until now, I couldn't find sufficient courage to...'

Daisy leans forward and looks hard at him. 'Don't be so stupid. Nobody's going to burn you at the stake for one wee fling all those years ago—silly old codger. For goodness' sake, chill out and get on with enjoying your daughter.'

A tear runs down Mr M's cheek—followed by the beginnings of a smile. 'You know?' he says, eyeballing me. 'I really should have consulted with

Daisy at the start—her counselling skills are without equal.'

Mr M and I laugh while Daisy tries to work out whether that was a compliment or not. He straightens, and a determined look enters his eye. 'Thank you—both of you. I have been a very foolish old man, but it ends here. Now—my only problem is how to get the news out quickly. I am a great believer in ripping the plaster off with one quick pull.'

Daisy grins at him. 'Hey, good as done. You've told Sam, haven't you...?'

39

'You've told Sam, haven't you...? What was that supposed to mean?'

'Relax. Wee joke—I was only trying to lighten the mood. Nobody would ever suggest you were a gossip.'

You did

Oh, I can't stay mad at her—not when I'm so relieved at having the "Mr M situation" resolved. 'Now we know she isn't a gold-digger, I'm suddenly seeing Kat for what she *really* is—a friendly, fun person.'

'Yeah, changes everything. Still finding it hard to believe Mr M did the dirty on his wife like that...'

'Daisy. We don't know the circumstances...'

'Rather not, thank you.'

We're halfway back to the hotel and it's even sunnier than before. Suddenly, I feel quite philosophical. 'Never were truer words spoken than: "Let he who is without sin cast the first stone."'

Daisy stops and stares. 'Sam—you got something to tell me?'

Then she laughs. 'Lighten up, wilya. Mr M's... well, Mr M again, and he's agreed to sort Keisha for us. The fairground caper's wrapped up—hey, meant to say. Saw Jodie on her way out this morning and asked if they'd released Ivor yet. Guess what—he'd already come up with an alibi.'

'So he's out?'

She giggles. 'Nope. Ivor's alibi was he spent Friday evening with a couple of mates—burgling a house. Its owners are away to Spain for a fortnight, so they practically emptied the place—took them hours. Ivor's fingerprints prove he was there and his *ex*-mates confirmed the time and date—eventually.'

I can't help laughing. 'So he's still going down? That should make Tina happy—when she gets out. What's Wilson charging her with—did Jodie say?'

'"Perverting the course of justice." Jodie reckons she won't get more than twelve months seeing as it's a first offence—probably be out in less with good behaviour. Jodie also told me Dobson looks to be a bigger fish than anyone realised. Now he's on the run and no threat to them, police snitches are talking for the first time—word is Dobson's fairgrounds are really launderettes.'

'But we saw the rides at his yard...'

She rolls her eyes and tuts. 'They're saying Dobson's a *money launderer*—you know, like in "Ozark" on the telly—for organised crime in Glasgow. That's the real reason he was so keen to get ahold of Paul's fair, with its great pitches. He would have used that to justify a huge rise in "profits"—and taken in more laundry. Hey, listen—you will not believe *this*. I spoke to Paul this morning, and the silly sod's taking Tina back—soon as she comes out of clink. Now that his contract with Dobson's invalid, the jammy beggar gets to keep the fair—but has decided he can't run it on his own.'

And Jodie called me a wimp

'Must be off his head,' is my immediate reaction. 'How could he ever trust her again?'

'Dunno—and it isn't my problem. Paul's history far as I'm concerned.'

'Was it the glasses?' I quip, but she doesn't seem to get it. (Don't people realise rectangular frames on a square face is the aesthetic equivalent of wearing green trousers with a red top?)

'He'd have been leaving soon anyway,' I try consoling her—not that Daisy's demeanour suggests she *needs* consoling.

'Oh, I could handle a long-distance relationship, but Paul's like Terry was—what he really wants is a mummy.'

"Long-distance relationship"—that could be my marriage if Davy and I go ahead. Because I *can't* hold Davy back from his "chance of a lifetime" as he put it—but neither can I leave Cairncroft.

I don't think...

'You look awful serious all of a sudden...'

Her eyebrows fly up. 'Oh, you're thinking about Davy. Hey, that's a good idea—let him go, you stay here, and the two of you can meet up at weekends.'

If only life were so simple as Daisy's view of it

She sees I don't want to talk about Davy and jogs me with her elbow. 'Listen, I've got to go and prepare—well, prepare Rebecca—for tonight's mid-week mystery. And catch up on a lot of other things—you must be the same with the hotel. What say we meet up later, after Jodie's home, and go up to her place with a bottle of wine or two—bring her up to date on Mr M and Kat?'

'Who's the gossip now?'

But she's right. Mr M probably *would* appreciate not having to go through another grand confession—plus, I was too dazed last night to thank Jodie properly. In fact, with that in mind, might make it a bottle of champagne.'

I could do with a good blowout before facing Davy tomorrow

40

Next morning, I oversleep. (Maybe we shouldn't have sent down for *another* bottle of champagne.)

It's not *that* late, though—only ten past nine when I stroll up the hotel drive. On a whim, I divert to the detective agency. Daisy was already gone when I got up—that's two mornings in a row. There's nothing I need to see her about, but it feels weird missing each other first thing. I'll pop in and touch base, maybe stop for coffee with her and Rebecca...

I'm surprised to find the front door wide open—yet, when I go in, Rebecca's chair is empty. Has she overslept, too?

But why was the door open?

The door to Daisy's office is ajar, and I hear a murmur of voices. Including what sounds suspiciously like a faint Irish accent. Moving closer, quiet as I can manage, the voices become clearer.

One of them *is* Dobson. I listen, spellbound.

Daisy: So you came here to shoot me? Makes a change from the last guy who sneaked in with a gun—*he* tried to top himself.

Dobson: 'Maybe him and me aren't so different. I've lost everything—thanks to you—so that was my plan, too. Nothing left to live for, you see. But I wanted to take you with me. I was hoping the posh one would be here, too.'

Daisy: 'Look, I'm every bit as posh as she is. Don't let the nose ring fool you... anyway, what's with the "nothing to live for?" You had 150 grand.'

Dobson: '"Had" being the operative word. Mickey vamoosed with that—just another rat on my sinking ship.'

   This is terrible. Dobson was obviously lying in wait for Daisy, and must have a gun. If Mickey's made off with his escape fund, Dobson's's got nothing to lose—and seems set on revenge.

Strangely, though my hands are trembling, I'm not frozen to the spot. In fact, when I slip sideways to the staffroom door, it's in a smooth, coordinated movement—left leg notwithstanding. Maybe I'm tired of people thinking I'm a wimp—or could it be that after last night, nothing will ever frighten me again? Whatever—I pad over to Daisy's equipment cupboard and ease it open. "Digby" and "Donna" take up an entire shelf, but what I'm looking for is on the next down.

Daisy's usual taser is a close-quarters, "contact" version—but the new version she loaned Rebecca is a different style altogether. Basically, it's a dart-firing airgun. The darts stay connected by a filament of wire, which transfers incapacitating voltage to whoever's unfortunate enough to have one stuck in them.

Although hearing she'd acquired another taser nearly made me blow a gasket, I'm glad now she did.

I'm even more glad she showed me how to operate the thing after Rebecca gave it back and that, despite my ire, I listened.

Right—take a little capsule of compressed air from the box beside it (think Daisy said it was actually nitrogen, but I don't particularly care *how* the beggar works so long as it *does*), insert appropriately, then press *this* button. (That starts the charging process, which takes about 30 seconds—confirmed by a low-pitched whine.)

Returning to the office door, I hear an ongoing murmur of voices—and feel weak with relief I'm not too late.

I'd *like* to kick the door open, but with a gammy leg… Instead, I take a firm grip of the doorhandle and shove hard, simultaneously stepping forward.

My heart's hammering harder than a drum on an Orange march, but icy determination carries me through cloying panic when it tries to block the way. Now everything depends on staying focused and moving fast—without hesitation.

My sweeping gaze confirms Daisy's behind her desk, picks up Rebecca in the furthest-away visitor chair—with Hector on her knee—then settles on Dobson, also seated and, conveniently, closest to me.

Letting go the door handle, I bring the taser up in a two-handed grip Cagney *or* Lacey would be proud of. Snippets of "Daisy advice" from past flirtations with firearms sound in my head. (We did visit a practice range once, but the gun was too heavy for me to hold—more recently, though, she talked me through a duck shoot at the fair and I won a, albeit pocket-sized, soft toy). Daisy's phantom voice whispers "point it like you'd point a finger" and "squeeze the trigger slowly but firmly".

There's a pop, the gun bucks against my hands, and Dobson screams. His head jerks crazily, then he tips backward—chair and all.

Strangely, as he flounders on the floor, his chair stays attached. Daisy and Rebecca, instead of applauding, are staring at me. Poor loves—the relief they must feel.

'Well,' I pronounce, not without a certain satisfaction. 'That takes care of *him*. Um, Daisy… aren't you going to tie him up before it wears off?'

Her expression suggests a missed vocation in teaching maths. 'He already *is* tied—to the chair.'

Then she holds up an automatic pistol, by its barrel. 'We're way ahead of you, Sam.'

'WELL, HOW WAS I TO KNOW?'

It seems Dobson *was* lying in wait for Daisy. He entered through the staffroom window, after forcing it.

Unfortunately for Dobson, Hector habitually attends to business before coming in with Rebecca each morning. She accompanied him around the back (at a discreet distance—Hector likes his privacy) and clocked the forced window, then intercepted Daisy and warned her.

Daisy went in by the same window as Dobson, collected the taser I just made such a fool of myself with, and threw a penny across the room to lure Dobson into the staffroom. When Dobson stepped through the door, Daisy tasered him.

First returning the taser to her equipment cupboard (sensible, with the police coming) and after Dobson had recovered sufficiently, my erstwhile friend used Dobson's own gun to make him walk through to the office. (Just in case a policeman should "accidentally" look in her equipment cupboard.)

There, she had Dobson sit quietly while Rebecca tied him up. (The success she had controlling him with a gun suggesting Dobson's previously-professed intention to commit suicide had slipped his mind.)

Daisy laughs and claps my back. 'Whatever you're on these days, I could do with some.'

Rebecca doe-eyes me. 'I think you're terribly brave, Sam.'

I won't repeat what Dobson said when he got his voice back

Inspector Wilson arrives soon after, with Jodie and two uniforms. Dobson predictably complains about Daisy's use of an illegal weapon. (And mine.)

'I feel an attack of déjà vu coming on,' Wilson murmurs.

Daisy sniffs. 'Want me to untie the beggar and show you how I took him down?' she suggests helpfully.

'That was your answer last time we had this conversation. No, a demonstration won't be necessary. But if I do ever catch you with a taser—the penalty's up to ten years imprisonment.'

'*Or* a fine,' Daisy puts in quickly. 'Up to the judge—how he feels about it.'

'Mm. You're on thin ice, lady. Nonetheless, you *have* saved the police a lot of time and effort—

every force in the UK has been looking for this blighter.'

On her way out, Jodie squeezes my arm. 'Nice one Sam, despite... sorry I called you a wimp.'

Guess she DID pick up I was miffed

As Jodie hurries to catch up with her colleagues a little grey-haired lady pops her head around the door. 'Mrs Struthers,' Rebecca calls, gesturing her in. 'What can we do for you?'

'I want someone to watch my husband. Now, I may be wrong—but think there's a possibility he's getting up to no good when my back's turned...'

THURSDAY EVENING, AND I'M ON MY WAY TO THAT FATEFUL dinner date. I still haven't decided what to do. Trouble is, I want it all—Davy *and* Cairncroft. But I can't stop him taking this job—that would undermine our marriage before it even began.

For years, I longed for a better life—now, suddenly, I've the choice of two. Both infinitely superior to anything I ever dreamed.

So if *I* won't leave—and won't stop *him* leaving—*and* don't want us to split up—then *what*? A long-distance relationship? Glasgow's not exactly "Seattle", but trying to make any semblance of living together at that distance could only result in sleepless nights.

Do long-distance relationships even work?

As usual, I'll agonise over this right up to the last moment—swinging wildly from one option to the other—then, when I get there, decide in a flash.

Wish I knew what that decision will be.

On second thoughts—I already know.

My heart is heavy, but it's the only decision I *can* make.

The Donstable Gazette

13th July, 2022

PRIVATE DETECTIVES NEARLY DIE ON FAULTY FAIRGROUND RIDE

Two local private detectives who have asked not to be named (for professional reasons) were involved in a death-defying incident last Tuesday night.
(See full story on page 2)

Inspector Wilson, of Donstable CID, confirmed those responsible had been apprehended and repeated his reservations about private investigation services. "Those poor lasses could have been killed," Wilson emphasised. "The police are far better equipped to deal with the sort of situation they were meddling in."

A spokesperson for the Cairncroft Detective Agency said: "Did he tell you who actually caught Dobson...?"

"Vertical Drop" ride
(Stock photo)

PUBLISHED EVERY WEDNESDAY
BY DONSTABLE PRESS LTD

NEXT IN SERIES

Things that go bump in the night...

... seem louder on Allhallows Eve

But when spooky turns to murder at the Cairncroft Hotel's Halloween party...

... you just KNOW who they're gonna call

ALSO BY A.J.A. GARDINER

I also write "The Con Woman" series of adventure stories

☆☆☆☆☆ "What a rollercoaster of a ride this is and what an absolute pleasure to read. I think you can tell that I really enjoyed this book!" (Goodreads reviewer)

ALSO BY A.J.A. GARDINER

☆ ☆ ☆ ☆ ☆ **"Must Read"**
"Loved this book" (Amazon reviewer)

Comedy meets drama in this cosy, heart-warming tale of a man, his dogs, and his dreams. Join Mark as he struggles with zany patients, gets fleeced by his ex-wife, and makes a friend called "Shovelhead".

"Eyes Up" is the story of a home-visiting optician, written by—a (former) home-visiting optician!

☆ ☆ ☆ ☆ ☆ **"The optometrist equivalent of James Herriot?"** (Amazon reviewer)

AUTHOR'S NOTE

Thank you for choosing this book—I hope you enjoyed reading it as much as I enjoyed writing it.

The best way to be kept informed of new books etc is to join my readers' club—when you'll get a free **Ebook** called "When Sam met Daisy", a short story telling how the girls met—it's yours by typing the following into your browser:

https://ajagardinerwriter.co.uk/free%20book/

You can mail me by writing to: alistair@ajagardinerwriter.co.uk – I'd love to hear from you. Or better still, visit my website where you can see ALL my books, sign up for newsletters, AND contact me.

www.ajagardinerwriter.co.uk

Thanks so much for reading my book - if you liked it, puh-lease tell your friends! ☺

I look forward to our next meeting.

AJAG

PS if your free book doesn't appear, check the SPAM folder. No joy? Mail me at alistair@ajagardinerwriter.co.uk
& I'll sort it out.

This is a work of fiction. Names, characters, places, and incidents either are the product of the author's imagination or are used fictitiously. Any resemblance to actual persons, living or dead, events, or locales is entirely coincidental.

Copyright © 2023 by A.J.A. Gardiner

All rights reserved. No part of this book may be reproduced or used in any manner without written permission of the copyright owner except for the use of quotations in a book review. For more information, email alistair@ajagardinerwriter.co.uk

First paperback edition August 2023

ISBN: 9798852658517

(Front cover design by Addison-Wright Publications)

Printed in Great Britain
by Amazon